THE STONE INITIATION

THE STONE INITIATION

DEBBIE CASSIDY

PAGE
&
VINE

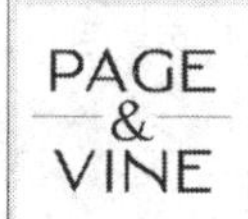

Page & Vine
An Imprint of Meredith Wild LLC

This is a work of fiction. Names, characters, places, and incidents either are the product of the author's imagination or are used fictitiously, and any resemblance to actual persons, living or dead, business establishments, events, or locales is entirely coincidental. The publisher does not assume any responsibility for third-party websites or their content.

The author acknowledges the trademarked status and trademark owners of various products referenced in this work, which have been used without permission. The publication/use of these trademarks is not authorized, associated with, or sponsored by the trademark owners.

Cover by Covers by Christian

Paperback ISBN: 978-1-964264-70-7

CHAPTER 1

CAMERON

There was a boogeyman in my closet. Again.

It was the third time this month, and I was losing my patience. I yanked open the door and stared at the mournful-eyed creature huddled in the corner of the dark cupboard.

"Seriously, Derek? Again?"

He moaned softly and hung his head.

"What happened now?"

"Eeee, oooow arghhh uuuuh." He sighed. "Grrrrr."

The sounds he made, although incoherent and downright frightening to anyone else, made sense to me. "Those bastards. I swear, if I get my hands on them, I'll extinguish the lot of them."

He looked up sharply. "Ungghh"

"I know. I know you want to be friends with them, but they're no good, Derek. You're better than them." I

He was. He was sweet and kind and totally not boogeyman material. But then he was mine. I'd created him, after all. He'd come from the mind of a lonely little girl in need of a companion, and now he didn't fit in with all the other monsters under the bed, and it was my fault.

I held out my hand. "Hey, you want some hot chocolate?"

"Ummm, urrrgh..."

"Yes, you can have marshmallows."

He took my hand and squeezed gently, his smile revealing rows of razor teeth. Gosh, he was the sweetest.

"Brrrgggh," he said softly.

"Yeah, I love you too, buddy."

BOOGEYMEN; THE THING in the lake; monsters under the bed and shadow men, they were all real, all the same thing—tulpas. A human's imagination could produce magic, and collectively...well, the evidence was all around us. Killing the creatures, however, was a little harder. It involved imagining a weakness into being, and then having the masses believe it. Back in the day, before the Gray messed up our world, the guardians had used the internet to keep these creatures under control. Feeding information to the masses that helped our stone protectors to take down these shadowy threats.

There was still internet, but now it was called the Vine. It was spotty and unpredictable and frustrating as heck. Cell service was also unreliable. But we were alive, and that's what mattered.

The details of the Gray threat that changed our world were spotty, but that was probably deliberate. The less humans knew, the less chance they would somehow imagine something similar into existence.

I led Derek into the kitchen, where the sun was making an arc through the sky, getting ready to sleep for the day. He had never quite caught on to the come-out-only-at-night part.

The huge kitchen clock showed it to be a minute after five. I had a date across town in a couple of hours. A small hunt organized by the locals that involved a nest of vampires that needed clearing out.

Tulpas weren't the only threat in our world. Vampires, werewolves, and other demonic things existed, but most of those inhabited the city beyond the rim lands, a place warded by powerful mageri magic. It was a safe place, filled with order and rules, but it was no longer taking admissions.

We were on our own out here in Old Town, and it worked just fine.

Derek made a sound of inquiry.

"Almost done, buddy." I shot him a smile.

Yep, I had plenty of time to give him a pep talk. He was my responsibility, and I adored him.

He waited patiently while I made his milky drink and popped it in front of him.

"Wnnngh argggh," he said.

"You're welcome."

"Bbbbrrf grunge beck."

"Yeah, buddy, it sucks. But that's what they're made to do. You can't change that. You can't make the others stop scaring kids."

He sighed and plucked a marshmallow from his mug before popping it into his mouth.

I could have extinguished him a long time ago. Being half gargoyle afforded me some abilities, and extinguishing tulpas was one of them, but aside from the fact that I loved the moany freak, using my abilities would expose what I was to the people of Old Town, and to my friends, and then it would only be a matter of time before the pureblood gargoyles found me. I was sure they kept tabs on spikes of power like extinguishing. I made sure that when I hunted, I did it the old-fashioned way.

It wasn't easy keeping my abilities in check when people around me needed help. But I'd learned to use the tried and tested methods to take down the monsters. They seemed to work on the creatures roaming the Rim, although I'd heard the variants that occupied the city were a stronger, ancient breed than the ones out here.

The only creatures we had no defense against were the graynites.

"Buuurg."

"Yeah, I was totally listening."

"Hnnng, errr."

I rolled my eyes. "Okay, so I zoned out for a moment. Sorry."

He reached across the table and placed his hand over mine. "Inggg arrrgh burrr Romi."

The mention of my brother made my chest tight. I hadn't seen him for almost eight weeks now. It was the longest he'd gone without a visit, and I was beginning to worry, which was ridiculous, of course.

"Romi's fine. He's always fine. He's probably on some secret mission for the guardians."

My gargoyle sibling was an elite. A pureblood. Part of the highest ranked unit in the Stonehaven Guardians. One of five, all born into the most powerful bloodlines.

He was older than me by a decade. But despite being busy training initiates, he'd taken care of me after my human mother died, finding me a home and checking in every few weeks. Until now.

He was fine. I was being ridiculous.

My phone rang shrilly. I snatched it up and answered quickly. "Hey."

"Cameron, where are you?" There was an impatient snap to Teri's voice that instantly had my back up, but I squashed my annoyance when I noted the time—still a minute after five. The damn thing had stopped, again.

The low-grade buzz of power in my limbs should have warned me that the sun had set.

A quick glance out of the window confirmed it. "Teri, I'm on my way."

"Liar."

I winced. "The clock stopped."

"Get a fucking watch."

"I'm allergic to nickel."

"Urgh, just get here."

"Give me thirty minutes. Do *not* go in without me."

"We're not suicidal."

No, they were savvy and smart, and they knew success against a nest required numbers.

I gathered my long, thick hair into a high ponytail and snapped a tie around it, then dropped a kiss on Derek's cloaked head. "I'll be back soon."

"Mmmurrg arrr buck."

"You want to come?" I arched a brow. "Will you help kill them?"

He hung his head and peered up at me. "Mung org arrr."

"No, snuggles won't help. Not unless you plan to smother them to death."

He looked horrified.

"Yeah, that's what I thought. I'll be back soon. Watch your favorite cartoons while I'm gone. There are some discs on the top of the pile by the TV stand."

I grabbed my keys and my backpack filled with stakes and holy water before heading for the door.

It was time to kick some fanged butt.

CHAPTER 2

CAMERON

The war had raged for a decade. A decade where our country had been decimated. Buildings brought down and the economy all but destroyed, but aided by the guardians, humanity had rebuilt. Still, there were parts of Old Town that were in ruins, the buildings too broken to be fixed, all that history and architecture wiped out. The only evidence of what had been, could be found in faded photographs and old documentaries.

But despite the ruins and the rubble, despite the patched-up windowless buildings, there was a beauty to this world, a defiance that gave the finger to any force daring to bring it down.

I took the underground passages, once occupied by whizzing trains and now a graveyard of rusted metallic frames suitable only for foot patrol. Brightly lit, these routes protected against the windy, stormy elements of our city. People trudged, shuffled, walked, and jogged through the tunnels. Homeless people pushed their belongings in trolleys, woolen hats pulled low over their eyes, pink swollen digits poking out from fingerless gloves.

It was cold in Old Town. Always so cold. But I'd heard that the north closest to the Fringe was sweltering.

Thanks to my half gargoyle constitution, I barely felt the chill. Still, I tugged my coat tighter around me, acting the part of pure human. People respected the guardians—pureblood gargoyles that protected the Rim—but a half human, half gargoyle, was something less tolerated. Especially females like me.

There were others like me, no doubt. Gargoyle males had high sex drives, or so I'd heard, but offspring with humans was rare. I'd never actually come across another hybrid, although Romi assured me they existed.

I took the stairs out of the tunnels and into the icy air of east side Old Town. Paper, plastic cups, and rumpled wrappers rolled across the ground in what I liked to call debris dust bunnies. People walked fast, heads down, eager to get to their destination. I hopped on a tram and jumped off two stops later outside a strip of stores that hadn't been open in some time. Business was not booming this side of town.

A van sat on the corner of the street. Teri's ride. She'd offered to pick me up more than once, but I'd turned her down with one excuse or another until she'd stopped asking. Truth be told, I didn't want them seeing where I lived. Didn't want them knowing I had my own apartment on the nicer side of town. They'd have questions about how I could afford it, and that would lead to lies.

I didn't want to lie to my friends any more than I already was.

The apartment was a gift from Romi. An expensive eighteenth birthday present that had gotten me out from under Ralph's roof—my legal guardian after my mother had died, and the only other person who knew what I was.

I banged a fist on the side of the van, and the door slid open. The smell of weed hit me in the face.

"Seriously? Before a hunt?" I glared at Fred, who gave me the peace sign.

"Just half a joint. I got this."

I looked to Teri, who shrugged. "Fuck him, if he wants to get killed, he can provide chow for the suckers and slow them down."

"Hey!" Fred sat up straighter, suddenly sober. "Not cool."

"Getting high before a fucking hunt is *not cool*."

Teri was badass for a human. We'd met two years ago when

I was tracking a wereboar; yep, someone had thought those up. Anyway, she'd been hunting it with Fred, and we'd linked up. We'd been working together ever since.

The growl of a motorcycle engine had my pulse spiking.

"Finally," Teri said with an eye roll. "When it comes to shit time-keeping, Levi takes the cake."

The bike engine cut out, and I stepped away from the van in time to watch him tug off his helmet. His sea-green eyes locked onto me, and the corner of his luscious mouth tugged up in a half smile.

"Damn, I must be late," he said.

I couldn't hold back my smile. "Fuck you, Levi."

"You wish," he drawled. But his eyes said, *later.*

Yes, I was looking forward to later because Levi was mine. Had been for the past eight months. Honestly, I hadn't expected us to last that long, which is why I'd asked to keep it a secret from the others. He'd started as an itch I'd wanted to scratch but turned into so much more, and now...now I had a choice. I could either let him go or tell him the truth about what I was. Either way, I'd probably lose him. Most humans steered clear of halfbloods like me. My kind were anomalies. Monsters to them, just as a shifter or a vampire might be.

Yeah...coming clean would mean losing him, both as a lover and as a friend. But breaking up with him would mean I might be able to keep him in my life.

But not yet.

I wasn't ready to let him go just yet.

Levi climbed off his bike and joined us on the sidewalk. He was a big guy. Tall and broad-shouldered, built to deliver and take hits. He'd worked for the guild up north where pockets of magic hovered over certain towns and villages, leaving others mundane and monster free. He'd chosen to come live in the thick of it, helping to keep Old Town clean, and stumbled onto our group.

We'd taken him in, and not long after that, I'd taken him to bed. Our connection was undeniable, and the fact the others didn't see it was a testament to our acting skills.

"*Both* of you need to work on your time keeping," Teri said, clearly irritated.

"I was catching some z's," Levi said. "Had a long night last night." He shot me a sidelong glance, and heat pooled low in my belly.

Yes, last night had been...something. Levi was the only guy I'd been with who could keep up with me in bed. His stamina almost matched mine, and that was saying something. We worked. We fit, and I couldn't wait to do it again.

"Are we going to do this or what?" Fred asked, looking from me to Levi.

Shit. I was staring at Levi. My gaze flicked to Teri to find her watching us with a frown.

Dammit. I reached for the pack in the back of the van and grabbed a wooden stake. "Let's just go and get this over with. If we're lucky, we'll catch them sleeping." I strode off toward the graffiti-covered block of flats down the street.

Our intel told us that the suckers had the basement level flats on this building. The rest were derelict and empty. Any poor, unsuspecting soul who wandered inside looking for shelter was in for a nasty surprise.

These kinds of issues never made it to the guardians' logs. They were allocated to whichever hunter party was responsible for the area. In this case, it was our ragtag motley crew.

After we finished with this nest, the flats would be cleaned up and used by people who needed them, and in Old Town, there were plenty of humans in need of shelter.

Teri led the charge, wooden stake in her leather-clad hand.

There were two kinds of vampire, the ones who adhered to the old novels, living in coffins and shunning sunlight. They quoted old poetry and made out like they were doomed to drink blood, blah, blah, blah. Then you had the modern breed who liked to blend in, using their human visages to live and work among us. They usually emerged in the late afternoon when the sun was going down. They took night shifts, or worked from home, mimicking the human life best they could. This latter kind were the worst. Hard to track and kill, because unless you could get close to check out their fangs and touch their skin, you'd never know they were monsters.

Holy water didn't work on this breed, and I was pretty sure it only worked on the old-style vamps because they believed it would.

The state of this building made me confident we were dealing with coffins and woe.

We entered through the busted door and made our way silently through the hallway to the basement access at the back of the ground floor.

This door was tightly closed, but the bloody handprint on the wall and the discarded shoe on the ground, told me we had the right spot.

Teri reached for the door and looked to Levi. He nodded. I braced myself, wooden stake held tightly, ready to get in between them and the vamp's fangs if need be. I couldn't morph to full stone skin like a regular gargoyle, but my body reacted to attack by instinctively turning the body part under threat to stone.

My ability had saved several lives over the past two years without the others ever realizing.

Teri yanked open the door, and the loud groan of hinges had us all wincing.

Fred set to work on those hinges, undoing them to take off the door completely. It would save us from getting trapped in the basement.

He stretched two iron wires across the opening, placing them at neck level, one slightly higher than the other, to account for height differences and catch any runners. We'd all have to remember to crouch and scramble when exiting.

Levi went first, his blade glinting in the gloom. He preferred decapitation to staking. I wasn't sure which was harder to be honest. Being stronger than an average human meant both required equal effort for me.

Bone was bone.

Stone steps led down to basement level, and weak lights flickered as we descended. There were apartments down here, too, cheaper than the ones above, but the nest would be clustered together.

Yep, coffins in a row in the entranceway. Doors to the flats all open.

Fred covered his nose. "It stinks."

"Decaying bodies do that." Teri pointed to the pile of body parts in the far corner of the room.

But alarm bells were going off in my head because despite what I had said outside about hoping they were still sleeping, it was way past sundown, and suckers didn't waste moonlight.

"Six coffins. All closed," Levi muttered. "Either these fuckers like to lie in or—

"Welcome to our humble abode." A male vampire dressed in a Halloween Dracula cape, dark hair slicked back, emerged from one of the rooms. "We've been waiting for you."

The coffins all creaked open at the same time, and six ratty-looking vampires sat up. The males wore capes and nineteenth century ruffled shirts, and the women were dressed in corsets and ankle-length dresses. Which fancy dress store had these fuckers raided?

I shook my head. "Like hell did you know we were coming."

He lifted his chin, attempting to look enigmatic. "I have my sources."

"Security camera," Fred said, peering past the vamp.

The leader growled. "You will pay for your trespass onto our territory."

"Pretty sure you're squatting, mate," Levi said.

"We do not squat. We conquer," he replied. "We are undead creatures of the night."

"Soon to be dead." Teri held up her stake. "Stand still and take it like a champ, will ya?"

That was our cue.

We rushed into the den, keeping to our assigned pairs. Teri and Levi, Fred and me following the usual routine.

Slam them down and punch a hole in them.

The first two went down easy, but then they fought back. Attacking with claws and fangs. Leaping and screaming. Messy stuff that might work on a regular human to shock them into submission or make them freeze in horror.

Not a seasoned hunter, though.

Three minutes later, six vamps were down, and the leader was running up the steps.

I tucked my stake into my belt. "Wait for it."

"Unggg." *Thud, thud, thud, thud, thud.*

Dracula wannabe's head landed at the bottom of the steps and stared at us accusingly.

"I'm hungry." Fred stepped over the head. "Anyone fancy pizza?"

I bit back a smile and followed the crew back up the steps. We'd log this with the guardians now because, like fuck was I doing clean up.

CHAPTER 3

Cameron

Pizza Delight did the best pizza in Old Town. The décor was cozy with leather booths, wooden tables, and soft, warm lighting. It was our go-to place after a hunt, and the owner, Keryanne, always threw in some extra garlic bread with our order. She knew what we did to help keep the streets safe. There wasn't an official hunter team allocated to Old Town, and small teams like us were all that the town had to rely on.

Huddled in a booth with three humans, it was easy to pretend that I was one of them. That I was normal. That these people I hung out with regularly were my friends. It was easy to push aside the truth while we sat, stuffing our faces with delicious cheesy pizza.

But the reality was, that I'd never have real friends while I was forced to lie to them.

"And then he kissed my feet!" Teri finished with a snort. "I mean, no. Just no."

Fuck, I'd totally zoned out, and now Teri was looking at me, waiting for a response.

Think, think. "I need to pee."

I slid out of the booth and headed to the washroom. Once I got there, I found that I did, in fact, need to pee. One less lie, I guess.

I washed and dried my hands while staring at my reflection in the mirror above the sink. "You're a coward and a liar." I closed my eyes. "If they're your friends, they won't care what you are. If he cares about you, *he* won't care..."

There was a knock on the door.

"Cam?" Levi knocked again.

Fuck. "Coming." I opened the door to find him leaning up against the wall opposite the washroom, his eyes dark with concern.

"What's wrong?" he asked.

"Nothing."

"You're lying."

He had no idea. "I'm fine. Honestly." The words tasted bitter on my tongue.

He held out his arms, and I stepped into them, laid my head on his chest, and closed my eyes. The steady beat of his heart soothed away some of the conflict in mine.

This was a side of him not everyone got to see. The caring, nurturing side that he reserved for me. For our time alone. To the others he was sarcastic and cocky, but to me he was just...my Levi.

"You know you can always talk to me, princess."

I swallowed past the lump in my throat, past all the things I'd love to say but was too afraid to reveal.

"I know there's stuff," Levi said. "Like why we've never hung out at your place..."

My expensive apartment in the fancy side of town would pose questions about my finances and my family. Things I couldn't... wouldn't talk about without the risk of revealing my nature and heritage.

I'd have to lie again. "You know I'm a slob."

He sighed and stroked my hair. "No, Cam, I don't know that. Because you've never invited me over."

"The others—"

"Need to know that we're seeing each other." His tone was

firm.

Panic seized me. I pulled away to look up at him, scanning his face to gauge the seriousness of his suggestion. "What? No. We agreed that we'd keep it a secret."

"That was six months ago, Cam." He sounded almost weary. "That was before I fell in love with you."

My heart stalled in my chest. "What..."

He cupped my face. "I'm fucking head over heels in love with you, Cam."

No, no, no. Why was he doing this? Why was he saying those words and making my heart beat so hard and fast that I was afraid it might burst from my chest?

"I don't expect you to feel the same way, but I need you to know that I'm in this for the long haul. This isn't just a fling for me anymore, Cam. I love you, and I want everyone to know."

I hadn't realized how much I'd wanted this until this moment. Hadn't realized how deep my feelings for Levi had grown until now, and the fear of losing this...losing us, swept over me in an icy wave. I pushed up on tiptoe and crushed my mouth to his, sinking my fingers into his dark, silken hair and breathing in his vanilla scent.

Why couldn't time stand still here? Why couldn't we just stop right here?

I broke the kiss and stood back on my heels. I needed to memorize his face before I did this next part: his dark winged brows, high, flat cheekbones, and the bump on his nose from the break that never healed properly. I'd kissed that bump so many times. I ran my fingers down the side of his neck, tracing the runic patterns of the tattoo that vanished beneath the collar of his T-shirt. The pattern was so familiar to me now I could trace it in my sleep.

"Cam..." There was doubt in his tone now, and my stomach knotted with anxiety.

Just fucking do it, Cam. Break it off. Tell him you don't love him. Do it or you'll lose him completely. "Levi, I—"

My phone buzzed angrily in my pocket. I should have ignored it, but it felt like a sign to shut my mouth.

"One second." I stepped away to take the call.

The caller ID showed an unknown number. I didn't usually answer those, but what if it was Romi? "Hello?"

"Hello, is this Cameron?" The voice was male, gruff, and not Romi.

"Who is this?"

"Is. This. Cameron?"

My stomach trembled. "Yes, who—"

"Romi's dead. I thought you should know." *Click*

I stared at the phone. This was a joke. It had to be. But who would do this? And how did they get my number?

The phone rang again, and the caller ID flashed *Ralph*. "Hello? Ralph, I just got the strangest call."

"Cam..." He sniffed. "I have some bad news."

"No."

"Romi's dead."

It was true.

It was real.

My brother was dead.

CHAPTER 4

CAMERON

Ralph opened the door and pulled me into a hug.

I shoved him away. Not wanting comfort but answers.

I'd run out of the pizza place so fast Levi's head was probably still spinning. He didn't know about Romi, had no clue I even had a sibling, so explaining my fear to him wasn't an option. But Ralph knew.

I stormed into his tiny kitchenette and stood hands on hips. "This can't be happening. This is Romi. He can't be... He just can't."

"It was all over guardian radio. Romi Basque killed in action."

Ralph worked for the local human police force. He also loved building shit and had stumbled across the covert radio frequency the guardians used several months ago.

I might have argued he'd misheard if not for the call I'd received.

"I'm sorry, Cameron," he said.

A bubble of grief swelled inside my chest, and I gritted my teeth, breathing shallow and fast to control it. "How? How did he die?"

"They don't say."

This was like déjà vu all over again. My mother, and now

Romi. "I need to know. Give me *his* number."

"Cameron, that's not a good idea."

"Give. Me. His number, now!"

Ralph pursed his lips. "Your mother didn't want you associating with that world."

"My mother is dead. My brother is dead. I'm done with the low profile. If Lionel Basque doesn't like it, he can shove it up his stone ass."

"Your mother signed a contract, Cam."

A contract that my paternal parentage wouldn't be revealed, and that Lionel wouldn't be liable for anything when it came to me. "Yeah, I know. But like I said. She's dead. Just give me his damned number."

Ralph nodded and left me alone in the room feeling like an ass for speaking to him that way.

My phone rang, and Levi flashed up on caller ID. I hit ignore.

Not now. I couldn't speak to him right now.

I pulled out a chair and sat with a thud. Romi was gone. Truly gone. A tear trickled down my cheek, but I dashed it away.

"Don't cry, little sister. You're not alone."

The memory rose to engulf me.

Rain lashing, battering my umbrella, and mud clinging to my new shiny black funeral shoes as they lowered the casket into the ground. My white-knuckled grip on the handle of the umbrella radiated an ache up my arm. A feeling I clung to because the rest of me was numb.

The handful of people who'd shown up for the funeral drifted away, but I stayed, standing beneath a sky that wept for me because I'd run out of tears.

The lady from social services stood a few feet away, clipboard tucked under her arm, ready to whisk me away to whatever home they'd found for me, because I had no one else. No family. No father. I was alone.

The ball of emotion in my chest pulsed, but I pushed it down. Mother would want me to be strong.

The woman took a step toward me, a signal that my time here was up, and rage starburst in my chest. She paused and looked over my shoulder, her eyes widening.

"Excuse me?" She hurried over. "Can I ask who—"

"No. You cannot." The voice was firm and authoritative.

I tipped my umbrella back to look up at the male whose shadow I now stood in. He was tall with golden hair and pale blue eyes, and he was looking at me like I was the most interesting thing he'd ever seen. There was something about him that told me I was safe.

"Excuse me," the woman said, indignant, "but I—"

"This child is under guardian protection," the man said. "I have the paperwork."

Guardians. This was a gargoyle in his human form.

The social worker blinked sharply then took the paper he handed to her. She skimmed it and nodded, backing away from us.

She was leaving? I wouldn't have to go to a group home? I peered up at my savior. "Who are you?"

The golden-haired gargoyle smiled, and my heart squeezed painfully in my chest because I knew that smile. I'd seen it in the mirror often enough. My vision blurred, eyes hot and stinging with the threat of tears.

He placed a hand on my shoulder. "Don't cry, little sister. You're not alone."

I surfaced with a sob and pressed my hand to my mouth. He'd been more than a brother. He'd been like a father. He'd been my best friend, and he'd found me a home here with Ralph. A man he'd trusted to take care of me.

Ralph and Romi were all the family I had.

And despite our ten-year age difference, Romi and I had been close. I'd longed to be a part of his world when I'd been younger, listening in awe as he told me tales of Stonehaven Academy. I'd wanted to be just like him, but reality had always hovered at the fringes of my consciousness. We were blood, but we'd never be the same. My humanity made me too weak to be a part of his world.

I was Lionel Basque's dirty little secret, the product of his illicit affair with a human. My existence was a secret, and my heritage had been a secret even to me until Romi found me ten years ago, after my mother died. I'd been ten years old. He'd taken care of me, finding me a home, and checking in every few weeks. Until now.

I'd loved him with all my heart, and now he was gone.

I had to know how and why.

Mother's death had been sudden too. A shooting at the store she worked at. But at least I'd known the details, even if the killer had gotten away.

I needed to know what had happened to Romi.

Ralph returned with a slip of paper. My mother's neat handwriting was printed on it. *In case of emergency only.* Then a phone number.

I'd found the envelope in her things after she'd died and given it to Ralph. He'd known the score by then, and he'd kept it safe. I could have used it back then, but she was gone, and the contract Lionel made her sign —the contract I'd found among her things—had made it clear that he didn't want me.

She'd signed away my claim to the Basque fortune. Made me illegitimate, not to protect his name, but to protect me from the gargoyle world. To shield me from being treated like a freak. Like I was worthless, and I'd kept her word even after her death. I'd stayed a secret, but no longer.

I dialed the number and waited, heart pounding because even though I hated the man who'd sired me, I'd loved his son. Even though I despised what Basque stood for, he was still the only blood relative I had left.

There was a soft click and then a male voice answered. "Geraldine?"

The world fell out from beneath me. Hearing my mother's name on his lips, hearing the tentative hope, the soft inhalation, confused me.

"No. This isn't Geraldine, it's Cameron, her daughter." *Her* daughter, *not* his. “Geraldine is dead.”

He was silent for several achingly long seconds.

“My mother left me this number for...emergencies.”

“Oh?”

Oh? That was it? I bit the insides of my cheeks and breathed through my nose. I couldn’t afford to lose my shit with him. I needed answers. “I want to know what happened to Romi.”

“He’s dead.” His tone was flat.

He didn’t ask me how I knew Romi, which told me he’d either known that Romi was looking after me, or he had an excellent poker voice.

“I know that he’s dead, but *how* did he die?”

“It was an unfortunate accident, and that is all I can tell you. This is not your world, child. Stay out of it and forget Romi. Get on with your life.” He hung up.

He fucking hung up.

“Cam. Are you okay?” Ralph asked.

I looked down at my trembling hands. The one holding the phone had gone gray and hard like stone. Shit. Breathe. I blinked back the red misty fog that threatened to eat away at my vision.

“He hung up.” My voice was a low vibration that bordered on a growl.

“I’m sorry.”

Sorry? Sorry, sorry, sorry. I hated that word. “I’m not having it. I’m not going to walk away like Romi never existed. You didn’t hear him when he told me Romi died in an accident. He sounded practiced. Like a fucking automaton. No emotion. No inflection. He’s hiding something.”

“Like what?”

“Like maybe Romi didn’t just die. Maybe...maybe he was killed.”

“Then why not just say it? Why call it an accident?”

“I don’t know, but I’m going to find out.” I tucked my phone into my pocket and headed for the door.

“Cameron.” Ralph grabbed my hand. “What are you going

to do?"

My smile felt tight and controlled. "I'm going to find out what happened from the gargoyles closest to him."

"But that means—"

"Yeah, I'm going to enroll at Stonehaven. I'm going to be a fucking guardian."

CHAPTER 5

CAMERON

Obviously enrolling at the prestigious gargoyle academy wasn't as easy as just wandering up to the front desk and filling out some forms. There were...tests and procedures before I'd be allowed through the hallowed arches of the gothic structure that housed our future protectors.

My gargoyle status had been kept off my birth certificate. My hybrid nature was a secret, which had been easy to keep because my abilities hadn't manifested until puberty, *after* Romi found me. How he'd found me was a mystery—one I'd probably never solve.

The first step in getting into Stonehaven involved signing up as a gargoyle at the nearest guardian registration offices in Denton, an hour's train ride from Old Town. This was one of the few places where gargoyle births could be registered, including any hybrids. This was where my mother *should* have brought me.

It was midday by the time I walked into the mundane red-brick building.

It looked like any other government office. Pin boards, plastic chairs, and tacky black-and-white checked floors. Pretty sure the staff here were all human too. Gargoyles had better things to do than grunt work. Most slept during the day so they could hunt at night. The ones that *did* work during the day, did so in human guise because sunlight prevented them from shifting to their stone monolith forms.

There was a woman in the queue in front of me, a scarf pulled up over her head. Was she gargoyle? I'd never seen a gargoyle female before and didn't know much about them. But this woman looked human. She was pushing a stroller. Could the baby be a halfblood like me?

From what Romi had told me, gargoyle babies looked human during the day and shifted at night. They also matured a lot faster than human babies, hitting puberty after five years and adulthood by ten. Romi had been twenty when he found me. Young for an elite.

But age worked differently for gargoyles, who lived for upwards of a century.

The woman handed in a form and left, but I didn't get a good look at her face.

It was my turn at reception, and the woman behind the counter looked down at my empty hands and around me at the empty space. "You must bring the child with you to register it."

I smiled thinly. "Oh, I have."

She arched a brow, gaze dropping to my abdomen. "It has to be born."

"It is." I jerked a thumb at myself. "I'm the child." I grinned at her. "Better late than never, right?"

IF MY MOTHER had been alive, she'd have been prosecuted for keeping my existence a secret. A hybrid was gargoyle property, able to be enlisted in any government role the guardians required. Once they'd taken blood and confirmed my nature, I was handed a batch of forms listing a number of roles I could serve in.

"We have vacancies here," the woman said with a kind smile. "The pension is good."

I flipped the page over to read the fine print. Then ticked the box I'd been planning to all along before handing it back to the woman.

She pressed her lips together when she saw what I'd chosen, then glanced about before speaking. "If you enroll, you have to take the entrance test like all the purebloods." She looked seriously concerned about that.

I didn't know enough about the gargoyle world to know what she was talking about, but I'd do whatever it took to get to the elite guard, and I'd find them at Stonehaven.

"I understand. I want to do the test. When can I take it?"

"Listen, the test isn't just something tha—"

"Is there a problem, Hattie?" A man appeared behind her.

Not a man, but a gargoyle male from the bulk and size of him.

Hattie straightened and smiled stiffly. "Not at all, Laxal. Everything is fine."

His gaze flicked to my application, then up to me. "A cadet, huh?" He looked back at the application, eyes narrowing. "A *halfblood* cadet?" His lip curled. "Halfbloods don't get to be cadets. Sign her up for an administration position at one of the outposts."

The way he spoke about me, as if I wasn't even there, as if I didn't matter, made me want to punch him in the mouth.

The woman shot me an apologetic look that held the edge of desperation. She feared this douchebag.

I locked gazes with him. "No."

He frowned. "Excuse me?"

"I said, no." I smiled, faux sweet. "I'll take the test to enroll as a cadet. Thank you."

He snorted. "Like I said, halfbloods don't go—"

"Is that a rule? A law?" Gargoyles were big on law and rules.

His eyes narrowed to slits.

"No," the receptionist said quickly. "It isn't."

I smiled thinly up at her boss. "Then sign me up as a cadet."

"Have it your way," he sneered. "Sign her up for the next run, which is"—he looked at something behind the counter that I couldn't see—"ah, tomorrow at sundown." The sneer turned into a smug smile.

"There's another in a week," the woman said in a small voice. "Maybe we co—"

"Tomorrow," he barked. "If she wants it so bad, she'll make it work."

He strode off into the back office, and the receptionist visibly wilted. "Oh...Oh dear. I'm so sorry."

"What for? It's just a test. I've taken plenty."

"Oh, sweetie, it's not the kind of test you're thinking of."

"What is it?"

"No one knows. We don't even know where it takes place. All I know is you either pass and end up on our system marked as a cadet, or your name comes up as deceased." She chewed on her lip. "Are you *sure* you want to do this?"

I'd be an idiot not to feel a stab of fear, but I never let fear stop me from going for the things I want.

Aside from Levi...

I shut down the annoying voice.

Right now, I wanted answers. I could either do this or spend the rest of my life wondering how my brother died. "I'm sure."

She tapped something into the computer, and the printer whirred and spat out some paper, which she folded and handed to me. "This is your ticket. The bus leaves from Central Station at two p.m. tomorrow. If you want your shot, you'll need to be on it."

I took the ticket and tucked it into my pocket. "Thank you, Hattie."

"You're welcome. And best of luck." She smiled wistfully. "It's about time one of us got into that place."

One of us? She was like me? A halfblood? She smiled and I returned it.

"I hope to see your name on my system," she said.

"I'll do my best."

I had no clue what was in store for me tomorrow, but I was one step closer to my goal, and that would have to do for now.

CHAPTER 6

CAMERON

The ticket wasn't just a ticket; it had a list of instructions on it too. Instructions that told me to pack an overnight bag with essentials and a change of clothes. That took me ten minutes. The instructions also said I had to leave my mobile phone behind.

I tugged it out of my pocket and stared at the four missed calls from Levi, and the knots in my belly tightened.

Derek moaned softly from the shadowy corner of my room. He'd stuck around as if sensing my agitation.

"Unnng arghh?"

"I don't know what they'll do."

"Mmmmg hugh argh usss?"

"No idea where the academy is. The location is secret."

He was silent, then moaned softly, words that made my heart ache.

"I'm sorry, Derek. I have to do this. I've got to go. But I'll try to come back for you if I can. I swear it. In the meantime, Ralph has a closet you can bunk in, or stay here if you want. The place is yours while I'm gone."

He groaned and then dissipated, leaving me riddled with guilt.

My phone rang. Levi again.

I owed him answers. I owed him some closure. I took a deep breath and answered the call. "Hey..."

"Cameron, fucking hell. Are you all right?"

"I'm...Can I see you?"

He was silent for a long beat. "Do you even have to ask?"

"I'll be there in thirty minutes."

I SUCKED ON Levi's bottom lip, fisting his hair and yanking his head to the side so I could get to his manly throat. He groaned as I sucked on his skin, hard enough to leave a mark.

This was bad.

This was wrong.

I hadn't come here for this, but I needed it. I needed this one last time with him before it was over.

"Fuck, princess...you make me so hard."

I hadn't wasted any time once I'd gotten here, stripping down in seconds, and climbing onto his delectable body. He was all dips and valleys of beautifully carved muscle.

Fuck talking. Fuck the breakup and the lies. He was mine for a little while longer.

His cock slid between my folds, throbbing and eager to be inside, but I wanted to play first. Nip, lick, and suck.

He groaned. "Harder, princess. Do it harder."

I bit down on his shoulder and sucked, making him swell further.

I wanted to ride him. I rose and adjusted my hips, widening my thighs so that his cock rubbed against my clit, sliding back and forth to leave me panting.

He watched me, lids heavy with desire, fingers digging into my thighs. "Fuck, yes, fuck. I need inside you. Now."

I took him deep, sinking down with a groan of satisfaction. We rocked together for a moment, adjusting, building the tempo.

He cupped my breasts, thumb flicking my hard nipples and

sending shockwaves of pleasure through me. "Pinch me."

He obliged, but not hard enough.

"Harder."

He increased the pressure, and my pussy flooded with heat. "Yes. Fuck. Yes." I rode him, slick and hard, our bodies slapping together until I crested the rise, coming with a growl that had him pulsing with his own release.

He held me afterward, stroking my hair as my heartbeat steadied. "Are you going to tell me now, Cam?"

Damn him and his insight.

A weight settled on my chest.

I'd come here to lie one last time. To tell him I didn't love him and that I couldn't see him anymore, but he deserved more than that.

It was time to tell him the truth. I owed him that much.

He didn't stop me from slipping out of his arms, as if he knew. As if he sensed that I couldn't be touching him when I told him what I'd come here to say.

I tugged my clothes on, ready for when he kicked me out.

"Cameron?" He sat up with a frown. "Just say it."

I shoved my feet into my sneakers, blinking back the threat of tears. "I'm not human, Levi." I looked up and locked gazes with him. "I'm part gargoyle, and I'm leaving to enroll in Stonehaven Academy tomorrow." He stared and stared for long moments. "Levi? Did you hear me?"

"A gargoyle, as in...a halfblood?"

I nodded. "Yeah."

He let out a bark of laughter and slumped back on the bed. "A fucking halfblood."

O-kay. I wasn't sure what to make of that reaction, so I grabbed my coat.

"Wait!" He swung his legs off the bed and stood, holding the sheets to his crotch. "It's okay. Please. Don't go."

"You're okay with me being supernatural?"

"Yes. Yes, I'm fucking okay."

No. This was all wrong. He was supposed to look at me in horror and disgust and... "What the hell is happening here?"

He was looking at me as if I was a marvel. "I knew there was a reason I was drawn to you."

I was so confused right now. "You have a thing for gargoyle chicks?"

"No, Cam. It's because I'm a halfblood too."

I'D SPENT MY whole life, until now, never having come across another halfblood, and now I'd met two in a single day. Levi was like me. Undeclared and hiding, except his sire had covertly provided for him until he'd turned eighteen.

"You can't go there," Levi said. "That place...it's fucking brutal, Cam. My mother used to work there. It's how she met my father. She told me about the training, the brutal beatings, the trials that ended up with so many gargoyles dead or injured beyond repair. These are purebloods, Cameron. What do you think that place will do to you?"

"I've got to go. My brother..." I swallowed the lump of emotion that rose up my throat. "My brother was pureblood. And he's dead. Someone killed him."

He puffed out his cheeks and shook his head. "I'm sorry to hear that, but what do *you* plan to do about it?"

I blinked across at him, momentarily stumped by his question. "What?"

"When you get there, if you find out what happened, then what?" he asked.

I hadn't thought that far, and it annoyed me that he was highlighting that fact. "Then I'll figure out what to do next, okay? I just...I need to know." My voice thickened.

He grabbed my shoulders. "Please, think about this, princess."

But I couldn't, because if I stopped to think, then reason and logic might get their claws into me, and doubt would set in, but

I owed it to Romi to find out the truth. If there was a cover-up, I owed it to him to expose it, but most of all, I owed it to myself.

I needed closure.

I tore out of Levi's grip. "I'm not your princess, and I'm not going to give up on the truth to stay here and play happy families with you, okay?"

He flinched as if I'd slapped him, but then his jaw tensed. "Do you love me?"

"What?"

"Are you in love with me?"

Yes. Yes, I was falling in love with him, but if I said it—if I allowed those emotions to flood my body—then they'd weaken me. They'd make me want to stay, and I'd forever wonder about the truth. Even if I *did* summon the courage to confess my feelings, then still left, the test to get into the academy could prove fatal, ending with Levi even more heartbroken than if he believed I didn't return his feelings at all.

"Cameron..." He took a step closer. "Answer me." His tone softened. "Do you love me?"

"No. No, I don't love you. This..." I waved a finger between him and me. "This was just sex. Really good sex."

He exhaled sharply.

I headed for the door, ignoring the hurt on his face, ignoring the ache in my chest. "And now it's over. We're over."

"You're lying," he called after me. "I felt it. I fucking felt it—"

I slammed the door, cutting off his words, and dashed away my tears. I had to do this. I had to go. And I had to make this a clean break.

Loving Levi was not an option right now.

But if we were meant to be, then we'd find each other again someday.

I had to believe that.

CHAPTER 7

CAMERON

There were two gargoyles on the bus. A female and a male. They looked young, but looks could be deceiving when it came to the stone-kind. The driver was also a gargoyle shifter in his human form. Easy to tell because even in human form the stone-kind were large and bulky, all around six-foot-five and built to take a punch. He had a mulish look about him, too, as if driving the bus was an insult. He practically snatched my ticket from my hand, then raked me over.

His lip curled in disgust. "You want to die?" he asked.

I smiled sweetly. "Nope. Do you?"

He balked, and the male gargoyle on the bus snickered.

"Your funeral," the driver muttered. "Sit down and hold on."

He hit the gas before I could park my ass, and I went flying. A strong grip on my arm stopped me face-planting the floor.

"I got you," a female voice said. She hauled me into the seat in front of hers because there was no room on her seat. Her long frame forced her to sit angled with her back to the window and her legs stretched across a seat that was built to hold two humans.

So, this was what a gargoyle female looked like?

Old Town was policed mainly by human hunters, and gargoyle intervention was rare. Their forces were concentrated east where the graynite issue was strongest, so I couldn't help but stare a little.

Her dark hair was cut short and tucked behind her ears, but you could tell it had a curl to it, even though she'd done her best to slick it down. The style accentuated her angular face. But sparkling hazel eyes, fringed in thick lashes, and a full mouth softened her sharp features.

"You're staring," she growled. "Rude."

The bus lurched, then whizzed around a corner, ignoring the speed limit. "I'm sorry."

She *harrumphed*. "He's right, you know. You're going to die today."

Wow. Blunt much? "You don't know that for sure."

"Yes, I do." She sat back and looked across the aisle at the male gargoyle. "Tell her, Touron."

Touron was more wiry than bulky, and he also sat with his back to the window—the only way for them to get their bodies to fit on a bus built for humans.

"The test will be designed to kill the weaker gargoyles," he said. "You're only half gargoyle, so you'll definitely die."

"Thanks for the vote of confidence."

"It's called reality," the female said.

The doubt and fear I'd been staving off pricked at my senses. Was this me committing suicide? Should I have listened to Levi?

Romi's face filled my mind. His smile, his laughter, the warmth of his hugs. I couldn't walk away. I *wouldn't* be a coward. "If I die, then I'll die trying."

The female side-eyed me. "The gargoyle way must be built into our genes."

"It's our curse," Touron said. "Sheer pig-headed stubbornness. *And* we never forget a slight. Trust me, if you piss off a gargoyle, you know you're gonna get served at some point. Might be icy cold by the time it gets to you, but it's gonna come. We're like elephants."

I arched a brow. "Bulky and gray."

He snort-laughed. "Nah, we never forget." He wagged a finger at me. "But good one. You know my name, and this brittle rock is Sharniza. And you are?"

"Cameron."

"Well, it's nice to meet you, Cameron." He grinned, but a moment later the smile dropped. "Shame we won't get to know you better." He slumped in his seat, as if the realization had taken the wind out of his sails.

"Maybe she's lucky that way," Sharniza said softly.

What did she mean?

The bus jolted and shuddered.

"Oh, here we go." Touron slapped the back of his seat. "Get ready forrrr—"

The world melted, colors spiraling and whirling. I was broken. Lost. Floating. I was gonna be sick. But before my stomach could eject lunch, the world righted itself, leaving me gasping a lungful of air.

"You don't hold your breath when going through a warp," Sharniza said, annoyed with me. "Don't you know anything?"

No. No I didn't. Because most of these things had been kept from me all my life. I was going into this blind. Stupidly and stubbornly. Mother would have kicked my ass so hard.

Panic formed a vise in my chest. No. Focus. I might not know much about the gargoyle world, but I was a fucking Basque. A halfblood, yes, but with the blood of one of the most powerful gargoyle families running through my veins.

If any halfblood could get through this, it was me.

I peeled myself off my seat. "I'm a fast learner."

Touron offered me his hand. "If, by some insane miracle, you make it through this, we are so gonna be friends."

I gripped his strong fingers, allowing him to pull me up.

"There are no friends at the academy," Sharniza said flatly. "Not until you qualify and find your pack. You're a fool if you think otherwise."

She pushed out of her seat, ducking her head so as not to smack it on the roof of the bus and stomped to the front.

"Don't mind her," Touron said. "She's an Aziza. She has a lot to prove."

Aziza? That name was familiar. Wait...It was one of the big five. Who were the others again? Halle...Mason and...shit...Albion, and of course, Basque. That was it.

I wasn't sure *why* they were the most powerful, though. Just that they were.

The doors of the bus squealed open, jolting me to focus on the world outside the windows. The twisty streets of Old Town had been replaced by rolling fields and forestland bathed in the orange and crimson hues of a setting sun. Scents of fresh earth and pollen drifted through the open doors, a far cry from the smoggy atmosphere of Old Town.

"Where in the Rim lands are we?"

"This is Stonehaven territory," Touron said. "Acres of land designed to test the next generation of guardians. But don't be fooled, there are threats here, too, threats that the next generation must control and subdue." He smiled, but it didn't quite reach his eyes. "At least that's what the induction manuals say."

I couldn't help but relax around this guy. "You got a manual?"

"Nope. But my brother did when he enrolled three years ago." He shrugged. "I got a peek at it when he.... Interesting stuff."

"So, your brother's a guardian then?"

The warmth left his eyes. "He was, yeah." He looked like he wasn't going to elaborate but then changed his mind. "He was killed a few months ago on a mission. Grotesque attack."

"Grotesque?"

"Used to be on the gargoyle team, but they work for the graynites now."

He'd lost his brother too. Telling him about Romi wasn't an option, not if I wanted to keep my identity a secret and root out the truth. If the gargoyles knew I was a Basque and if there was some cover up, then they'd clam up even more.

"I'm sorry for your loss."

He smiled at me with sad eyes, then tipped his head toward

the exit. "Come on, we should go."

The driver was gone, but there were three other buses parked on the grass outside, and more gargoyles climbing out of them.

They cracked their necks and stretched, obviously pleased to be out of the yellow metal contraptions much too small for their bulks.

I caught sight of our driver huddled with three other large males wearing driver uniforms.

Sharniza stood alone in a clear spot, away from the other gargoyles who seemed to have formed their own little groups.

I felt their gazes on me, heard whispers of half-blood and bait, and my blood simmered. Romi had hinted how it would be for a halfblood. Explained the derision the pureblood had for my kind, and how fraternizing between human and gargoyle was frowned upon. But seeing it...feeling it firsthand, was a stomach-turning experience.

It made me feel lesser. Dirty somehow, and I hated that.

"We're not all assholes," Touron said. "But it looks like this month's quota is full of them."

I couldn't help but smile. "Yeah?"

"Gargoyles come from all over the rim lands," Touron said. "From each major settlement, not just from Arcadia."

I knew this one. "The home of the power five?"

"And a few other houses affiliated with them through mate bonds. Arcadia is a stronghold, but if we have another dark event, I doubt the rabble will be allowed in."

"Aren't gargoyles supposed to be protectors of humanity?"

"Oh, yeah, and I'm sure they'll save enough of the humans to stop them going extinct."

"Figures."

"Some gargoyles are traditional in their views. They believe in the cause. Believe that humanity is worth saving." He frowned at Sharniza. "Some don't even want to be here."

Wait a second. "You're saying it's compulsory?"

"Honor and duty are always compulsory," Touron said, fist to his chest. "But yes. It kinda is."

"You're very...*relaxed* for a gargoyle."

Shadows formed in the depths of his forest-green eyes. "Yeah, I need to work on that."

The air crackled and popped, and another bus appeared a few meters away.

This was insane. "How do they know where to materialize?"

"It's a warp zone," Touron said. "This whole area." He made a circle with his hands.

There was so much to learn. "So, now what?"

"We wait," Sharniza said, joining us again.

"Not for long, though?"

A shadow fell over the world as the sun finally set. Touron made a strange rumbling sound, and Sharniza's hazel eyes flashed green.

"Now we're talking." Her voice dropped an octave.

She stepped away from us, her body morphing and changing, growing a foot until she was looming over me, her gray stone-like form dwarfing mine. Around me, the other gargoyles were doing the same, shifting and changing until I was surrounded by hulking winged gray creatures with tails, wings, talons, and feet built for gripping ledges.

There were two other females aside from Sharniza and me. They stood together, their stony, muscular frames encased in leggings and crop tops that left their eight packs on show. Sharniza's and Touron's clothes were also intact. They'd stretched to accommodate their new frames.

Touron grinned down at me, fangs glinting. "Cool, huh?" He flexed a bicep, and his T-shirt strained but didn't rip. "Lastonflex material. Best invention yet."

Gargoyles weren't made of stone, but their bodies could shift to become stone if need be. Their skin was hard as nails, and tough to pierce either way, though.

Wings snapped at the air as the gargoyles stretched their formidable appendages, and an empty pit of loss opened inside me. A feeling of incompleteness. A longing for something more.

Sundown affected me, too, giving me heightened senses, speed, and strength, but none of that equaled what it did for a full-blood gargoyle.

“They’re here!” someone bellowed.

All eyes were on the sky and the two figures flying toward us. Each Gargoyle’s wingspan had to be at least twelve feet, and their speed probably a hundred miles an hour, and shit, they were descending. Silver lines glinted on their black uniforms.

The colors of the elites.

The colors of Romi’s team.

CHAPTER 8

CAMERON

The elites landed with a thud that shook the earth and sent soil and pebbles flying. They were massive, with arms and legs like tree trunks, thick necks and hands that could snap a person like a twig.

It made sense that they'd belong to the five-strong gargoyle shifter team that Romi had been a part of. Had Romi looked this huge when in gargoyle form? Had he had a tail like these two? Did *all* gargoyles have tails?

A quick glance at the potential cadets confirmed that every gargoyle here certainly did. But not all the tails were the same. Some were smooth and thick with bulbous ends made for smashing. Some were barbed with arrowhead ends. Others simply swished back and forth, reminding me of an elephant trunk. Touron's tail was smooth and thick with an arrow tip, and Sharniza's was serrated. They both looked lethal and dangerous and standing between them, it was hard to not feel like a piece of limp lettuce.

My pulse thrummed hard in my throat as the elite strode toward us.

These males had known my brother.

Romi hadn't spoken about his work or his team in detail, but he'd mentioned them in passing, and I'd latched on to the information, greedy for any nugget about his life when he was away from me.

He'd mentioned Serath, the team leader once, and someone called Prasan, who he'd said was super intelligent. He'd dropped the name Orix, too, and talked about the kick-ass female on the team whose name I couldn't recall. Which of the three males were these two?

The moon was high and bright, allowing me to get a good look at them. One had golden hair streaked with silver, and the other's long locks were such a deep brown they looked black in the moonlight.

The dark-haired one was slightly taller than his companion, and for some reason, I couldn't take my eyes off his commanding frame. He stepped forward and lifted his strong chin to survey us. Moonlight caressed the hard, flat planes of his brutal face, lighting up the scar that ran from his temple over his eyelid and down his cheek. What could have done that? What could have scarred a gargoyle?

My gaze dropped to the gold chain around his neck and the heart-shaped pendant that hung from it. I couldn't see the design, but I knew what it was. It was the elite symbol. Romi had owned one too. The silver-haired gargoyle also sported one. I had no clue why the elites wore the chains, Romi had always changed the subject when I'd asked.

The dark-haired elite's gaze skimmed over each entrant but stopped when it landed on me. A fission of awareness shot through me, and my breath locked in my lungs. His eyes were beautiful, light blue, ringed in black. Husky eyes. They bored into me, pinning me to the spot for achingly long seconds before dismissing me to move on.

I exhaled. My whole body thrumming so hard my head felt light.

What the heck was that about?

"You're all here because you chose to be," he said.

My pulse kicked up at the sound of his voice—a gritty, abrasive vibration that seemed to rub against my senses.

"You're here because you think you're worthy of a place at Stonehaven," he continued. "Worthy to serve. To be a guardian, maybe even an initiate."

Initiate units answered to the elite team. The only way to make it into one of those high-level units was to rank high enough during basic training to get into the initiation program.

My stomach fluttered with nerves because when I laid it out like that in my head, it seemed impossible.

No. No doubt. Not now. Not here.

"But before you can be allowed through the hallowed gates of Stonehaven, you will need to prove yourself worthy," he said. "You will be tested. A minor test of skill and endurance." His lip curled around the word minor. "Although, it might be too much for some of you?" His gaze flicked to me and settled there. "Some of you will fail before you start." His gaze lingered and heat filled my chest—annoyance and something else I couldn't define. "So, I'll make an exception on this *one* occasion and offer you the chance to leave." He was looking at me, and now everyone was staring.

My cheeks heated, shame and anger making my breath come fast.

The silver-haired gargoyle growled softly. "Serath?"

Serath? The leader. Romi's leader.

This was him.

Serath ignored his companion and continued. "Walk away now. Get on a bus and stay there, and you will be taken back to your lives. There is no need to die today."

There was no doubt he was speaking directly to me, even though he was sweeping the crowd again.

Murmurs skimmed across the gathered, and sharp smiles were thrown my way.

"Shit," Touron said. "Maybe you *should* go, Cameron."

He was right. This was my chance to walk away. Go back to my life and forget about the truth. About Romi. I could go back to Levi and tell him how I truly felt.

I closed my eyes and fought the panic, the human survival

instinct, my mortal weakness that screamed at me that I couldn't do this. That I was making a mistake. Instead, I focused on my gargoyle nature, on the part of me that killed monsters for a living. The part of me that could run faster and hold my breath for longer than any of these fuckers. The part of me that was a Basque.

Then I opened them and stared Serath straight in the eyes. "I'm not going anywhere." I spoke under my breath, for Touron to hear, but the flare of Serath's nostrils and the narrowing of his husky eyes told me that he'd heard me too.

He grunted, turned on his heel, and shot up into the night sky, as if he couldn't wait to get away from us.

The silver-haired one's smooth, rumbling voice replaced the gritty growl of his leader's. "Follow me and keep up."

His powerful thighs bunched, and then he launched himself into the sky after Serath, wings flaring, snapping, and catching to sweep him high.

It never failed to amaze me how these powerful beings managed to stay airborne. I'd asked Romi once, and he'd explained it with aerodynamics and magic. But it had all gone over my head.

Gargoyles shot into the sky all around me, and my stomach dropped.

How the heck was I going to follow them?

Sharniza shook her head with a knowing look. "You should have taken the bus home."

She broke into a jog, then leaped into the air to join the others.

"It's all right," Touron said. "I don't know what we'll have to do once we get to where we're going, but I can carry you there."

Relief made my knees weak. "Thank you."

"Turn around," he said. I planted my back to him, and he wrapped one huge hand easily around my waist. "Don't wriggle."

My feet left the ground, air whooshing over me, raking through my hair and stealing my breath as we climbed into the night sky. Euphoria swelled in my chest as Touron's wings splayed to catch the updraft, taking us higher. I let out a whoop, and Touron's laugh rumbled through me.

"Pretty epic, huh?" he said.

"It is! It so fucking is!" This was what I was missing. This power and freedom. But I'd take what I could from this moment and sear it into my mind. "Thank you."

"Don't thank me yet. Who knows what's in store for us."

But in that moment, I didn't care. In that moment, my senses were in overload, taking in the vista of moonlit fields and silver-kissed canopies of forestland below. The scent of ozone filled my head, and the symphony of beating wings surrounded me. In that moment, I was a part of something bigger. In that moment, I was one of them.

It helped that the gargoyles who had stared and sneered at me were now too focused on what was to come to pay me any mind.

Moths spawned in my belly, and I breathed through a sudden wave of anxiety. I could do this. I had to do this.

We flew past acres of forestland and a spattering of buildings clustered into a small village, and farther, toward a mountain range. The air grew cool and misty, and the distinctive sound of rushing water drifted up to us.

The elite led us into a valley in the mountains that morphed into a ravine housing a rushing tide of water. Rapids churned and flowed, hard and fast.

The elite flew higher and perched on the closest side of the ravine. They crouched, bodies bunched and ready to leap, waiting for us to join them.

The ledge was wide and deep with plenty of room for us all to land.

"Tuck in your legs," Touron instructed.

I bent my knees and held onto the hand wrapped around my waist as we took a dive toward the ledge to join the others. Touron set me down gently, ignoring the sneers and growls the other gargoyles threw his way.

They were angry that he'd helped me?

Seriously?

"Weakness should not be shouldered," a gargoyle with dark

blue hair snarled. "Weakness can infect us all." He closed in on us, and two other gargoyles joined him, trying to pin Touron in. "She doesn't belong, and you showed weakness in feeling sorry for her."

Rage starbursted in my chest. "Back off." I slipped between Touron and them, hands bunched into fists, body vibrating with anger. I didn't give a shit how much bigger than me they were, didn't care that one flap of a wing could knock me off the ledge. All that mattered was smacking down the bully, and I didn't need huge fists to do that, just a little wit.

I relaxed my fists and crossed my arms affecting an unintimidated air. "Aren't guardians meant to protect humans?"

His eyes narrowed. "Of course."

"Hello, half human here." I jerked a thumb toward myself.

Blue-hair's sneer deepened, menace radiating from every inch of his body. "You're either human or you're not. There's no *half* about it."

I held my ground, tipping my chin up to look him in the eye. "Yeah, well you obviously flunked genetics class, didn't you?"

Touron choked back a laugh.

"You think that's funny, Lomax?" blue boy asked. He shook his head and turned away. "Did you think it was funny when your brother got taken down by a grotesque?"

Touron went as still as stone behind me, and the air spiked with murderous intent.

"Look me in the eye and say that again," Touron said.

Blue boy turned to face us, his wide mouth cocked in a smug smile. "I said—"

"Back off." Sharniza shot forward and shoved him hard enough to force him to take a step back. "You make me sick, Curi. You're a fucking stain, and if you open your mouth again, I'll wipe you clean off this ledge, you hear me?"

Curi dropped low, his muscles rippling and bunching with tension as if he wasn't sure whether to attack or retreat.

Sharniza stood over him, hands on hips, unfazed.

Curi hawked and spat. "You're making a mistake, Shar. You

need to stick with your own kind."

Sharniza snorted. "I don't need to *stick* with anyone. I got this. Solo."

"Then why are you standing up for him?" another gargoyle asked. "He's a no one."

"Because I don't like bullies or assholes, and Curi..." She snorted in derision. "He's the best of both."

"Enough!" Serath called from a ledge above us.

How long had he been up there, watching, and why hadn't he intervened?

"It's time to start the test." Once again, his piercing husky eyes looked past everyone and focused on me. "There will be no aiding another potential in completing this task. You may work together, but you must complete the task under your own steam, using your own faculties."

Shit, what was he going to ask us to do?

"Your task is simple. To get from this side of the ravine to the other."

Curi chuffed and flexed his wings, and my heart sank.

This was a test of flight?

"Your path won't be uninterrupted," Serath said.

A horn blared so loud it made my teeth rattle. When the blast ended the world was muted and eerily silent. But that silence was soon broken by angry screeches coming from across the ravine.

A dark cloud rose to skim the bottom of the full moon before spiraling down to circle the chasm.

"Terror hawks," Touron said. "Fuck."

Huge birds with long sharp beaks swooped and flapped in agitation. "What are they?"

"Evil fuckers that'll take a chunk out of anything," Sharniza replied.

"You have an hour to make it across," Serath said. "You'll either succeed or end up as terror hawk bait."

Bait.

That's what they'd called me.

He launched himself into the air and vanished from view.

"You want to go solo, huh?" Curi said to Sharniza. "Try getting across solo in this task." He chuckled cruelly as he joined two other gargoyles.

They put their heads together to strategize.

"I'm sorry," Touron said to me. "I'd fly you across if it were allowed. But he said to get across under your own steam."

I swallowed past the dry lump of dread in my throat. "It's fine. Thank you for getting me this far." I didn't want to ask what happened to those that stayed on this side of the ravine. We were in the middle of nowhere, surrounded by wilderness and goodness knew what kind of creatures.

"We need to work together," Touron said to Sharniza.

I couldn't blame them for dismissing me. They had a task to complete. A place to bag at the academy, and I was dead weight right now.

The receptionist had been clear on one fact. *No one* came back from these tests. You either got enrolled or deceased.

I did not want to be deceased.

Think, Cameron, think.

The crash of water far below interrupted my thoughts and sent them spiraling. Because there *was* a way across for me.

It just wasn't by air.

It was by water.

"Hey, guys." I stepped between the two gargoyles. "I need a favor."

"The rules are clear," Sharniza said, impatiently. "We can't carry you across."

"I know. But dropping me into the water isn't carrying me across, is it?"

CHAPTER 9

CAMERON

"That's insane," Touron whisper-hissed.

"No." Sharniza kept her voice low too. "It's brilliant." Her lips curved in an approving smile. "Perfect, in fact. We can completely avoid the terror hawks if we swim across the ravine."

I grinned up at her. "You're gonna take a dip with me?"

She matched my grin. "I'm a strong swimmer."

Touron looked between us. "The current is lethal down there."

"Not as lethal as a riled-up flock of terror hawks," Sharniza pointed out. Then to me. "I'm in. I'll get you to the water, but then you're on your own."

"Fine by me."

Touron ran a large hand down his face. "I suppose it's not breaking the rules. He said not to assist anyone across the ravine and dropping you into the water is hardly an assist. More like murder." He winced. "Are you sure?"

"We're sure," Sharniza and I said in unison.

"Okay...Okay." He strode to the edge of the ledge to look down at the churning, frothing river.

"See you on the other side," Curi called out. "If you make it."

He and his minions sprang off the ledge and into the sky,

flying in a kind of crisscross formation to evade the terror hawks. The other gargoyles followed suit, and the air filled with the angry flap of wings and hungry caws.

The flock converged, attacking with a vengeance. The gargoyles evaded as best they could, dipping, then rising to get past the threat, but the terror hawks were faster, and screams and bellows ripped the air as they sank their beaks into what they considered prey.

"Stone skin doesn't work that great when in flight," Touron muttered to himself. "Shit."

A gargoyle fell, then another, but terror hawks zoomed across the ravine, catching them with snapping razor beaks before they could get close to the water. The crunch of bone was almost too loud.

"Fuck it," Touron said. "I'm in."

I tugged off my boots and yanked off my top layer of clothing. It was going to be freezing in the water, but my gargoyle nature would keep me warm, and my skin would harden as I hit the surface, protecting me from serious injury.

"We'll have to shift once we hit the surface," Touron said to Sharniza.

"I know."

Touron reached for me, but Sharniza beat him to it. "I've got her."

I looked up at the female. "Don't drop me on a rock, okay?"

She gave me a crooked grin. "If I thought you were serious competition, I'd be tempted."

"Um...thanks?"

She wrapped her hands around my torso. "Hold on until I tell you to let go."

"Got it."

My feet left the ground as she carried me to the edge. The wind howled and battered my frame, but she tucked me against her body, shielding me with her powerful bulk.

I glanced across at Touron, but his attention was on the waves below. "On the count of three," he said. "One, tw—"

Sharniza dove, taking me with her.

My stomach dipped hard as we fell like a boulder, hurtling toward the water.

Fuuuuck

Her wings unfurled with a whoosh, catching air and slowing our descent. "Now!"

I let go of her and forced my body into a dive formation as I fell toward the dark waters.

Cold spray hit me a moment before I crashed into the river. Ice engulfed me, shocking the breath from my body.

I sank like a stone, legs kicking, arms reaching desperately for air. By the time my head broke the surface, heat was racing through my veins, and my body was in protection mode.

The rush and crash of water was so loud it was impossible to focus on anything else but this mighty element. I defaulted to the front crawl, swimming *with* the current not against it. It would take me a little longer to get across, but I'd save energy. Waves of ice water battered me, trying to break my momentum, trying to force me to fight back, but I succumbed to nature, riding each wave, and following the current.

The world above seemed far away, and a bubble of self-awareness formed around me. It was just me and the water. Just me and the other side of the ravine.

Long minutes passed, my limbs ached, the shield around me was failing. Needles of chill pricked my skin.

Come on.

Don't fail me now.

The other side was so close and wait...there was someone there. A figure waited on the other side. Another one joined it a moment later.

Had Sharniza or Touron made it across already?

I went under briefly, coming up sputtering and choking. Shit. Something brushed my hip and a chill, unrelated to the icy temperature shot through me.

There was something in the water with me.

CHAPTER 10

SERATH

"Look at them," Orix says. "Eager. Hungry."

"Are we talking about the gargoyles or the terror hawks?"

"Both." He shakes his head. "I always find this part distasteful, don't you?"

It doesn't matter what I think. This is how it is. These are the rules. "We all had to take the test. The first of many."

These potentials have no idea what they're in for. What happens at the academy stays at the academy. It's the only way to ensure the tests and trials aren't compromised. The only way to ensure that anyone who passes and climbs the ranks deserves to be there.

We perch on the ledge, low down where the ravine takes a turn. From this vantage we can watch the trial take place and count the number of gargoyles that fall. The terror hawks will retreat in an hour or so. They'll need to rest their wings, but until then, the gargoyles will have to fight to get to the other side.

Flight is a vital part of our role as guardians. Aerial combat is essential. Which brings my thoughts to the half human, tiny and fragile, still on the starting ledge. Two gargoyles remain with her. What are they planning?

"She won't make it across," Orix says. "Shame. She has spine.

I wonder who sired her?"

"It'll be on her application."

"It isn't. I checked. It says *father unknown*."

"Bastard, whoever it is." I have no time for absent fathers. For males who don't take responsibility for their spawn, hybrid or not. She's one of us, even if she doesn't belong in the guard.

The way she stood up to the Mason boy was both stupid and admirable. He could break her easily. Hurt her easily.

My anklet heats.

No. I'm imagining it.

This is a stressful time.

Wait, what are they doing?

The female gargoyle grabs hold of the halfblood.

"Well, what do you know." Orix chuckles gruffly as the trio drops off the ledge and dives into the water.

My breath catches.

She's in the water. The fool is in the fucking water.

"Smart move for the gargoyles," Orix says. "Not so much for the halfblood."

I can't move. I can't breathe, and the heat from my anklet stings my skin. Where is she?

She surfaces a moment later, and the rush of relief leaves me dizzy. Move you fool. Swim.

She does so with strong, sure, strokes, working with the current, not against it. Smart woman.

A shadowy fin slices through the waves toward the swimming trio, and my chest tightens. Come on. Faster. You can do it.

"She's a strong swimmer," Orix observes. "Faster than the other two." He crouches on the ledge, gripping stone with his feet and leaning forward to watch the race.

The race, not between halfblood and gargoyle, but between halfblood and raptor fish.

If she's bitten, she's as good as dead. There is no cure for their venom.

She goes under briefly, and my anklet burns my skin. I bite back a hiss.

"Serath?" Orix asks. "What is it?"

The raptor is almost on her now. "Dammit, woman can't you go faster?"

"Serath? Hey!" Orix says.

I'm already airborne, flying stealthily and low enough to skim the water with my feet. I land on the ledge opposite.

Where is she? There. The raptor coming up behind her. My heart slams, and my ankle flares with heat again.

Dammit.

Orix lands beside me with a thud. "Please tell me this isn't what I think it is."

"Shut up." My words are a growl.

There's something else in the water coming up fast to her left.

A river snake.

Not poisonous but lethal if it gets a grip on its prey.

My wings flex, desperate to take flight.

"Dammit, Serath," Orix growls. "Let her die. You have to."

Yes, that would be the wise move. The sane move.

The raptor bumps the female, and I grip the stone ledge so hard that rock crumbles.

"It'll be over soon," Orix says. "Stay strong."

Because that first brush is a tease, the second will be a bite, then it'll drag her down and hold her there until she suffocates. Even if she manages to get away, the toxin will kill her before she reaches the shore.

Doing nothing is the wise choice for me.

The raptor fin circles back and cuts toward her. But it looks as if the snake will get to her first.

It'll be over.

I need to let it be over.

My anklet sears my skin, fighting to keep me in check, but primal instinct is too strong. I make to launch myself into the air.

"No!" Orix slams into me. "I won't let you do this."

"Let me go. She'll die. Dammit, Orix. She'll die."

"I know," Orix says. "I'm sorry."

CHAPTER 11

CAMERON

Of course, the waters would be infested with something. Probably something equally as dangerous and hungry as the terror hawks.

My lungs ached, my muscles threatened to seize, and the urge to swim against the current to get to the other side faster gnawed at my chest, but I quashed it. I could do this. I was so close, but now I knew that there was something in the water my senses were alert to it.

It was coming for me. Shit. I wasn't going to—

Something slammed into my side, then a vise gripped my thigh, and the river swallowed me.

Down, down, into the depths.

No. Fucking hell, no!

I twisted and kicked out at the thing clinging to my thigh. Stone skin had activated, so I couldn't feel its bite, but it had me.

It was too dark to see. The water churning and wild. But I got the impression that the creature was huge. I had to pry it off me. I grabbed at its head, and the pressure on my thigh increased.

How far down were we?

I kicked again, but the thing rolled me, and the next moment there was pressure around my legs, holding them together. No. Shit.

A snake? A river snake? Fucking hell.

I slammed my fist into his head over and over, but the water slowed the momentum, making the blows ineffectual.

My body hit the riverbed, and the snake tightened its grip. Panic swelled my lungs, and the need to breathe was almost overwhelming.

No. I had to hold on.

Find something to fight back with.

I swept my hand across the riverbed and grazed something hard and jagged. A rock. Yes! The river snake was crushing my leg. Stone skin wouldn't hold much longer. I brought the rock down on its head and pushed as hard as I could until I felt something give.

The snake's grip slackened, and I kicked myself free, lungs burning with the need for oxygen. I needed air. I needed it now!

I pushed up to the surface. How deep was this damned river? Please. Gods, please. My vision darkened.

No.

Please...

I broke the surface and sucked in air like it was the nectar of the gods. Fuck...oh fuck.

I was alive.

I could make it across

The two gargoyle figures I'd spotted earlier were still on the ledge on the other side of the ravine.

I wasn't so sure they were Touron and Sharniza any longer, though.

SERATH

I FIGHT TO get free as the halfblood goes under, but Orix has me pinned. My wings are trapped. I can't break free.

"It's okay," Orix says. "This is for the best. You know it is."

My chest burns as if it's me under water. As if I'm the one

drowning.

"It's over," Orix says. "It's over." He releases me, and I shove him away hard enough to make him stumble.

"You bastard."

He nods. "I know."

I look out at the river, at the spot where she went under, my insides in knots. I'm sorry, little one. So sorr—

Her head breaks the surface, and she takes a lungful of air.

"What the fuck?" Orix says. "How the fuck?"

Triumph blooms. The little halfblood has claws. But she's not safe yet. The raptor that lost her to the snake has spotted her again. It's beelining toward her.

"Don't," Orix says softly.

She looks my way. Looks right at me. Her beautiful gray eyes wide with shock.

Fire circles my ankle, and my thighs bunch, my body working on instinct.

"Serath, don't!" Orix makes a grab for me, but too late this time.

I'm airborne.

I arc through the air then slice into the water, diving and rocketing toward the raptor. I slam into it before it can reach her. Down into the depths we go. It struggles and bucks, but I grip its jaws and tear it in two. The fire circling my ankle ebbs and dies.

She's safe.

For now.

But me...I'm fucked.

CAMERON

A SHADOW SLICED across my periphery and vanished into the water.

Wait...

One of the figures from the other side was gone.

Had the gargoyle jumped into the water?

Not my problem.

Focus.

Swim.

There could be more eels, more dangers in the river.

Imminent threat galvanized me, adding fuel to my waning fire and acting like a butt rocket to push me over the finish line.

My fingers grazed rock.

Oh, gods. Yes.

I gripped stone and hauled myself up the rock face notch by notch until I felt the lip of the ledge proper. A sob broke from my throat. Muscles screaming in protest, I dragged myself up and over, then rolled onto my back to stare up at the night sky still teaming with terror hawks and desperate gargoyles.

I'd made it.

Ha, take that, purebloods! If I weren't so wiped, I'd have gotten up and twerked. Maybe in a moment. Just one more minute.

A shadow blocked the moon, and ocean-blue eyes stared down at me from beneath ruffled silvery hair. This elite had sharp, clever features with winged eyebrows. It was a pleasant gargoyle face, almost handsome, if you could call gargoyles handsome.

"Hi." I grinned up at him, still swimming in euphoria at my win. "Wanna help me up?" I held out my hand.

His eyes flinched, and he gently gripped my palm with a hand that could have crushed every bone in mine if he'd wanted to. But he didn't pull me up, and the first trickle of unease filtered through my bubble of elation.

"What's the—"

He yanked me off my feet and grabbed my neck. "I'm sorry for what I must do." His voice was a low, apologetic grumble.

Terror tightened my scalp. "What are you—"

"Orix!"

Serath smashed into Orix, who released me abruptly. My ass hit the ground, and pain shot up my tailbone.

Orix slammed into the rock face with Serath's hands around *his* neck. The elite leader's teeth were bared in a mask of fury. "No!"

Orix grabbed his shoulders. "You're a fool!"

The gargoyles tussled for a moment before shooting into the air.

What in the actual fuck?

"Can't believe you beat us," Sharniza said as she climbed onto the ledge in human form. She stood and slicked back her hair, squeezing out the water.

Touron joined us a moment later. "Now *that* was a rush." He shook his head, dislodging droplets of water.

I stared numbly at him, and his smile dropped. "Cameron?"

"Hey?" Sharniza snapped her fingers. "What's wrong with you?"

I blinked up at her, finally piecing together what had almost just happened. "I think...I think an elite just tried to kill me."

SHARNIZA SCANNED THE sky, searching for the elites, but there was no sign of them.

"Why would he want to kill you?" Touron asked.

"I dunno. When I see him again, maybe I'll ask."

He flinched, looking hurt by my sharp tone. "There's no need to be mean."

"I'm sorry. Look. I don't know why. Maybe because I made it across. Maybe because they don't want me at the academy, and now they have to let me in?" The numb shock was gone, and I was pissed.

Fuming.

In fact, I was surprised there wasn't steam coming off my body. "If they think they can get rid of me that easily, they're delusional. I did not just fight a river snake and pass this fucking challenge to get my windpipe crushed by an elitist bastard."

"There was a river snake in there?" Touron asked, eyes wide.

"Fucking huge. I almost died, but I didn't. I made it across, only for him to try and finish the job. No. Hell no." I reached for my neck, still sore from the attack. "He would have succeeded, too, if Serath hadn't intervened."

"Calm down," Sharniza said to me. "If what you say is true—"

"*If*? I think I know when someone is trying to kill me."

"Okay, if they want you dead, then they'll probably try again."

"Gee, thanks for that."

Her mouth turned down. "You say Serath *stopped* Orix."

Orix, my wannabe murderer. "Yeah, he was furious."

"So, Serath *doesn't* want you dead," Touron said.

I pinched the bridge of my nose, casting my mind over the events of the last few minutes. The swim to get to the ledge, the thing in the water. "I saw two gargoyles on the ledge further down. Then something bumped my hip in the water, and I panicked. After that, the snake got me and I went under. I came up, and I think...I think maybe there were more of those things coming for me, but something flew into the water. I think one of the gargoyles..."

"You think one of them jumped in?" Sharniza chewed on her cheeks.

"Was Orix wet when he grabbed you?" Touron asked.

"No...but Serath... I think Serath was. Water splashed me when he grabbed Orix."

"So, Serath was in the water." Sharniza's eyes narrowed.

"It's obvious there's something strange going on here," Touron said. "We need to stick together."

"We?" Sharniza scoffed. "No. This isn't my problem." She shifted into gargoyle form and shook out her wings. "I'm headed to the top and victory. I suggest you do the same," she said to Touron.

"We might not have gotten across if not for Cameron's idea," Touron said.

"And I'm grateful," Sharniza said to me. "But that's where our association ends." She leaped up, latched onto the wall, and began to climb, her epic body moving with sinuous grace.

Touron sighed. "I feel bad for her. The pressure must be intense."

"Aziza blood?"

"Yeah, big five and all." He gave me a crooked smile. "At least you and I don't have to worry about living up to the family name."

A needle of guilt stabbed at me, but I shook it off. "Nope, I just have to worry about living."

He frowned. "Sharniza may not want to be friends, but I do. I've got your back."

"Why? Because you feel sorry for me?"

He shook his head. "Nah. Because you remind me of my brother."

I arched a brow. "Seriously?" I looked down at myself. "Your brother?"

He chuckled and reached out to ruffle my hair. "You're mouthy and feisty, and you don't quit, just like him. He got on my nerves, but I loved him. Maybe hanging with you will make me miss him less."

My throat thickened. "Yeah, okay. Friends." I gave him a cheeky grin. "Does that involve a lift to the top of the ravine?"

He shifted into his gargoyle form and rolled his neck on his shoulders. "I think that can be arranged."

We were partway up the wall, with me clinging to Touron's back like a rhesus monkey, when the spot between my shoulder blades grew hot.

I looked over my shoulder, across the river to the other side of the ravine, at the ledge where the task had begun. A figure crouched there, dark hair whipping in the wind. And although it was too far for me to be sure, I was certain that it was Serath and that he had his gaze fixed on me.

CHAPTER 12

CAMERON

Only seven gargoyles made it across the ravine, ten if you included us. They stood about with droopy wings, catching their breath while their cuts and scrapes healed.

Curi crouched by a boulder, knuckles grazing earth, blue hair hanging lank against his cheeks. Sweat dripped off his chin and hit the ground.

Of his two minions, only one remained.

The twin females had made it too. They'd shifted back to their human form and were leaning against a tree, looking wiped out.

Shocked gazes tracked me as I joined them, flanked by Sharniza and Touron.

Curi snarled, unfurling his body to stand tall, hands curling into fists. "You cheated." He glared at me, then at Touron. "You carried her."

He'd obviously been too busy trying to stay alive in the air to see how we'd crossed.

"We swam," Sharniza said. "Cameron's idea."

"Fuck," one of the twins said. "The water...of course."

"Clever," the other twin said, looking at me with an appraising glance.

They had identical features, but one's face was slightly more angular than the other's, and her hair held a wave to it.

"S'pose wits are all she has," Curi said, derision dripping from his tone.

"Well, we can't all be big and dumb," Sharniza retorted before I could reply.

"So much for staying out of things," Touron muttered in amusement.

The air beyond the big old oak fizzed with blue sparks, and a man materialized out of nowhere. Dressed in dark blue jeans, a T-shirt, and thigh-length jacket, he looked chic but casual. Designer stubble covered his strong jaw, and a cigarette hung from his bottom lip. He pinched it away from his mouth and exhaled. A tendril of smoke curled from his perfectly formed lips as he raked us over. His brows flicked up when he got to me, and he shook his head as if in dismay before taking another drag of his smoke.

"Doorway to your dreams awaits," he drawled. "Direct to the gates. In you go."

"Who the fuck are you?" Curi demanded. "Where are the elites?"

The man's eyes flinched, and a muscle in his cheek jumped, the only visible indication that Curi's tone bothered him. "The elites are back at the academy, which is where this magical doorway, that I so kindly created for you, will transport you now."

"How do we know this isn't another test or a trick?" Curi demanded.

The man gave Curi a flat look. "Oh, I don't know, maybe the fucking archway behind me that says Stonehaven?"

Yep, there was indeed an arch visible through the doorway he'd opened.

"It could be a trick." Curi looked to the others for support.

The man sighed and pinched the bridge of his nose, muttering something that sounded suspiciously like, *I don't get paid enough for this.*

With the ability to open a portal like this, he had to be mageri, but what was he doing slumming it in the rim?

From what I'd learned, the mageri had no authority out here. Guardians and humans ruled, so if he was here, then he was working for them. Were there other mageri at the academy?

I'd come here for answers about my brother's death, but there was no denying my curiosity about how the world on the other side of that portal worked.

It was time to find out.

I strode forward. "We just go through?"

He fixed his golden, hooded eyes on me. "Yeah, pretty simple." His attention flicked to my wet hair and clothes. "You crossed via the river. Nice."

"Yep. And I'm gagging for some dry clothes, so..." I strode past him and stepped through the portal.

A light fizz of power skimmed over my skin, but the world didn't shatter or tip. The breeze blew me an icy kiss, ruffled my hair, then filtered through my wet clothes to chill my skin. If I'd been full human, I'd have caught pneumonia by now.

The heat from the other gargoyles' bodies pressed in on me as they came through the portal behind me, and the air, which had been downright frosty a moment ago, no longer felt like it was trying to slice through my clothes. But my attention was on the austere stone arch that rose about fifteen feet tall and fifteen feet wide.

Iron gates blocked our path, the metal so thick I'd struggle to wrap my hand around the bars. A wide gravel road, bordered by woodland, stretched out and vanished into frosty mist.

There was a rush of air, and the portal behind us closed with a snap.

"Welcome to Stonehaven," the mageri said. "Someone will be here to let us in momentarily."

"Or we could simply fly over the wall," one of the gargoyles said.

"You could try it," the mageri replied. "If you want your guts to explode." He pushed out his jaw and exhaled, creating a veil of smoke over his features.

I caught the whiff of licorice and cloves.

"Wards?" Touron asked.

"Powerful ones," the mageri said. He looked impressed but not smug. Which meant...

"Not your work?"

He looked sharply my way. "No."

He didn't elaborate.

"Are there more mageri here?"

He snorted. "Hardly."

Movement on the other side of the gates called my attention, and a woman appeared out of the mist. How had her boots not made a sound on the gravel path?

"Good evening, new recruits." She surveyed us from the other side of the arch with dark, fathomless eyes set in a face created for the silver screen. Her hair was a deep burgundy, parted in the middle and falling in carefully styled waves to just above her shoulders. She looked to be in her mid-thirties, dressed in an odd ensemble of skinny jeans, ankle boots, and a waistcoat thing with a cream shirt underneath. One look at her told me she was no gargoyle, but she wasn't human either, and it wasn't just the fact that she didn't seem to feel the cold that gave it away. There was a preternatural stillness about her that screamed supernatural. But what kind?

"Remi, you were supposed to wait for me." Another woman appeared from the mist. She looked around the same age as the first. Her cheeks were flushed, eyes bright behind round spectacles, and a chunky coat covered her from neck to mid-calf.

Human. No doubt.

"Remi. You promised to...Oh, hello there. Ha, aha, new recruits. How lovely." She clasped her gloved hands together. "Miss Travani, the gates if you will."

Remi rolled her eyes, a slight smile tipping the corner of her mouth. "Yes, of course Mistress Carter."

She pointed her hand at the gates, and they slid back into the stone wall.

"In you come," she drawled lazily.

We trooped through the gates onto the gravel path.

"Thank you, Mr. Willowman." She inclined her head in the mageri's direction.

He gave her a jaunty salute and vanished.

The gates closed, and we huddled together, waiting.

"Congratulations." Mistress Carter beamed. "You passed the first test, and you are all now officially enrolled at Stonehaven. My name is Regina Carter, headmistress of Stonehaven and—"

"Headmistress?" Curi growled, incredulously. "A human?"

"Very observant, Mr. Mason." There wasn't a hint of sarcasm in her tone, although I couldn't help but feel her comment *was* sarcastic.

Curi's eyes narrowed. Yeah, he felt it too.

"You're wondering why a human would be running an academy that trains Gargoyle guardians?"

"Something like that," Curi said warily.

"Yes, well the answer is simple. Gargoyles have better things to do than cover the administration of Stonehaven. If you're here, then I'm sure you're aware that there's a war raging. One that shows no signs of ending, and every able-bodied guardian must be free to fight against the dark power that threatens our world." Her gaze skimmed over us, settling on me for a moment before moving on. "A threat larger than the tulpas, the blood rats, or the rogue shifters that roam the rim."

"Graynites," Touron said softly. "Graynites and grotesques."

The headmistress looked at him and nodded. "That's right, Mr. Lomax." She smiled sadly. "I'm sorry for your loss."

Touron swallowed hard. "Thank you."

"The graynites are our most formidable adversary yet, and inside these walls you will be taught everything we have learned about them. Things like the fact they cannot procreate with humans or other supernaturals, which has helped in our fight against them as their numbers remain all but the same. You will be taught how to vanquish them and how they *could* vanquish you." She lifted her chin. "I am your headmistress because I'm a symbol of the species that you must protect, and I am also damn good at my job."

Mistress Travani bit back a smile before speaking. "Thank you, Mistress Carter." She focused her attention on us. "You'll come with me. I'll show you to the cadets' dorm. You'll be housed there for the next few weeks while you train for the practical exam that will determine whether you progress to initiate training, general forces, or fail and enter an administration post, here or in the Rim.

If you pass, you'll take the stone oath binding you to become a guardian. Initiates are our front-line guardians, and if you're deemed worthy, you'll learn more about how they operate directly from our elites."

"But in the meantime," the headmistress continued. "Please get some rest. The kitchens are open until dawn if you're hungry."

Of course, gargoyles were most active at night, preferring to sleep in the day, although they barely needed three to four hours of sleep to function. With my half human nature, I needed a little more than that, but I'd figure it out so as not to miss the important stuff.

"This way." Travani stalked off down the path, and Carter ushered us to follow.

She gently took my arm as I passed. "Come see me anytime in my office if you have any issues." Her smile was filled with genuine warmth. "This program is designed with purebloods in mind, and although I admire you for wanting to do your duty, it won't be easy. If you change your mind, I'll do my best to sign you off."

She was offering me an out, and once I had the intel I needed, I'd take it. "Thank you."

I rejoined the others, sliding into place between Touron and Sharniza.

"What did she want?" Sharniza asked.

Curi answered for me. "Offered her a way out if things get

too rough for her." He looked down his nose at me. "You should take it. Save us all the embarrassment of making you eat dirt." He walked off with a chuckle, leaving me with the urge to punch him in his blocky head.

"I didn't think gargoyles could be such assholes."

"They're not," Touron said. "Not all of them anyway. Curi is simply a bad example."

"No, he's not," Sharniza said. "Not when it comes to qualifying for initiate, which is what every gargoyle who comes here wants. There are no friends here, only temporary allies, because everyone, and I mean *everyone*, is your competition for those coveted initiate spots."

This was news to me. "The spots are limited?"

"Damn right. Twenty spots a year. They take five gargoyles every eight weeks and training is intense. We're the last batch of cadets for this quarter, which means we're already three weeks behind in training."

"Wait...we don't all get the same amount of training time?"

"Evert man for himself," she said coolly. "Adapt and learn, or die."

"It's not that bad," Touron said with a nervous laugh. "At least it doesn't have to be. We can work together. Allies, if not friends?"

Sharniza exhaled. "I'll think about it."

I'd been so focused on the conversation that it was a surprise when we came to a stop outside a large gray stone building four stories high with huge gleaming windows and a ledge running beneath the third and fourth floor windows.

A ledge for gargoyles to land on and get into their rooms without going through the building.

"Kitchens are on the ground floor," Travani said. "The dorm master will assign rooms and provide you with maps of the academy grounds and an induction manual."

Movement on the ledge above caught my eye. A figure in a white nightgown stood looking down at us, her pale, bare feet hung half off the edge of the platform.

"Hey, get back!" I stepped forward, waving my arms at her.

"What is she doing?" Touron said.

"She's not a gargoyle," Sharniza added. "She's going to—"

The woman tipped forward and fell off the ledge.

CHAPTER 13

CAMERON

Curi was the first to get to the spot where the woman had fallen, but the ground was clear of a dead body.

"What the fuck?" He looked up at the ledge, then back down again, his heavy brow furrowed in confusion. "Did you see that?"

"I apologize for the fright, cadets," Travani said. "I'd forgotten about our resident spirit. Miss Parker likes to frighten the new arrivals. Jumping out of closets and hiding under their beds, but this...This one is new." She sighed as if the whole thing was a minor nuisance. "You'll soon get used to her."

"You have a ghost?" the wavy-haired twin said. "Why haven't you extinguished her?"

"She's not a tulpa, or a demonic force, Miss Hunter. She's the soul of a deceased person who chooses to remain earthbound. Yes, it's a nuisance, but there is little we can do about it."

"She was human." I looked up at the window.

"Yes, Miss Walker, she was."

It was impressive how she knew all our names. "What was she doing here?"

"Working. We have human staff here. They're perfectly safe. A guardian can't harm a human. It's against our genetic code to do so."

"Then how did she die?" the wavy-haired twin asked.

"Ginia!" Her sister nudged her, widening her eyes in warning.

"What?" Ginia retorted. "We have a right to know."

"Yes, of course you do," Travani said. "And it's good to ask questions. She killed herself." She clipped toward the doors. That was it? That was all we were going to get? "Now, in you go. Get rested. Tonight, we tested your bodies, but tomorrow you'll have a chance to orient yourself with the grounds using the maps provided, and you'll have your induction class where you'll get a rundown of what will be expected of you here—classes, behavioral policies, etc.—and believe me when I tell you, that your minds will be tested."

The double doors to the dorm opened, and a gargoyle male in human form greeted us.

"Over to you, Mr. Raffi." Travani drifted off and vanished into the mist.

Raffi harrumphed. "Get inside. I'm dorm master. Come to me with questions after the induction tomorrow not before. For now, collect your welcome packets from the table by the door. Room numbers and keys are inside. There's a fully stocked kitchen down the hall to the right if you need food."

"We have to cook?" Curi asked.

Raffi fixed a cool gaze on him. "Guardians are self-sufficient. If you want to eat, you cook. You have an injury, you treat it. If it's bad, then we have a medic, or you work with your assigned team to fix it."

"Team?" Sharniza looked confused. "We'll be put into teams?"

Sharniza frowned, probably realizing her *every man for himself* theory was put into question.

"Eventually, yes," Raffi said. "Teamwork is essential to the success of the guardian operation. Units of five is how we operate. Those that qualify will be matched. That's all for now." He turned and limped away. My gaze dropped to his foot, to where it was twisted at an odd angle.

Gargoyles were hard to hurt, and if you managed it, they healed super-fast, so an injury that would last, that would disable a gargoyle, wasn't something to take lightly. There was no doubt in my mind that Mr. Raffi's guardian status had been taken from him because of this injury, and now he was stuck taking care of every generation to come.

How many more Gargoyles like him would I find here? And how many might know the truth of what had happened to my brother?

Touron passed me a large brown envelope. "Miss Walker."

I tore it open and poked around inside to find my keys. "Room four two zero."

"Four one nine," Touron said, peering at mine. "Right next door."

"Four one eight." Sharniza groaned.

"What are the odds?" Touron said. "This alliance was meant to be."

As we headed for the stairs, it was difficult not to wonder if the powers that be had put me with these two gargoyles for a reason, because if I was going to survive this place long enough to find the information that I needed, I'd need all the help I could get.

THE DORM WAS made of wide corridors and high ceilings to accommodate a gargoyle in both human and natural form. The staircases were also much wider than any I'd ever seen, and almost every window backed onto a landing ledge.

The architect had thought of everything.

We climbed the stairs to the fourth floor, losing gargoyles the higher we went, until it was just Sharniza, Touron, Curi, and me.

Looked like the abrasive male was going to be on the same floor as us.

He growled with displeasure when he realized this, then stomped off in the opposite direction to us when we got to our floor.

"At least his room isn't next to ours," Touron said. "I bet he snores."

"He probably fucks loudly too," Sharniza said coolly, coming to a standstill outside her door.

"With commentary," Touron added with a shudder.

Sharniza snorted in amusement. "I dated a goyle like that once. Wouldn't stop telling me what he planned to do, or how good it all felt. I ended up shoving a pillow over his face until I was done."

Pindrop silence followed her disclosure.

She grunted and shoved open her door. "Night." She slammed it shut, and Touron and I exchanged glances.

"She likes us," he said. "She totally wants to be friends."

It wasn't until I was in my assigned room that it hit me I had no personal effects with me. My bag was back on the bus, and even then, I'd brought only one change of clothes and some toiletries.

But my bag sat on my bed, waiting for me.

O-kay, the academy was certainly organized. Made me wonder what happened to the effects of all those gargoyles, or goyles, as Sharniza called them, who didn't make it.

I unzipped my small holdall and sighed. At least the bed was made. I'd need more stuff, though. Clothes to fill the dresser for starters. I tugged open the top draw and found it neatly filled with T-shirts and vests.

I lifted one, and the label glared at me. Lastonflex. It looked my size. And there were more clothes—pants, socks, and some sports bras. The wardrobe had a couple of pairs of leggings and two joggers and zippy tops all made with the same material. They even had Lastonflex sneakers.

One size could fit all. It explained why they didn't ask you to bring loads of stuff. They had it covered.

Khaki, gray, and brown.

Looked like these would be my colors for the next, however long it took to find what I'd come looking for.

But where to start? I hadn't thought beyond getting into the academy. The next step would have been getting close to Romi's elite team. But Orix's reaction to me, his whole trying-to-kill-me thing, meant I needed to tread carefully there. I needed to figure out what his problem with me was, and whether it was more than him trying to keep a halfblood out of Stonehaven. Because honestly, murder was a little excessive. There had to be more to it, but I wasn't about to do the dumb thing and corner him to ask.

Serath saved me once, but there was no guarantee he'd be around to do so again if Orix decided to finish the job.

Serath was my obvious entry point.

The thought of the elite shifter made my chest tight. There was something undeniably compelling about the male and the way my body had reacted to him...

I didn't know much about the mating habits of gargoyles, but I knew when I was attracted to someone, and I was attracted to the elite, and something in the way his gaze had lingered on me in the warping circle told me he was intrigued by me too.

I didn't need this. I had Levi.

I was falling in love with my halfblood boyfriend, and although I'd broken it off with him before coming here, part of me hoped we could patch things up once I got the closure I needed. That is, *if* he waited for me.

My heart sank at the thought of Levi with someone else.

The attraction to Serath was a fluke. Too much adrenaline and the whole fight-or-flight situation must have messed with my senses.

But if he was attracted to me, then maybe I could use it to my advantage?

He'd jumped into the water to save me from whatever monster had been about to take a bite out of me. Pretty sure that was a breach of the rules, and not something done lightly. So, either he couldn't bear to see me hurt or...Oh shit! Maybe he knew who I was and felt compelled to save my ass.

Either way, he was my target. If I could get close to him and earn his trust, I might finally get to the truth of Romi's death.

Whatever I decided, it had to be done before the initiate exam. Before I was officially contracted as a guardian. There was no way I could pass that exam. I'd be delusional to think otherwise, and once I failed and got put into administration, any hope of getting close to Romi's team would be gone. Any hope of answers wiped.

I sat on the bed, and my ass thanked me. I was exhausted. My stomach growled. Hungry too.

I lay back, mind swimming with plans that seemed to slip away the heavier my limbs got.

My eyes drifted closed. Was that a face hovering over me? Curious gray eyes and...

CHAPTER 14

SERATH

Orix leans against the wall by the observatory window, his muscular arms crossed over his chest, eyes burning with the fire of betrayal.

The wounds I inflicted on him have healed, but there's a bruise between us now. This is the first time we've fought, the first time any conflict has arisen within our unit, and it's all my fault.

The observatory, the pinnacle of our residential tower and a place that has always been a sanctuary, feels tainted by the negative flow of energy between us, but although my chest aches to make amends, rage at his actions continues to simmer in my veins.

I'm a male torn.

He's called this meeting.

This is an intervention, and I have no choice but to sit here and listen.

"We need to tell the Stone Council," Orix says.

"No!" I curl my hands into fists. "I won't be responsible for an innocent female's death." My eyes narrow. "And neither will you."

"It's the beast that needs to be kept in check," Selas says from her perch on the sill opposite Orix. Her pale eyes look out at a night she cannot see, but she feels the moon and hears the sounds of nature that we miss. Her senses are twice as heightened as ours.

"The anklet can be strengthened."

"Yes," Prasan says from his spot by the bank of computers. "Until then, you can't be near her."

It's his job to monitor our units and organize the patrols when the graynites go to ground. When it's quiet like this, we get to come home and focus on training the goyles that will take over once our stone bodies are worn and exhausted, or if one of us gets taken down. Like Romi.

We're a fractured unit right now. Weakened by his loss. I can't let this unexpected turn of events break us...Break me.

I've worked too hard to be here. To be a part of this team.

"I'm sorry, brother," Selas says softly, her pale eyes looking over my head. "I truly would not wish this on any male."

Selas Mason is the best of us. Our anchor and lynchpin and having her here, on my side right now, soothes the acid burn in my chest.

"Thank you."

"You'll stay away," Orix says again, wanting my vow.

I can give him mine, but the beast's vow? That's a separate issue.

"He can't stay away," Selas says. "He's the elite leader, and he has a duty to the cadets. To shirk that would do them a disservice, not to mention questions will be asked as to why, and if the truth comes out... Well, we know what will happen to the halfblood then."

"We can help," Prasan says. "One of us can be with Serath at each training session that he's meant to attend."

I hate that they need to monitor me like this, but I'm not fool enough to deny that it's needed.

Orix growls low in his chest. "And what about after? What about once the initiate test is over?"

"Then we'll stick her in an admin post far from here," Prasan says.

My chest rumbles in a warning growl. I bite it back. He's trying to help. Trying to prevent a potential tragedy. I refuse to lose my temper.

"If she makes it that far," Orix mutters.

My chair clatters to the ground as I leap to my feet, all resolution gone and a warning snarl on my lips.

"Fuck you, Serath. Seriously?" Orix says. "She's a fucking halfblood. What do you think is going to happen over the next few weeks?"

I want to hurt him. I want to tear the words from his mouth along with his tongue. But that's the beast thinking. Not my gargoyle self but the other monster hidden deep inside me. A monster, unique to my bloodline.

Selas places a hand on my shoulder, and calm radiates through me. "Let it happen, Serath. It'll be a blessing for you both if you do."

She's right, and yet the burning, gnawing in my gut screams otherwise.

I rake a hand through my hair and stand. "I need some air."

Orix pushes off the wall. "I'll come with you."

The beast surfaces violently, pivoting my frame to face my friend and morphing my body into goyle form with a roar that vibrates the whole room.

Orix's chest heaves as he battles with his own beast. I roar again and he raises his hands in submission—the alpha bowing to the sigma.

It shouldn't be this way. We're equal in status, the only difference being how we lead. How we function. I prefer solitude and my thoughts. I prefer to meet my expectations my way. Not stagnating. Not following the herd. Even though we both have a respect for authority, we do our duty in different ways.

Right now, my nature is trying to find a loophole. Some way to both follow the rules and break them, while Orix is determined to keep me grounded.

Shame grips my throat because he's right to want to watch me. Right to think that a part of me, even now, wants to find her.

But I won't. Because to do so would ruin us both.

I force a smile to my lips. "I'd be grateful for the company, friend."

CHAPTER 15

CAMERON

I woke to the smell of coffee, and sure enough, there was a steaming mug on my bedside table.

How had that gotten there?

And how had I gotten into bed?

I'd passed out on top of the sheet with my legs dangling off the mattress.

Someone must have been in here.

No. I'd locked the door.

But ghosts didn't need keys to get into rooms, did they?

A chill swept up my spine as I gave the mug a wary look.

Had the ghost gotten me coffee? "Hello? Miss Parker? Are you there?"

Nothing.

Damn that coffee smelled good. Fuck it. I took a sip and sighed. It was just the right temperature and sweetness for a morning wake up. Good stuff. But now I needed the loo.

Thank goodness for ensuites.

I hadn't had a chance to examine the bathroom last night, but the academy hadn't skimped in here either. The shower stall was massive, all slate and tiled with one of those power showerheads. There was no bath, though. Shame, because I loved a good soak.

Wait, was that my shampoo and shower gel on the shelf in

the stall?

My toothbrush sat in a holder by the sink.

I'd barely had time to unpack my bag last night before I'd passed out, so this had to be the ghost's doing.

I wasn't sure whether to shout thank you or warn it to stay out of my stuff. But the coffee though...That was sweet of her. Fuck it, who was I to turn my nose up at a little help?

I shut the door and stared at my bedhead in the bathroom mirror. I looked like I'd wrestled a rhino in my sleep. My white-blonde hair was a halo around my head, and the skin around my eyes was slightly red, making the blue flecks in my slate-gray eyes stand out.

"If you're in here, I suggest you leave. Trust me, you do not want to see what happens next."

Silence greeted me.

A thirty-second warning was enough. I really had to go.

Bathroom business complete, I went back to my coffee. No sign of the resident ghost, Maybe, she only hung out at night?

There was a knock on my door. "Walker, you up?" Touron called.

I unlocked my door and tipped my head back to look up at him. He'd donned a set of sweats and smelled of citrus body wash. His forest-green eyes brightened when his gaze fell on my mug.

"You made coffee?" The hope in his tone was almost potent enough to be guilt-inducing.

"Sorry. Nope. A ghost got it for me."

His brows flicked up. "Parker? No way."

"Yep, *and* she unpacked for me."

He peered into my room cautiously. "Is she...in there?"

"I don't think so." I studied the wary lines of his face. "Touron, are you...scared?"

He balked. "*Pfft*, Scared? Gargoyles don't get scared. We have the power to extinguish terrors."

"Uh-huh, we do, we do, but ghosts aren't terrors. They're untethered souls."

He rubbed the back of his neck, looking surprisingly sheepish. “Ghosts give me the creeps. My aunt has a couple at her estate.” He shuddered and then his eyes widened. “What if she comes to my room?”

I bit back a smile. “You can come get me. I’ll protect you.”

He exhaled through his nose. “You know what? I refuse to be embarrassed about this. Everyone has some aversion. Mine happens to be ghosts and odd socks. I can’t stand it when people wear odd socks.” Another shudder. “I’m heading down to the kitchens. There’s some pasta left over from last night. You want some?”

It hit me that I had no clue what time it was, or when induction would take place. “What time *is* it?”

“It’s early, like eleven. Class is at four. The others probably won’t be up for a while. We went to bed a couple of hours ago. I did knock for you when I made pasta, but you didn’t answer, and Shar pointed out that with your half human constitution you probably needed more sleep.”

“I thought she’d gone to bed.”

“Nah, she showed up in the kitchens last night and devoured three tins of tuna, two plates of pasta, and a jug of juice.”

Goyle metabolism was a bitch.

“I’ll have to work on getting my body clock in sync for this place. But pasta for breakfast sounds great. I’ll see you down there. I got to shower and change.”

“Sure.”

I closed the door and stifled a yawn. I needed more sleep than a pureblood, but five hours usually was enough for me, except last night I must have slept at least ten. That was not normal, and it was totally not like me.

The trial must have taken a lot out of me.

And there would be more. So, I needed to toughen up and get on with it.

Starting with pasta for breakfast.

Yum.

SHARNIZA WAS IN the kitchen with Touron when I arrived. It was a spacious room with long wooden tables and benches for seating. There were two double ovens and three stoves, along with plenty of pots, pans, and cupboards filled with dried goods. The fridge was fully stocked, and so was the freezer, mainly with meat, eggs, and fish. Gargoyle staples.

I heated some pasta in the microwave and joined the others at the table. The food was meaty, saucy, and delicious. We ate in silence for a while.

"Touron says Parker paid you a visit?" Sharniza said.

"Yes. She brought me coffee."

"Be careful," Sharniza said. "I've heard that she can be temperamental."

"I'll try not to piss her off."

The twins entered the kitchen, rubbing sleep from their eyes. Ginia's wavy hair was pulled up in a high ponytail today while her sister's poker-straight locks were loose.

"Any pasta left?" they said in unison.

"Plenty," Touron said around a mouthful of food.

"You'll make some omega very happy someday," Ginia said, almost wistfully.

They grabbed plates and served themselves.

I looked across at Touron. "Omegas?"

Sharniza sat back in her seat with her frown. "You really are clueless, aren't you? Your mother must have known she was bedding a gargoyle. Did your sire not teach you *anything* about this world?"

My mood dipped at the mention of my father. "My sire wasn't around. I don't know who he is." The lie tripped off my tongue easily but left a bitter taste in my mouth. "My mother died when I was a child. So, yeah, I didn't really give a shit about this world until..." I'd said too much.

"Until?" Touron prompted.

I speared some more pasta with my fork. "Until I decided to find out."

"By becoming a guardian?" Touron looked equally impressed and confused. "Talk about immersive education."

Sharniza was watching me with a shrewd expression. I'd messed up, and she'd picked up on it. My story, my reasoning for being here, was flimsy, and I mentally kicked myself for not preparing better. This was my Achilles heel—the lead with my heart and jump in before thinking things through. Romi had warned me about this time and time again.

But his death.

His loss.

I'd been completely focused on one goal. Getting here. Now that I'd succeeded in that, the rest was uncertain.

Sharniza was still watching me, waiting for me to elaborate. If there was one thing I knew, it was that the best lies were built on a foundation of the truth. So, that's what I'd give them.

"Look." I sat back in my seat. "I didn't care about this world before because I had a life and a family outside of it, but a week ago, I lost my half-brother." They'd think I meant my fully human sibling. "After that I was alone, and I needed something. A connection. I was grieving so..." I threw up my hands.

"You acted impulsively and signed up to enroll at the academy," Sharniza said.

I nodded. "I figured it was the quickest way to find out about my heritage."

"And maybe who your father is?" Touron added.

Ooooh, good cover story. I smiled thinly, letting them believe that lie.

"I'm sorry," Ginia said, joining us. "Gargoyle males can be bastards."

"Hey!" Touron looked offended.

"Not all of them," she added quickly.

I'd side-stepped a tricky situation. "So, what's an omega?"

"Any female that isn't us," Ginia said with a tight smile.

"There are two kinds of female gargoyles," her sister explained. "Alphas and omegas. The alphas are built to fight, protect, and lead. History says that in the old days we were the warriors that protected the camps when the males went hunting or to war. Then our world perished, and we came to the human world. We made alliances with the humans and took an oath to protect them in exchange for refuge. And we played our part, but the world changed, and magic dwindled, and our aid was no longer required, so we slept in stone for centuries until the Gray came."

"What is this? Story time?" Curi entered, trailed by two other gargoyles. "If she doesn't know about our history, then she doesn't deserve to be here."

"None of us knew about our history until we were taught it," Ginia's twin said sharply.

"Palia, don't even bother," Ginia said. "He's not worth it."

"No," Curi said. "It's your kind that aren't worth it. Females who can't reproduce so pretend to be males. You're all just walking cu—"

Sharniza's fist was in his face before he could finish the slur.

Curi staggered back, hands flying up to cup his nose.

A low growl that promised pain ripped through him, and his body bulged as his beast begged to be free. But he shut it down and slowly raised his head, looking at her from beneath heavy brows. "You'll pay for that, Aziza."

Sharniza crossed her arms, her stance relaxed and unaffected, but the tense lines of her shoulders told me she was ready to react if Curi attacked. "I'll be waiting, Mason."

He turned on his heel and strode toward the exit, shoving his minions aside to get past. They looked momentarily torn, as if they wanted to stay.

"Move it," Curi called.

They quickly followed.

Sharniza picked up her plate and took it to the dishwasher.

"Let's load up and get going. Induction starts in two hours. We should check out the grounds and orient ourselves before then."

Touron nodded. "Okay, sure, we'll just gloss over the last minute then, shall we?"

Sharniza shot him a sharp glance, and he held up a placating hand.

"Mind if we tag along?" Ginia asked.

Sharniza shrugged. "It's a free world."

We cleaned up and headed out. It looked like our trio had just grown to five strong.

CHAPTER 16

CAMERON

We'd all gotten maps and induction books in our packages, but only Palia had brought her map of campus with her. We spent the next hour taking a tour of the grounds. Orientation would take place in the main building in the center of the academy grounds, so we didn't bother checking it out. We could do that when we went to our first class later.

We passed more dorm houses as we headed north. These were larger buildings with more stories than ours. There were several iron-framed towers visible, too, with platforms high up. Perches for observational purposes no doubt.

There was a running track and a trail that led into the forest to the northwest.

We were headed toward a redbrick two-story building when a Gargoyle pushing a cart laden with tools crossed our path. He was muttering under his breath but stopped short at the sight of us.

His back was hunched, and he peered at us through milky eyes. He was the first old gargoyle I'd ever seen. I hadn't realized they could look so aged.

"New," he said. "Something new, you are." He blinked and shook his head. "Can't be here. Can't be walking here."

"Oh, we're so sorry." Ginia stepped off the path onto the grass to let him pass, but he didn't move, just continued to stare at us, his gaze continually flicking back to me. I guess I stuck out like a sore thumb in this world of six-foot-and-over males and females.

"Are you all right?" Touron asked him. "Can we help with anything?"

But the man with the cart had gone eerily still and silent, his gaze almost blank.

"Should we get someone?" Palia whispered.

The man blinked sharply and then glared at us. "Got to weed the gardens. You're in my way."

We all stepped aside, and he trundled off down the path.

"Weird," Touron muttered.

"Varsa is harmless." A man joined us on the edge of the path.

A woman trailed behind him, shooting us a tentative smile.

They looked young, probably only a few years older than me. Their eyes were golden irises rimmed in black, similar to the mageri who'd transported us here. Were they related to him?

"He's the academy caretaker," the man said. "He's a survivor. One of the only gargoyles to survive a Graynite siphoning."

Had he said siphoning? "A what?"

"They won't know yet," the woman whispered. "You're jumping ahead." She dropped her gaze when I looked her way.

"Ah, yes, I have a tendency to do that," the man said. "Which is why I have you, little sister."

She peered up at him with a soft smile. "Shall we go to class and set up?"

"Yes." He arched a dark brow our way. "Induction in twenty minutes. Don't be late. I do hate tardiness in my students."

He looked older in that moment. Wiser. He gave us a nod, then strode off with his sister in tow.

"What are they?" Ginia asked.

I shrugged. "No idea, but I'm sure we'll find out."

We passed a building that was marked *Gym*, and then walked by an outdoor area divided into cement, sand, and grass pitches. The sky above was clear, but storm clouds hung low over the grass pitch, spewing sheets of rain that soaked the hulking gargoyles in combat. They clashed and smashed, tails swinging and slamming into the earth to throw up huge chucks of grass, feet sliding in the mud as their stone bodies collided. A male and female stood off pitch watching the action.

The woman had her back to us, her long mahogany hair, tied in a high ponytail, whipped about in the localized storm. Her dark clothes molded to her muscular form. Black and silver—the elite colors. This was the elite female Romi had told me about. But who was the male that towered over her?

His dark hair was long enough to get blown about but short enough to expose the back of his corded neck. His Lastonflex shirt looked like it was being tested by being stretched across his wide muscle-rounded shoulders. There was something familiar about him. Something that made me stop in my tracks and stare. A gust of wind hit my back, and tendrils of hair escaped my braid, the wisps flying forward as if reaching for him.

His shoulder muscles rippled, and he turned, offering me the shaved side of his head. He looked like the images of Vikings of old. Strong nose, hard jaw, defined lips, and dark brow drawn low.

I wanted him to turn all the way and look at me so I could see his face, because my pulse was pounding, blood rushing through my veins in excitement, and I needed to see. I needed to see his face.

He shifted on his feet, swiveling his upper body. He was going to look!

But the woman stepped closer to him and placed a hand on his arm. Fire lanced through my chest. How dare she touch him. How—

"Cameron, are you coming?" Touron asked.

The strange hold on me snapped. What the hell had just happened?

"Cam?" Touron looked down at me with concern.

"I'm good. Let's go." I glanced back at the pitch. The woman was still there, but the man...The male was gone.

CHAPTER 17

CAMERON

Palia pulled her welcome packet from her satchel and studied it. "It says lecture hall three is on the first floor."

I needed to be more prepared, but I hadn't thought to bring a pack or satchel in my essentials bag. In fact, now that I took a moment to properly study the twins, their dark blue sweats and black sneakers finally registered.

Not the same colors as I'd found in my cupboard. "Is there a color code for clothes here?"

They looked at me in confusion.

"They gave me brown, gray, and Khaki stuff like Touron and Sharniza."

Palia made an *O* with her mouth, but it was Ginia who responded.

"Our luggage arrived this morning. Mother's super organized, and she was confident that we'd get in, so we have our own clothes already. But your things should be here in a couple of days." Palia elbowed her, and Ginia looked horrified. "Oh. I'm sorry. You probably...it's probably..."

Yeah, I had no one to send me stuff. No one who had connections to this world.

"It's fine." I shook my head with a smile. "Honestly. I'm sure I can speak to someone about ordering some things. You know, stuff that isn't Lastonflex." I smiled and she relaxed.

"I suppose you don't need it," Palia said kindly.

"Nope. I like my regular fabrics."

The main building loomed, huge and imposing with its many windows and turrets. Stone steps led to a patio that wrapped around the structure, and several goyles in human form sat reading or talking. They glanced up briefly as we passed, and although their gazes lingered a little longer on me than on the others, it wasn't uncomfortable or intrusive, and everyone quickly went back to doing their own thing.

We swept through the main doors and into a cavernous foyer. The ceiling was braced by pillars set at spacious intervals, and archways led off into corridors.

"Which way now?" Touron peered over Palia's shoulder at the papers in her hand.

"I don't know. I don't have a map of the building."

I spotted one on the wall by the door. "Here we go." It looked complicated. "Okay...We need to go left, then up a flight of steps to the first floor. The room we want is the second door on the right."

By the time we got to the room we needed, several gargoyles were already waiting to be admitted. Some I recognized from our dorm, but others I'd never seen before.

The door was closed, and everyone crammed into the corridor.

"Out of the way." Curi shoved goyles aside to get closer to the entrance.

Sharniza tensed, and Touron stepped closer to me, shielding me with his body.

But the doors chose that moment to swing open, and the corridor emptied as everyone flowed into a lecture room large enough to hold us all. The seats were spaced out to accommodate gargoyle frames in ascending rows. Several took the steps up to the back of the room, but I opted for a seat at the front. Sharniza, Touron, and the twins joined me. Curi stomped past us with a scowl.

"What is his problem?" Ginia muttered. "I've met his cousin, and she's super nice. You wouldn't think those two were related.

"You have?" Touron asked, sitting forward. "You know Selas?"

"Not know, but we hung out for a bit at some event a year ago. She's so pretty and talented. You know, she wasn't born blind, right? But she's adapted, and she managed to make the elite team."

Now I was intrigued. "Selas is on the elite team?"

"Yep," Palia said. "The only female to ever make it in."

The female I'd seen on the training court with the male...It had to be her. And the male...had that been Serath in his human form?

The golden-eyed man from earlier entered the room, followed by his sister. She closed the door and took a seat at the end of our aisle.

I shot her a smile, which she returned before ducking her head so her dark wavy hair fell forward.

Golden-eyes placed himself in the center of the room and looked us all over. "Welcome to Induction 101. I'm Mr. Yarrow, and my sister and I are here to induct you into Stonehaven." Mutters rose behind us, but Yarrow ignored them and continued. "Some of you have been here for a couple of weeks already, and I apologize for the delay in setting up this class. But my sister and I had important business in the north. I'm told Mistress Travani filled you in on the basics. However, I'd like to take this opportunity to elaborate and answer any of your burning questions, which"—he held up a finger—"I'll take at the end of the class. You'll also get your timetables for the next few weeks then. The weeks leading up to the initiate exams." Everyone broke out in murmurs, and he allowed it for a moment before intervening. "It may seem unfair that some of you get less time to prepare for the initiate tests, but that assumption is incorrect. Training officially begins tomorrow, for all. Those of you who arrived in the first wave will have had more time to become accustomed to the grounds, and yes, you'll have completed the academia side of your training, but the arcana and physical training begins tomorrow for everyone."

"Arcana?" someone asked. "Magic? Gargoyles don't do magic. We *are* magic."

Yarrow smiled. "No."

"No?" The gargoyle asking the question looked confused.

Yarrow smirked. "Gargoyles are *not* magic. They are creatures of *arcana,* and in arcana class you will be taught how to harness that power and not just exist within its grasp."

"But—"

"You'll wait till arcana class," Yarrow said firmly. "Miss Yarrow, and I will explain it all to you then. For now, we'll go over the Academy basics and...hold your questions until the end." His expression was stern.

The lights dimmed, and a map of the academy bloomed on the wall behind him.

"I'm sure you've all made it a point to take a wander with your maps, so you'll recognize the schematic behind me. However, there are a few rules that must be followed. The omega den is off limits to everyone but the staff that reside there and the omegas themselves. You will steer clear unless you have an invitation to enter. Greenwood Forest is open to all for jogging or whatever other exercises you wish to participate in, except on an omega moon."

I wanted to ask what an omega moon was, but he'd said to leave questions until the end of the class, so I filed that one away.

"You are not to, in any circumstance, attempt to leave the Stonehaven grounds. There are wards in place for a reason. You will be transported outside the walls by warping for certain classes and for set periods, which you will adhere to. If you fail to return to a warp point by the assigned time, you will be left outside the walls, and your fate...Well, it won't be pleasant."

His sister leaned forward in her seat and whispered, "The observatory."

"Ah, yes," Yarrow said. "The observatory is out of bounds also." He pointed at the towering structure on the map. "This is the elite residence, accessible only to the elite and their guests. You'll see the elites from time to time as they monitor first-year cadet training. If you show promise and get into initiate training, then you'll be fast tracked with one year of intensive combat and strategy training. The tests are dangerous, and the survival rate is low. If you make it into general forces, then the training lasts two years, but you will be called to active duty after the first year is up, patrolling the eastern settlements and cleansing them of localized tulpa and supernatural threat."

So, like the human police and hunters then.

"As general guard, you'll liaise with local human enforcement."

That made sense.

"Classes," his sister prompted in a whisper.

"Classes," Yarrow echoed. "There will be four kinds. Arcana. Combat, history, and once you've taken the initiation exam, dance will be added to your timetable."

Dance? What the heck?

"Questions?" His eyebrows flicked up as several hands shot up, mine included. "Hmmm, I didn't expect so many. You." He pointed at someone at the back.

"Why do we need dance classes?"

He shrugged. "You'll have to ask Madame Pontiere." He pointed at another gargoyle. "Yes?"

"When does the testing start for the omega moon," another goyle asked.

Laughter skittered across the room.

"You'll be informed," Yarrow said with a shake of his head.

Like, what? What did that mean?

My hand went back up again, but he picked someone across the room.

"Why do you smell wrong?" I stiffened at the sound of Curi's voice. Gruff and almost accusatory. "I met a mageri once, and you don't smell like one."

"Wow, well..." Yarrow steepled his fingers. "My scent, as you so indelicately put it, is not mageri because I am *not* mageri. I'm a witch."

Silence greeted his declaration, and my stomach quivered because witches had been wiped out by the Gray, and mageri had risen to take their place. Everyone knew that.

Yarrow smiled thinly. "You'll learn more about my kind in arcana class. In the meantime, feel free to speculate, because that's always fun." He clapped his hands together, and the lights came back on fully. "If there aren't any further questions, then Miss Yarrow has your timetables."

But I had a question. The burning question I'd come here to solve. I raised my hand high and waited for his golden gaze to settle on me.

"Yes, Miss Walker?"

Shit. My mouth was dry. I licked my lips and cleared my throat. "There are five elite guard, right? They organize the alpha teams?"

"That's correct."

"But I've only seen three of them. Are the others out on the frontlines..." I let my question hang.

He pressed his lips together. "I assume you're fishing for information on the unfortunate accident that occurred a few weeks ago."

Silence had descended, thick and heavy, as everyone focused on Yarrow and what he was about to say.

"Mr. Basque was killed in an unfortunate accident on a routine sweep of one of the further eastern sectors."

Unfortunate accident.

I was sick of hearing that crap. I gritted my teeth. "An accident? What kind of accident?"

His eyes narrowed. "An unfortunate one."

Rage flickered in my chest, but I breathed through my nose to temper it. "I'm just wondering what kind of *accident* could kill an elite gargoyle, that's all."

Touron tensed beside me, and Sharniza sat forward slightly, as if eager to know the answer.

"I wish I knew," Yarrow said. "But that information is above my paygrade."

He was lying. I could feel it.

But the others seemed satisfied with the answer, and no one pushed for more. *I* wanted to ask—push—but doing so might come across as odd. I mean, who was I? Some half-blood getting in his face about an accident that happened to an elite, someone so far removed from me and my life that I shouldn't even care.

But I did. I cared all too much, and it took everything I had to snap my mouth closed and sit back.

Yarrow watched me for several beats before turning his attention to the class. "Stay seated until Miss Yarrow calls your name, then collect your timetable, and you're free to go."

I guess question time was really over now.

His sister hurried to take his place at the front of the class, but she kept her head down, rummaging in her satchel for a sheaf of papers. She fumbled, and the papers slipped from her grasp and fluttered to the ground. Someone laughed, and she flinched.

"Who laughed?" Mr. Yarrow's golden eyes glowed as he stepped forward to scan faces. "Who. Laughed?" The air was suddenly heavy and charged with energy.

His sister grabbed his hand. "It's okay, Blake. I'm fine."

I slipped off my seat and grabbed a couple of the timetables that had floated my way, then handed them to her.

"Thank you." She smiled shyly.

"No problem." I helped her pick up the rest before returning to my seat.

"Palia Lambert," she called.

The next few minutes flew by. I was one of the last cadets to get my timetable, and Mr. Yarrow intercepted me at the door.

"Miss Walker, a word, please."

My stomach dropped. I must have pushed too hard, and now he was about to quiz me on why.

"You'll find an extra arcana class on your schedule," he said.

I took a quick look, and sure enough there were two arcana

slots in my week, one at sunset and another mid-afternoon. The knot in my stomach eased, and I gave him a questioning glance.

"You're a halfblood, and you'll need a little extra help. Miss Yarrow will work with you in your mid-afternoon sessions. She's an excellent teacher but does best one-on-one."

My chest warmed with gratitude, but there was also a prick of unease because this highlighted how out of my depth, how unprepared, I was.

I didn't belong here. "Thank you. I appreciate it."

His half smile was almost wistful. "Don't thank me. It was Flora's idea. You can thank her at your first lesson later this week." He looked down the corridor where Touron loitered, waiting for me. "I'm glad you've made friends. Despite the popular belief that's been spread by the elders, unity is important, not only once you qualify, but from the start. What we're fighting...It will try to tear us apart, and out there, your team, your loved ones, and your friends are all you'll have to hold on to."

His words sent a shiver of unease down my spine, but then reality set in, reminding me that I wouldn't have to deal with any of this, because I would never make guardian.

I was here for one reason and one reason alone.

To discover the truth behind Romi's death.

The rest...Not my problem.

CHAPTER 18

CAMERON

My stomach was rumbling by the time we left class. There were kitchens in the main building, but the place was packed with second years, so we decided to head back to the dorm and cook a meal there.

Night time was active time at the academy. The dorm windows were bright spots in the distance, and gargoyles trekked back and forth from the main building to residences.

Many were in their final year of training for general forces, and according to Palia's research, there were written exams as well as practical ones, so the study here was intense.

We decided to take the scenic route past the training grounds.

I wanted to get a better look at them and figure out how they'd gotten it to rain over just one pitch, but as we got closer, the roars and bellows of encouragement drifting toward us told me that the grounds were still occupied.

The grass pitch had been abandoned by the gargoyles, and Varsa, the caretaker, sat on a small tractor-type vehicle which slowly flattened the grass while he sprinkled it with something.

It was the sand pitch that was occupied.

Gargoyles, in beast form, stood in a loose circle, watching something that was blocked to us.

My height disadvantage made it impossible to see what was going on, and the bulky frames of the goyles left no gaps to peek through. All the stomping and cheering made me want to know what was happening beyond the wall of muscle.

I hopped up and down. "Touron, what's happening?"

He craned his neck. "I can't see...One moment." He morphed and instantly shot up by several feet. "Better, but still can't get a proper look." He shot me a toothy grin. "Fancy a lift?" He crooked his arm, offering me a seat on his muscular bicep.

Why the hell not? I hopped up and wrapped my arms around his neck.

Sharniza made a sound of exasperation before morphing, too, and the twins followed suit. The excitement emanating from the sand pitch was too enticing to ignore.

Touron stretched his wings, body coiling, and the next moment we were airborne, high enough to see over the crowd. To see the monoliths in the center of the ring duking it out.

Serath and Orix circled one and another, lunging and grappling, hitting the sand, rolling, and then springing apart in a dance of combat that had my heart fluttering at the beauty of it. These huge monolithic beasts were light on their feet one moment and shaking the ground with stomps the next.

Orix leaped back to avoid Serath's grapple. But the elite leader spun counterclockwise on his heel, turning the missed grapple into a tail swipe that knocked Orix's feet from under him. Orix went down and Serath pounced, pinning him easily.

"Yes." The world was barely a whisper, an explosion of breath, nothing more, but Serath's head whipped up, and he looked right at me, his husky gaze searing me and squeezing my lungs until I couldn't breathe. An aroma spiked in the air, musky and sharp, twisting me in knots and making my heart lurch with primal need. I arched toward him.

"Cam!" Touron grabbed me tight against him to stop me falling off his arm.

Serath's gaze locked on him and darkened with fury. He

bared his teeth in a fresh roar aimed at my friend. Orix forgotten, his body bunched ready to launch into the air.

At us!

"Serath!" Orix grabbed him around the waist and yanked him back, pinning a thick forearm across the leader's neck. Serath growled, snarled, and bucked, his gaze flicking from Touron to me.

"What the fuck?" Touron said.

I caught the flash of Orix's ocean blues, filled with a storm and aimed at me. "Go!" The command had the initiates backing up, but there was no doubt in my mind that the order was for me.

Touron must have come to the same conclusion because he took us higher, swerving toward the dorms, his arms wrapped tightly around me.

We landed on the lawn in front of our residences, but Touron didn't set me down straight away.

"You're shaking," he said. "And...you're warm." His grip on me tightened a fraction, his green eyes darkening as he tracked across my face. "You smell...so good." His voice dropped an octave, thickening with emotion that made my insides thrum.

"You need to put her down," Sharniza said. "Now!"

Touron blinked sharply and shook his head before carefully setting me on my feet. Palia was there to brace me when my knees gave way.

Touron took a step back, exhaling mist as if to clear his senses. "Damn. That was..."

"Um, Touron, you might want to..." Palia waved a hand toward his crotch where the fabric of the Lastonflex was working exceptionally hard.

He looked down and cursed. "Fuck. I'm sorry."

My mind was fuzzy, my body throbbing in the strange needy way it did when I needed to get off but multiplied by ten. "What just happened?"

"It makes no sense," Sharniza said, "and it shouldn't be possible for you *or* for him. Serath's a sigma after all, but I think...I think you're his mate."

❧

THE KITCHENS WERE occupied by a couple of gargoyles I didn't know but we'd seen in class. They were busy cooking chicken on the stove. Sharniza snorted in annoyance.

"I know where we can go to talk," Palia said. "There's a library with a study room we could use."

"Trust you to have found the books," Ginia muttered.

Palia led us through the entrance hall where we slipped beneath an arch onto a dingy corridor. A wooden door halfway down opened into a booklined space dotted with seats and a couple of study tables.

"There's a room over here." Palia crossed to another door that hid a smaller room housing two tables and adjustable lamps.

We squeezed inside and Ginia shut the door.

"How are you feeling now?" Sharniza asked me.

How was I feeling? "Confused." My mind reeled, processing emotions and sensations that Serath had somehow evoked, not to mention Sharniza's conclusion that he was my mate.

"This makes no sense," Palia said. "Sigma's don't have mates. They never have."

"Never doesn't mean they can't," Touron added. He leaned across the table and cracked open one of the windows. "It's warm in here, right?"

"There is no other explanation for Serath's reaction to Cam," Sharniza said, eyeing me with interest. "Maybe your half-blood genes make you...different somehow."

"Halfbloods don't conform to alpha, beta, or omega status," Palia said as if quoting from a textbook. "In fact, not much is known about them at all." She looked deflated, as if she'd let us down somehow.

"I'm hardly the only half-blood out there? Surely if sigmas could mate with halfbloods, it would have happened before now."

"They don't come through Stonehaven often, so maybe sigmas don't usually come across them," Palia suggested.

"So, you think a sigma *needs* a halfblood mate?" Ginia looked perplexed. "He'd break her with his huge—"

"Ginia!" Palia looked shocked.

"It's true," Touron said sagely. "Gargoyle males have mammoth di—"

"Touron!" Palia turned pale, like she was about to pass out.

Ginia sighed and put an arm around her sister. "Palia has an aversion to crude language. It's her personal defect."

Palia shot her a glare. "There is *nothing* wrong with a little decorum."

"You so should have been an omega."

"The guardian world could use a little class." Palia raised her chin. "Who said that gargoyle females have to be all grrr, argh and crush?" She made a crushing motion with her hands.

"The guardian world said so," Sharniza said dully. "But we're veering off the point. Cameron is Serath's mate."

Panic wrapped its hands around my throat. "We don't know that for sure." Mates meant an unwanted commitment. It meant being bound to this world. Mates meant mystical shackles. It meant giving up Levi. "It doesn't mean anything." My tone was weak and unsure, and I wanted a redo. "It can't mean anything. I have someone. I love him."

"You can't," Palia said softly. "Fated mates are...they're sacred. They're twin souls."

"No, they're pheromones and primal lust. What Levi and I have is...It's more than that. We have an emotional connection."

"Levi is your human boyfriend?" Ginia asked.

Levi had shared his halfblood status with me, but it wasn't fair of me to share it with anyone else so I simply nodded in response.

"Yeah, that connection won't hold a candle to a fated mate bond."

"Once the bond has hold, no other male will matter." Palia looked apologetic.

I scanned the others' faces, and they all gave me variations of the same look.

I dropped my face into my hands. This was bad. This was the last thing I needed. Entanglements with a male gargoyle, expectation and...wait...Maybe this could work in my favor. If I *was* his mate, then it would mean getting close. It could lead to disclosure and...sex. No. I couldn't do that. I wouldn't. No matter how much the bond made me want to. If I caved it would cement our bond. So...no sex, but I could get close to him and get the information I needed, then leave. Get far away from him and this world and—

"...no sense why he hasn't approached you yet?" Palia said. "Alphas *always* approach their mate once they find her. Sigmas would be the same. It's such a big deal. There is no choice when it comes to a fated mating. You just belong together, end of. It's not like the omega moon."

The damned omega moon again. "What happens at this omega moon?"

"It's like a mating run," Palia explained. "The omegas run through Greenwood forest and get chased by eligible males, and if they're caught, they can choose to engage in coitus and in some cases mark the male as theirs. The forest is warded that night and only omegas and the invited males can get in."

"But if you're fated, there are no runs," Sharniza said. "Just one mate for life." She gave me a stern look. "You need to speak to him."

I balked. "How? He's an elite. Not exactly accessible, is he? Besides, if what you say is true. If he is my...my fated mate, then he'll find me, right? He'll come to see me."

They all exchanged glances.

"She has a point," Touron said. "But it was strong...The pheromones...So strong." His gaze snagged on mine for a moment, and I caught the dark longing in them before he dragged it away. He rubbed the back of his neck and looked sheepish. "I think I'm going to go for a run. Burn off some tension."

He left the room quickly.

Shit. "I think he's uncomfortable around me now."

"He'll be fine," Palia said. "You must have been emitting some strong pheromones. He just needs to clear his head."

"He'll experience worse on an omega moon," Sharniza pointed out. "The air will be soaked with pheromones."

"Okay, can we stop talking about pheromones?" My stomach growled. "I need food." I headed for the door. "I'm thinking steak and potatoes. We'll save some for Touron." Anything to take the focus of me and my *pheromones.*

"Sounds good," Ginia said.

And when Touron got back I'd speak to him, and things would be back to normal. None of this pheromone bullshit.

I hadn't known him long, but he'd quickly become a friend. I didn't want this weirdness to ruin our dynamic.

I wouldn't let it.

CHAPTER 19

TOURON

I stay in human form as I run for the forest. I need to clear my head of Cameron's floral scent. A scent that didn't bloom for me. It's not mine to savor, and until it saturated my senses, I hadn't looked at Cameron in that way.

I still don't, not mentally anyway, but my primal senses are confused right now. I need to reset them.

Running helps. It's always helped when my senses have been overloaded. When they told me Garth had been killed, I ran ten miles without stopping. Ran and ran until the tears dried and stiffened on my face. Until my chest burned, and my muscles screamed *enough*.

The forest closes in around me, and the earthy scents of nature press in, filtering into my lungs. The winter evergreen aromas slowly wash away Cameron's scent, and the tightness in my crotch ebbs.

It's okay. Everything is okay.

I slow my stride, ready to turn back, when something crashes through the canopy above. I skid to a halt as Serath lands in front of me in his gargoyle form.

My skin pricks, primal instinct calling to my beast, but I hold it back, raising my hands in a placating gesture instead.

Serath slowly straightens from his landing crouch. His pupils are so large that the pale blue is all but gone.

I know what this is, and fuck, I'm in deep shit.

"My actions were not a challenge." I keep my voice even. "There is *no* challenge to your mating."

His chest vibrates, and he tips his head to the side.

He's not in control right now, and I'm in danger, because there's no way I can fight an elite in primal challenge mode. Because that's what this is. He saw me with Cam. Saw me holding his mate while she leaked pheromones, and now his beast is riled up and needs to beat me down.

This is the nasty side of our breed. The side of us that operates on instinct only. I need to snap him out of it.

"Cameron and I are just friends."

He advances, and I lock my knees. Running will be an invitation. He stops a foot away and looks down at me, pupils contracting and dilating as he struggles to control his need to challenge me.

Mist plumes from his nostrils as he breathes heavily. His eyes go wide, the whites bleed to black.

Oh fuck.

Her scent.

It may be out of my head, but it's all over my clothes.

His fist meets the side of my head in a crack that shakes my brain. The world goes dark, and my body vibrates as it hits the ground.

"Serath, no!"

The sound of grappling is followed by the beat of wings.

Fuck...I need to get up, but I can't move.

Cool fingers kiss my brow, and the thunder raging in my head ebbs to a throb. I crack open my eyelids and peer up at the angel hovering above me. She looks down at me with eyes that glow white in her smooth brown face.

Oh wow, she's...wow... "I'm dead, aren't I?"

Her mouth fights a smile. "You'll live, cadet, but you'll have a hell of a bruise. It'll take a few hours to heal."

Wait...she's... "Selas?"

"Touron, right?"

"You know my name?"

The smile breaks through. "I do. I knew your brother. He was a good warrior, and he will be missed."

My throat tightens. "Thank you."

She moves away and stands, looking down at me. "Get back to your dorm and put some ice on that." She turns away.

"Wait. What about Cam? He's her mate, isn't he?"

Her shoulders tense.

"That's why he acted like he did before. It's why he attacked me." I pull myself up. "Why hasn't he spoken to her about it?"

She turns to me with a sigh. "Sigmas aren't allowed to take mates. It's Stone law. Has been for...forever. Tell Miss Walker that she's safe. Serath will keep his distance."

She takes a step, then launches herself up through the canopy, vanishing from sight.

Well at least we have confirmation now, even if it came with a bruised face.

CHAPTER 20

CAMERON

Sharniza slid steaks off the grill while I mashed potatoes. The room smelled meaty and delicious, and my stomach rumbled in eager anticipation.

Palia and Ginia grabbed plates, and I glanced over at the door. We'd held off on cooking, wanting the steaks to be warm when Touron got back. He'd been gone over half an hour now. Surely, he should be headed back by now?

He arrived a moment later, as if summoned by my thoughts. His sandy hair was dappled with dirt and mussed, and his face...

"Oh, God, your face!" I dropped the masher and rushed over to him.

"I'm fine." He held up his hands to ward me off. "Seriously. I just need some ice."

Palia passed him a pack of frozen peas. "If you tell me that you tripped and fell..."

He gave her a wry smile. "I did. After Serath punched me in the head." He pressed the peas to the side of his face and winced. "That goyle hits hard."

"He hit you?" A bubble of rage expanded in my chest. "He fucking hit you? What the fuck?"

"Why did he do that?" Ginia asked, confused.

"I was up close and personal with his mate, that's why."

"No." I shook my head.

"Sorry, Cam. Selas confirmed it," Touron said. "He was in the grip of primal rage. It's a male goyle mate-thing. Selas says he'll leave you alone, though, because sigmas aren't allowed to have mates. Stone law or something."

"I've never heard of such a thing," Palia said.

But I couldn't take my eyes off the swollen bruise on my friend's face, couldn't shake the growing indignant rage that ate away at my lungs. "So, he hit you, then what did he do?"

"I think another elite grabbed him and made him leave," Touron said. "Not sure, I was semi-conscious at the time. But Selas told me that—"

"He just left?" My voice rose an octave. "He hit you and left? No apology. Nothing?" My eyes sizzled with anger.

"It's all right, Cam." Touron said, smiling with the half of his face not busted up. "He's not going to claim the mate bond so—"

I headed for the exit.

"Cam, wait," Sharniza called.

But I was already out of the door because bond or no bond, he had no right to act like I was a piece of meat. No right to hurt my friend and act like he owned me.

He'd barely said two words to me since we'd met.

It was time I changed that.

It was time I said several choice words to his face.

YARROW WAS CLEAR about not accosting the elites at their residences, but one of them had tried to break my friend's face. So, that rule could go suck it.

I stormed out of the dorm and down the path.

"Cam, stop and think about this." Palia strode beside me, the voice of reason I didn't need or want.

"Cam, leave it!" Touron called from behind me. "It's done."

"Like hell! He can't just attack you and get away with it. I won't, argh!" I leaped back as something large and gray swooped at me, and the next moment I was in its grip, boots off the ground and airborne.

"Cam!" My friends' cries drifted away as every sense in my body focused on the thing...the creature that had me in his grip.

Serath held me against his body. Thick muscled arms crushing me to him.

"Don't struggle," he said. "I don't want to drop you."

Struggle? I couldn't think, let alone struggle. His woodsy scent, his arms around me, his body pressed to mine...

Overload.

"Breathe," he said with a soft chuckle. "Just breathe."

I hated him for hurting Touron. I wanted to punch him in the face to even things out. I'd do that as soon as he put me down. As soon as he let me go.

That was right.

That was the plan.

I exhaled and inhaled in quick succession, then regretted it because his delicious aroma flooded my mind and my traitorous body melted against him.

"Fuck," he said under this breath, the word vibrating against me like an intimate invitation.

We landed in a clearing, nature pressing in around us, cocooning us as he continued to hold me. His heart beat like a drum against me.

I was so mad at him. So fucking pissed off. Fuck, this feels good. It felt right. I rubbed my cheek against his pectoral, and he made a soft vibrating sound like a purr.

What was I doing? "What are *you* doing?"

"Having this moment," he said, his voice a low-grade rumble.

I lifted my chin to look up at his monstrous gargoyle face. To trace the strong lines that made up the features that were both frightening and compellingly beautiful. The combination made my heart ache, and the urge to reach up and trace his scar rushed through me so strongly that my fingers were hovering at his jaw before I managed to catch myself.

I clenched my fists. I was here for a reason, and this...This wasn't it. This was hormonal, pheromonal, needy body bullshit. "You hurt my friend."

"I know. I'm sorry."

Dammit, why wasn't he being an asshole? I gritted my teeth. "Tell *him* that."

"I will. I swear it. I will. And after this moment." His throat bobbed. "After this moment, I'll stay away from you. I won't touch you. I won't covet you. I'll let you be. I just...I need this *one* moment."

There was an aching throb to his words that echoed inside me. My eyes heated with the threat of tears that made no sense. I swallowed past the lump in my throat. I didn't want to mate with him. I didn't need a fated lover, but my body didn't seem to agree. It yearned for him. Longed to stay here, like this. Enveloped in his heat, so even though I didn't want it, I found myself asking.

"Why? Why can't you—"

He gripped my jaw and forced my head up. "Don't ask it. *Never* ask it."

My mouth went dry while other parts of me grew slick with need.

He took shallow breaths, eyes rolling as he inhaled. "Fuck..." He continued to sip at the air, sip at my scent. "Fuck me."

He swelled against me, hard and thick, and oh God, in that moment I wanted to. In that moment I wanted to straddle his huge frame and find a way to make him fit. Make us fit, impossible as that might be with him in this form.

How could we be possible? How could he be mine? Why did I want him so badly?

"Don't..." He engulfed my wrist with his hand.

I'd been touching him without realizing it, tracing the hard line of his jaw and his full bottom lip.

He moved suddenly, and my back hit bark so that I was pinned between him and the tree, feet dangling high off the ground. He dipped his head and ran the tip of his nose along the column of my neck.

"This is mine," he said under his breath. "This was made for me." He drew back, husky eyes bright, pupils large and hungry. "I would have been a good mate, Cameron Walker."

I could barely speak past the pinching in my throat. "Why? Why can't you? Why is there a law? Tell me."

"I can't." He inhaled me again. "I wish I could, but I can't, and after this moment we will never speak of it again."

A fracture cut a path across my heart, and confusion clouded my mind. These feelings, these sensations—strong and sudden—made perfect sense, even though they shouldn't.

"Your friends know what this is, but they cannot tell anyone else. The Stone Council cannot find out."

"What happens if they do?"

He closed his eyes as if the answer pained him. "We won't need to find out because this...This won't go any further. You'll be safe." He set me on my feet and moved away, each step slow and deliberate, as if he were fighting himself, as if the distance were physical pain.

I took a step forward.

"Don't." The word was a warning growl.

I froze.

"Goodbye, Cameron Walker." He shot up into the air and vanished beyond the canopy.

"Cam! Fuck, Cam!" Touron came bursting out of the underbrush, Sharniza and the twins in tow. "Where is he?"

"Gone." I pushed the word past the constriction in my throat. "He's gone."

And the goyle part of me, the beast that had never been permitted to grow, quietly mourned.

CHAPTER 21

SELAS

"You shouldn't have let him do that," Orix says.

Let him? "When do we ever *let* Serath do anything?"

"The new cuff works," Willowman says. "The Yarrow siblings channeled into it too. He won't lose control and claim her."

Willowman might as well be an elite. He spends so much time in the tower that he might as well live here. He's our go-to guy when we need help recharging our psychic shields. The man is an enigma, and we've learned not to probe into his past too much.

It's enough that his power is on our side.

"He needs this," Prasan says from his spot by the computers. "It's closure not just for him, but for her too."

"A halfblood... It makes no sense," Orix says.

I don't have to look to know that he'll be sprawled across one of the armchairs. It's his hangout spot when we come up here to meet.

"It makes sense to the cosmos." The moon is an almost full disk in the shadowy expanse of my vision. I can see the forests and mountains beyond the wall as clearly as if it were day, not with my eyes, but with the schematic my mind has captured from my many flights. My sight was taken, but the powers-that-be blessed me with a sonic awareness, a new way to see, and in some ways it's truer than any picture I could ever have seen with my eyes.

It's a deeper seeing, one that investigates a person's heart and feels what they feel. Serath has been broken and torn in the past, but he's always healed and come back stronger. Not being able to claim his mate will be a test of his will and his belief. I suspect that this female has the potential to either be his salvation or his ultimate undoing.

Only time will tell.

But we must let the cards fall where they may.

Another face fills my mind, sandy-haired, bruised, and bloody, but still beautiful in the planes and lines that make it up. He carried *her* floral scent, yes, but *his* was stronger, reaching for me in waves.

I'm dead, aren't I? His words, said with awe when he looked at me. A smile tugs at my lips. I wonder if he'll make initiate. I shut down the thoughts. Alpha females rarely find mates, and if we do, they often leave us for omegas. We don't have fated mates like male alphas, and as far as I know, no alpha female has ever been another alpha's fated mate. We are born for war, and we take our pleasure when and where we wish. Maybe I'll take it with the sandy-haired cadet...

"Selas, are you even listening?" Orix asks.

"No. I was daydreaming."

He huffs in exasperation. "I have a meeting tonight, so I can't be on hand to babysit."

"By meeting you mean a sex date, right?" Prasan says. "I just want to make sure we're on the same page here."

I turn away from the window. "Isn't that the third this week?"

"Are you keeping track?" There's a smile in Orix's voice.

He thinks I'm jealous. We fucked once. It was stress relief. He likes to think it was more. Typical, after all, what has he got to lose? "Yes, I keep track. It's my job to keep track of you. All of you. But right now, Serath needs us, so cancel your plans. As soon as he gets back, we're heading out on patrol."

"Reports of a werewolf den in Night Town," Prasan says.

"Three locals have gone missing. Human law enforcement called it in."

"What about the local hunter unit?" Willowman asks.

"Not responding," Prasan said.

"This is a job for general forces," Orix says.

"Which is why we're cleared to do it," Prasan says with a shrug.

We're a frontline team. One of the strongest forces that the Stone Council have against the graynites. Our five bloodlines are bound to create one fist of power, but we're a finger short.

With Romi gone, we're weakened, and the next Basque in line is just a child, so for now, we're stuck here at the academy. Unable to go to the outer sectors and patrol like we usually do. For all we know, the graynite threat could be growing to take advantage of our inactivity.

I can't just sit here and do nothing.

This minor case is perfect for us. And the fact that it's not too far east means we're cleared to take it on as a quad.

Orix rolls his neck on his shoulders with a sigh. "Fine. Sex or a rumble, either will do. I'll suit up."

My nape prickles, and I turn to the window, pushing out my sonar.

Serath blooms to life in the air and a weight settles on my chest.

He's back, and a rumble is exactly what he needs.

CHAPTER 22

CAMERON

"You'll be okay," Palia said. "You can do this."

I sat on the floor, back against my bed with my head in my hands. My senses were still in overload. My heart twisted and broken over a male I didn't even know.

"This is insane. No one needs to feel this way." *Urgh.* I tugged at the ends of my hair. "I want it to stop." I wanted the storm that leaving Levi had brewed inside me, not this raging tornado that being away from Serath spawned.

"As long as you keep your distance from Serath, you'll be okay," Sharniza said from her spot in my dresser chair. "Look. It's shitty. But you came here to be a guardian. Focus on that."

But I hadn't come here to become a guardian; I'd come here to find out about Romi, and Serath had been my way into the elites, but now...The truth was on the tip of my tongue, but I bit it back.

"We have two hours of training tomorrow," Touron said. "Focus on that. Focus on your goal."

My goal was fucked, but I smiled. "Yeah, you're right."

"You can trust us," Palia said. "No one will find out about this."

I believed her. I believed them all, and even though I'd only known them for a couple of days, I trusted them. But after this fated mate secret, telling them about Romi would be putting another weight onto their shoulders. Another secret. It wasn't fair to drag them into it.

I'd need to figure this out for myself. Ask around and make it look casual. I was sure Yarrow knew something but wasn't telling, and I had no doubt there were others like him here. What I needed was for someone to slip up, but supernaturals were a wily bunch and...Wait a second...Not everyone in a position of power here was supernatural. The headmistress was human. *And* she'd given me an open invite.

The weight on my chest lifted.

"Um...Cam?" Touron said. "Why are you smiling like that?"

I dropped the smile that had crept onto my lips unawares. "What? I'm not."

"You were," Ginia said. "And it was kinda creepy."

"Sorry, I was thinking about Derek." It was the first lie that popped into my head.

"Derek?" Touron asked. "I thought your boyfriend's name was Levi?"

"It is. Derek is the boogeyman that lives in my closet." Silence greeted my declaration. "Never mind."

"Hell, no," Touron said. "You can't say something like that then ask us to forget it."

"Fine. I created Derek when I was a child. I used to have these awful nightmares. There was this voice..." A shudder passed through me. "Anyway, I created Derek to protect me. To make me feel safe, and he did. He's wonderful." Guilt gnawed because I'd left him behind to come here. I'd left him alone when he'd always been there for me. "I left him behind." I exhaled. "He's all alone." Shit.

Levi and Derek.

I'd left them both.

"Cam, it's all right." Touron lowered his frame onto the floor next to me and nudged me with his shoulder. "It's okay. I'm sure he's okay."

I needed that to be true. I needed him to be okay. "I wish I could have brought him with me."

"I doubt he would have gotten past the wards," Sharniza said. "You did the right thing leaving him behind. An Academy filled with gargoyles is no place for a tulpa."

"And I'm sure Levi will move on," Ginia said with a wave of her hand. "He'll find a nice human to settle down with."

My stomach hollowed at the thought. I was a mass of contradictory emotions right now.

Sharniza rose out of the chair. "You should get some rest. Sun will be up soon, and we have a long afternoon of classes ahead of us."

She left, and Palia and Ginia followed, but Touron lingered, waiting for the door to shut before speaking.

"I'm sorry about earlier," he said.

"About what?"

"Getting all weird on you when you released your phe—"

"Don't say that word."

He pressed back a smile. "Okay. But it wasn't intentional, and I don't...I don't see you in that way."

"Gee thanks. I'm so flattered."

He shook his head, smiling and looking at the ground. "You know what I mean. I want us to be friends. I like you, Cameron, and I don't want things to be weird between us."

"They won't. They aren't."

"So, friends?"

"Friends."

He dropped a quick kiss on my temple and headed for the door. "Sleep well, Cam."

"You too."

I had more than training and arcana class tomorrow. I had to wangle a meeting with the headmistress and subtly interrogate her about my brother.

It was going to be a long day.

CHAPTER 23

SERATH

Willowman closes the portal behind us, and outpost three vanished from view. My stomach feels off, just as it always does when we take a warp. And we took one from the academy to outpost three less than ten minutes ago. Portals aren't so bad, but warpings make me sick.

"Drink." Willowman hands me a small bottle containing a tincture to settle my stomach.

I take it and glug. "Thank you, Marcel."

He nods grimly and tucks the bottle into a pouch on his belt. The witch is a walking collection of potions and tinctures. It's a hobby of his, and one we benefit from. If only he could make a tincture to stop the ache in my chest or the longing in my loins. The cuff on my ankle mutes the beast's primal need to rut when I'm near my mate, but my chest is still tight with a grief-like sensation for having left her. For knowing I can't touch her. Be close to her.

I want to know her.

But I can't.

I need to focus on the task at hand. Blow off steam in the only way allowed.

A decent kill.

The settlement before us is silent and asleep. Tiny slate-topped houses sit in a bowl of land surrounded by woodland with desert beyond that. To think this was once a lush isle of rain and rivers, and now the terrain and weather contradict each other at every turn.

Being burned by otherworldly magic can do that.

It's almost one in the morning, and the sparsely populated village isn't one for nightlife; even so, three souls have been taken by werewolves. Three humans devoured, and it's our job to prevent any more losses.

Human populations are low in the Rims, but they thrive in the southern sectors, safe closer to the Fringe. But here, on the outer eastern lands, supernatural threats are widespread and many, and the nightmare nights are a breeding ground for creative imaginations to spawn even more horrors in the form of tulpas.

At least tulpas are easy to extinguish. They always come with a weakness for hunters to exploit and a gargoyle can burn one up with a single touch. Once we catch it of course.

Prasan takes the lead into town. The male carries maps of every settlement and town in his head, and we instinctively follow. Our dark clothes allow us to blend into the shadowy night as we make our way toward the human law enforcement office.

The streets are narrow and filled with dips and hollows, and the buildings seem to sag as if in defeat. There's an air of despondency about this place that puts my teeth on edge.

The enforcement office is a small run-down affair with peeling paint and a half-starved feline loitering on the steps. It peers up at us with desolate eyes the color of peridot. Orix clicks his tongue and holds out his arm. The creature darts forward, leaps up and clambers up his arm, coming to lie across his broad shoulders like an inky, ratty scarf.

"Hey there," Orix says in his soothing baritone. "You're safe now. I've got you."

The cat purrs softly, clinging to him as if he's the lifeline the feline has been waiting for.

"You can't adopt them all," Selas drawls.

"Why not?" Orix reaches across to stroke the cat's head, and it purrs louder and closes its eyes.

I've never visited his cat sanctuary, but I've heard it's a wilderness area on the outskirts of Arcadia, filled with feral cats. Once upon a time, these furry felines were domesticated by humans and kept as pets, but now they roam free, most of them starving. The sanctuary is a safe place for them to thrive.

This cat is lucky Orix found it.

The door to the building opens, and a woman steps out. She's tiny, maybe five feet tall with wild brown curly hair and angry eyes. "*Now* you come," she snaps. "Where were you three days ago when I put in the call, huh?"

I arch a brow at Prasan. This is, after all, his department.

"The call went to your local hunters," he says smoothly, "and only came to us when it wasn't marked as actioned. We came as soon as we could."

But she is looking at us with fresh eyes now, and they go round as realization dawns. "Are you the elite team?"

"Yes," Orix says with a charming smile that showcases his fangs. "We're here to help, so point us in the right direction, and we can get your werewolf problem cleaned up right away."

"Werewolf?" She frowns up at us. "You think we have a werewolf problem?"

"That is what the message said."

She pinches the bridge of her nose and exhales. "Darn it, Bertie."

"What?" someone calls from inside.

She looks over her shoulder. "Did you report our problem as a werewolf issue?"

"Sure did. We got us some werewolves, ain't we, Jude?"

She grits her teeth and peers up at us. "We certainly do, but did you let them know those werewolves also happen to be our local hunters newly turned. Did you do that, Bertie? Did you submit it to the emergency channel?"

"Um...I submitted it."

To the regular route, which would have sent it to the local hunter's inbox, the very hunters they were trying to report. Shit.

Selas steps forward and puts a hand on the woman's shoulder, looking down at her with a reassuringly calm expression. "Okay, start from the beginning and tell us exactly what happened."

"SO, THE HUNTERS went in, and they never came back out," Jude says. "And when I went to investigate, I barely got away." She blows on her coffee mug and takes a gulp of the milky concoction. "Adam, the lead hunter, held the others off so I could escape. He was turning, but hadn't..."

"Become a monster yet?" Selas provides.

"Yes." She looks up at us, and I notice the red veins in her eyes for the first time, the dark smudges that speak of lack of sleep and the tightness of her mouth that tells me she's determined to keep her people safe.

Humanity, for all its sins, is a tenacious beast indeed.

"Mutts are unpredictable," Willowman says. "But they don't usually turn humans. They're more about feeding, and more mutts mean more competition for food, so this makes no sense."

"Tell me about it," Jude drawls. "But it's happening so... Help me."

I take a breath and speak for the first time. "We will."

She glances at me and nods.

"Even beast born wouldn't turn a whole group like this," Orix mutters under his breath.

Beast born are selective about who they let into their packs. They prefer order and rules. We don't know much about them, because they keep to themselves, and we rarely have to deal with them. Most migrated to the city, into the wards, when the mageri offered sanctuary, and those that stayed in the Rim kept off the radar, hunting mainly game.

Mutts...well they're a different breed. A hybrid bloodline,

whose genetics are questionable. They sleep in the day and hunt at night, so they'll be active now. We can take them down.

I focus on the woman. "How many?"

"Five hunters, and...I don't know how many mutts," she says.

Prasan shrugs. "Mutts aren't an issue. Newly turned mutts, who were once hunters, might be a challenge." He grins, revealing jagged teeth.

And it's a challenge I need. I match his grin and nod. "Let's go smash some skulls."

THE CURFEW THE local sergeant has set means that the streets are empty, doors locked, curtains drawn. The people of this settlement are frightened, and rightly so.

But not for long.

Power fizzes through my veins as we fly over the streets, searching for the fallen pylon which marks our location. There's an old, abandoned stately home to the west of it. Mostly ruins, its roof partially missing. That's where the creatures are holed up. Woodland borders the acres of land that once made up this estate.

People lived here at one time. A family. Noble bloods maybe. But it is now an empty shell holding no spark of its former glory.

We land silently on what was probably a landscaped lawn previously but is now an untamed garden of nature.

There are only four of us now, since Willowman remains at the station with Orix's adopted cat. Although he sometimes accompanies us on missions, he isn't cleared for combat and must stay back to provide arcanic assistance from afar if required.

So now, for the first time in two decades, the elite team is missing a member. Our strength is diminished until that elite is replaced.

This time I take the lead. We make a circuit of the house, noting boarded up windows and missing walls. The place is a step away from crumbling. There's no way to pen the creatures in. If they want to escape, there are plenty of places to slip out, and we can't cover them all.

I look to Orix and indicate the sky.

He nods and backs up, ready to launch himself into the air and keep an aerial watch. He'll attack any mutt that runs out.

The rest of us climb into the building through a hole in the wall.

It's quiet inside. Too quiet for a mutt den at this time of night. Moonlight dapples the cracked wooden floors and broken tile as we pick our way across the ground. It's impossible not to make a sound. Our bodies are large, our feet built to grip and hold our weight. But our objective now isn't stealth.

They'll know we're here. They'll either attack or run.

Either way, we'll hear them.

Prasan shoves a table out of the way, and Selas crunches over broken plates and glass.

We move into single file down a corridor. The sky peeks at us through gaps where the windowpanes have fallen out.

An arch leads us into a large chamber, and the smell of blood and gore hit me.

It takes a moment to process what I'm seeing. and when it does, the scene makes no sense.

Several bodies are sprawled on the ground, either gutted or with their throats ripped out. And the remains of several more are piled into a corner. Some of the bodies are in partial shift.

The mutts.

But others are in human form.

Prasan points at two of the bodies. "They're marked."

There are two types of hunter. The civilian hunters and the marked. The marked are rumored to have druid origins somewhere in their bloodlines and work in packs. Each pack has their own mark, a symbol that they tattoo onto their bodies, probably related to their druidic ancestry. Two of the four males have visible marks, and I wager the other two are somewhere in this mess of dead bodies also.

Someone got to this nest before us.

What is this?

A shadow shifts, my scalp tightens, and a growl swells in my chest. "Come out. Now."

A man steps out of the shadows across the room, wiping blood off his face with a handkerchief.

"You made it. I was wondering when you'd show up," he says.

My skin hardens, an automatic response to a serious threat. But this male looks human. Smells human. Barely six feet in height with a medium, wiry build, he's hardly a threat, and yet I have no doubt he's responsible for the carnage here.

"Who are you?" Prasan asks. Ever the information gatherer.

"Ah, introductions. How civil. Not at all what I've heard about your kind."

"Then you know we don't have the patience for small talk." I take a step forward and the air crackles in warning. The familiar scent of sulfur hits me, and my stomach hollows.

Because that smell only accompanies one type of creature. "Graynite."

He smirks.

"He can't be," Prasan says. "He's human."

"Am I?" His eyes flash yellow, the gleam of a graynite's eyes. "Sorry about the mess. I was trying a little experiment. Didn't go so well. Turns out hunters don't take too well to the wolf curse. They die in excruciating pain, so I did the right thing and put them out of their misery, and once they were dead...well...the mutts didn't matter anymore." He tucks his hands into his jeans pockets and lifts his shoulders. "So sorry you got dragged all the way over here for nothing."

I have no idea how he exists, but there's only one way to find out. We need to capture and interrogate him.

The others have come to the same conclusion. I feel it in the fizz in the air and the throb in my blood. We take one unified step toward him, then dash.

I aim straight for him while Selas and Prasan flank him.

His eyes flare wide as he realizes what's about to happen. Regular gargoyles can't move this fast, but we're not regular gargoyles.

I make a grab for him. My fingers graze the cotton of his shirt, and victory rages through my blood, but in the end, I grab only air.

He's gone.

"Fuck!" Prasan punches the wall and brick and mortar crumble to the ground.

"We have to report this to the Stone Council," Selas says. "This...this could change everything."

Yes, because until now, graynites haven't been able to procreate with humans. It's what's kept their numbers in control. But if what we just encountered was a Graynite-human hybrid, then we're all in big trouble.

CHAPTER 24

Cameron

You never know when the last time you'll see someone will be. Like the last time I saw Romi. We had been sitting on the couch, feet up, popcorn bowl between us, getting ready to watch a selection of old movies he'd managed to get his hands on.

I'd never seen a movie before Romi introduced me to them. We didn't have a movie player. I still couldn't believe that acting had once been a profession, and that there'd been a whole industry around making stories into film. Romi had said they probably made movies in the city, that they probably still had actors, but here in the Rim we made do with books and whatever had been left after the exodus.

At least we still had publishing presses and writers and the news was on three times a day.

"I'll be gone a few weeks this time," Romi had said, taking the popcorn bowl from me as the title credits began to play.

I'd hit pause and twisted my body to look up at him. "How many weeks?"

"Four...Maybe six."

My heart sank. "Oh..."

"But when I come back, I'll have two weeks off, and guess what?"

"You're going to spend it with me?"

He grinned. "Nope. *You're* going to spend it with me. I've met someone, and I want you to meet her too."

"Wait, you have a girlfriend? You're actually going to introduce me to another gargoyle?"

He shook his head. "No. Miranda is...She's not a gargoyle. She's human."

A human? He was seeing a human despite what he knew his father...our father would say about it. "Romi, are you sure you want to do this?"

He smiled, his eyes taking on a dreamy look. "I've never been so sure in my life. I love her, Cam, and I know you will too."

We'd talked and watched movies and eaten way too much, and when he'd said goodbye, I'd had hope in my heart. Hope that he'd become a larger part of my life now that he was in love with a human. Hope that maybe I could become more a part of his.

But none of that was to be.

And in my shock and grief over Romi's death I'd completely forgotten about the woman he'd planned to introduce me to.

Poor Miranda. She'd never know what happened to the male she fell in love with.

I lay in bed, pondering, running that memory over in my mind and looking for clues. Anything else that might give me an idea of what his mission had been those weeks, or who this Miranda was. But I came up blank.

Thoughts of Levi filled my mind. I'd told him I was leaving but not when. I should have left him a note. Something to soften the awful goodbye. But then, what would I have said? It wasn't like I could promise to come back to him. And poor Derek. I'd created him and left him to fend for himself. This trip. Being here...It had to amount to something meaningful or else I'd have hurt them both for nothing.

I had class in an hour.

Time to get up.

I showered quickly, then hurried into the bedroom to dress.

A mug of coffee sat on my bedside table. "Hello? Ghost?" Nothing. I grabbed a sticky note and scrawled a message to the spirit.

Thank you so much for the coffee. Wanna hang out?

Cam x

I stuck it by the mug, pulled on my clothes, then downed the drink before heading out.

TOURON, SHARNIZA, AND the twins were already in the kitchen, finishing up breakfast. Touron pushed a plate of bacon toward me, but I shook my head. I didn't have much of an appetite this morning.

"Eat it," Sharniza said. "We have physical training first off today. You'll need the energy."

"She's right," Palia said before shoving a crispy slice into her mouth and chewing with gusto. "So good."

I snagged a couple of pieces and ate them quickly, barely tasting anything.

"That's it?" Touron frowned.

"I'll grab something more later. Let's go."

I wanted classes over so I could see the headmistress and sneakily interrogate her. Training and arcana were just in the way of my main objective for the day. I might have gone earlier if I hadn't been sure she kept late hours like most of the inhabitants on campus.

"Someone's eager," Sharniza muttered.

"She's right, though," Palia said, getting up quickly. "We should get going. The class is being taken by Master Farnell, and he's a stickler for punctuality."

"Total hard ass," Ginia said.

"Ginia!" Palia snapped. "Language."

Ginia rolled her eyes. "Ass is not a cuss word. It's a part of the body, and also an animal."

"Not the way you were using it," Palia said primly.

They continued to bicker as we made our way to the training hall.

We got there just as the doors opened. I caught the top of Curi's blue head. He was right up front and the first through the doors.

We trooped into the room laid with mats and lined with weapons racks. The ceiling was high but not high enough for aerial combat. I supposed that took place mainly on the outdoor training grounds.

A gargoyle in human form stood to one side of the room. He was stocky and solidly built, standing so still I almost mistook him for a weapons rack. His gray hair was buzz cut, accentuating the squareness of his head. Metal bands on his wrists caught the light and winked at me.

His attention was on Curi and his minions, who stood whispering with their heads together. His glare must have penetrated their little bubble because they straightened quickly.

The gargoyle's gaze settled on me next. He stared long enough to put my teeth on edge. I'd have looked away if I hadn't been held hostage by his ice-blue peepers.

He finally released me with a blink.

"Why was he looking at Cam like that?" Palia whispered.

"Farnell is all about survival of the fittest," Sharniza said. "We aren't told about the trials and tests that take place here, but I've heard about Farnell. You don't pass his class if he considers you weak."

Good thing I didn't give a shit about passing his class. I just needed to get past it so I could get on with the real mission for the day.

Touron stepped closer to me. "Stick with me. If we're asked to spar, you can be my partner."

Damn, he was a sweetheart. "Thank you."

"Or mine," Sharniza said. "I'll make it look real when I take you down."

"Er...thanks?"

Palia and Ginia giggled, and Farnell's head whipped around, drilling them with that ice-blue gaze.

Fuck.

This was not going to be fun, but we'd get through it.

"My name is Master Farnell, and my class will be fast-paced, unrelenting, and brutal."

Fabulous.

"I'll test your endurance, your stamina, your strength, and your mental fortitude. Fail in any of those and you fail my class. Fail my class and you go straight to the admin bin. You do not pass go. You do not collect any fucking money. Do you understand?"

A chorus of "yes, sirs" filled the room, and I found him staring at me once more.

"Do you understand?" he said again, aimed at me.

Unlike the others, I wasn't frightened of the admin bin. I wasn't here for his approval; and I didn't like the fact that he seemed to have made up his mind about me already.

I crossed my arms and met his gaze coolly. "I understand, but feel free to repeat yourself if it makes *you* feel better."

Several gasps filled the room, but Master Farnell wasn't fazed. In fact, his lips curved into a thin smile. The kind of smile I'd expect to see from someone accepting a challenge.

"A smart mouth won't save you from a graynite, halfblood. But feel free to exercise it to your heart's content if it makes *you* feel stronger."

Ouch.

He turned on his heel and strode to the main doors to close them. "Today, you will be put into pairs, and you will fight. There is only one rule. No death. Once you've had enough, stay down and your opponent wins. Simple." He turned to face us. "This will allow me to assess your abilities and separate the adept from the inept." He lifted his chin. "Medic time will be allotted to those who may need it." He looked right at me when he said that.

Bastard.

I hated this guy, and I barely knew him.

He started calling names and pairing us up. The first pair were gargoyles I hadn't spoken to yet.

"Palia and Sharniza."

Palia grinned at Shar.

"Touron and Dayn," he continued.

One of Curi's buddies stepped forward and cracked his knuckles. He was no bigger than Touron, but he was stockier. Touron rolled his shoulders and bounced on his feet, ready to rumble.

He called out two more names. Two males paired up, leaving me, Ginia, Curi, and another male gargoyle, unpaired.

Ginia looked over at me and smiled. Looked like we were going to be fighting, but I felt sorry for the other male. He wasn't as stocky as the other goyles in his human form. I'd seen him around the dorm, and he hadn't looked at me in disgust, which gave him points in my book. It sucked that he was going to be paired with Curi, who was a total bastard.

"Ginia and Saffe," Farnell said.

Wait, that meant...

My pulse went wild.

"What?" The word exploded from Touron's lips.

Curi grinned, cold and evil, and my stomach clenched.

Oh shit. I was about to fight Curi.

CHAPTER 25

CAMERON

"I'll take Curi," Touron said quickly. "Give Cameron to someone else."

Farnell stared at him flatly. "You'll fight who I assign to you. You follow orders. That is what a guardian does."

"With all due respect," Touron bit out, "Curi is a sadistic asshole."

"I'll be the judge of that," Farnell said.

He was doing this to make a point. Hit me hard and illustrate that I didn't belong here. But the joke was on him. I already knew I wasn't guardian material. I just needed to be cadet material for long enough to get what I came for.

Sharniza took a step forward, but I cut her off with a look.

"It's okay. I'm fine."

Sharniza's lip curled in a silent snarl aimed at Curi, but she didn't say a word.

Touron on the other hand wasn't done. He rounded on Curi, his voice dropping an octave. "I know where you sleep."

Curi smirked. "Anytime."

I was so done with the male posturing. "Let's just do this."

Romi had trained me for years in self-defense. I could handle myself well enough against a human or a supernatural, but I'd never gone up against a gargoyle. Romi didn't count because he'd always held back in training, afraid to hurt me. Still, there was a first time for everything. I wasn't holding out hope of beating Curi, but I could evade, get in a few punches, then hit the mat when I was ready for time out.

"Take to the mats," Farnell said to Curi. "We'll get you over with first."

Over with, because he didn't expect me to last long. Indignation flared in my chest and the stupid stubborn part of me that didn't like being outdone reared its petty head.

No. No. I'd stick to the plan. Evade, get in a couple of blows, then hit the mats.

Touron walked right up to Curi, and for a moment it looked as if he was going to smack into him, but he swerved at the last moment so that only his shoulder bumped the goyle.

Curi shook his head, a dry smile on his lips, and when his eyes locked with mine that smile widened.

"You ready to rumble halfblood?" he asked.

"Sure, blue boy, let's do this." Nerves be damned. I wasn't going to make this easy. I wasn't going to go down like a fool. Romi hadn't trained me for nothing. I'd make him proud.

The other gargoyles moved back and surrounded our mat.

I kicked off my sneakers and bounced on my feet, rolled my shoulders, and did a few stretches like Romi had taught me.

"Are you done dancing?" Curi growled.

I smiled sweetly at him. "No, Curi, I'm just about to get started."

Curi lowered his head and charged.

My stomach dropped, and then a calm settled over me. *Hold.* Romi's voice filled my head. *Hold. Let him run at you then use his momentum against him.*

Now.

I side-stepped, ready to spin so I was behind him, ready to shove him, but his tree trunk arm slammed into my chest, knocking the wind out of my lungs and the feet out from under me.

No. He'd anticipated my move.

Up, Get up. Move.

I rolled in time to avoid being crushed. Fiery claws dug into my scalp tearing a scream from my lips.

He had me by the hair.

Shit.

I twisted, and grabbed his thick wrist, digging in my nails.

He laughed. "That might work on a human's skin, but I'm not human."

Tears blurred my vision as he hauled me up by the hair, his grip so tight that if I tried to break free, I was sure he'd tear it from the roots.

He drew me close. "You want to hit the mats, hmmm? Admit defeat?"

That had been the plan, but his hand in my hair and his hot breath in my face had fury bubbling through my veins. My vision darkened at the edges as I struggled to breathe past the rage. The primal part of my nature always hovered out of reach, hidden in the shadowy recesses of my mind, but the bond with Serath had nudged it, brought it out a little, so now, with this oaf's fist in my hair, his face up close and personal to mine, she finally stepped out of the shadows.

"You might not have human skin, but every male has one weakness."

"Oh? And what is that?"

I grabbed his balls and squeezed with everything I had.

He let out a pained groan, mouth parting on a whimper. He was supposed to let go, but his grip on my hair tightened, leading me to squeeze harder.

"Ungh!" His inverted roar vibrated between us, then cold fire exploded against the side of my head.

The world tipped and the mat hurtled up to meet me.

CHAPTER 26

SERATH

"This is a bad idea," Selas says as we make our way to the new cadets' first combat training class. "You should skip this one. I'll square it with Farnell."

Not happening. "He asked me personally a week before the cadets arrived. I've got to be there. I owe him."

"You owe yourself," she says.

"No, Selas. Not in this case." My hand goes up to graze the scar on my face. It burns sometimes. Reminding me of how I got it, but it could have been so much worse if not for Farnell.

The training building looms, and Selas opens the door.

Cameron's scent hits me. Not sweet and inviting like usual, but metallic and sharp like iron filings. She's in danger.

"Serath, no!" Selas grabs my arm with a steely grip. "Calm down. Now. Damn you."

Cameron on the ground. My mate is on the ground. *Bleeding.* There's blood, and a male hovers over her in a menacing stance.

She's not moving. She's not *fucking* moving.

Blood rushes to my head, my vision bleeds crimson, and I'm about to tear myself from Sela's grasp when Cameron slowly raises her head and spits blood.

"Is that all you've got mother fucker?" Her voice is a deep

resonance that calls to the beast inside me. Her eyes flash green.

Oh fuck, she's beautiful. So fucking beautiful. Power emanates from her tiny frame, saturating the air and filling my every breath. I want to join her. I *need* to join her.

"You can't." Selas's grip on my arm is a manacle reminding me of my duty. My vow, and the risks to the female that was created just for me.

I breathe through my nose to calm my base instincts and watch Cameron gather herself. The side of her face is purple and bruised. Her lip is bleeding, but her eyes, gods, her eyes are emeralds of lethal intent as her gargoyle nature comes to the fore. Even though I know she's no match for the Mason boy, even though I know he'll eventually overpower her, I also know my mate will go down swinging.

She wipes her mouth with the back of her hand and falls into a crouch before making a bring it gesture with her fingers.

The Mason boy's thighs bunch. He's about to attack. If he touches her, I'll kill him. There is no other outcome.

A rumbling fills my chest. "Selas..."

"Master Farnell!" Selas strides forward, and Farnell notices us for the first time. "I'd like to take this opportunity for a teaching moment, if I may."

The Mason boy stands down and turns to look our way, but I have eyes only for her.

Cameron locks gazes with me, and her skin flushes. The metallic scent of danger spikes with a sweet undertone, and now I need to cross the room for an altogether different reason.

The cuff on my ankle heats and tightens as it attempts to mute my susceptibility to her pheromones, but it barely takes the edge off.

Selas is still speaking, but I scarcely register her words. I'm locked in a battle with my primal self because my prize is so close. So fucking close.

"Get off the mat, Miss Walker." Selas blocks my view of Cameron, and the hold on me relaxes. I exhale and take a step back to compose myself.

I'm an elite. A leader. An example.

Cameron joins her friends, and Selas turns to the Mason boy. "Hello, Curi," she says softly.

He's gone still and silent. Staring, simply staring at his cousin.

Selas smiles, but with her milky-white eyes, it looks more like a threat. "There's a technique to taking down an opponent larger than you. As a female gargoyle, it's one I've honed to perfection. And now, with the help of my lovely assistant, I will demonstrate how." She cants her head. "So, Curi, are you ready to attack me?"

His fists clench. "No."

Murmurs skim over the gathered. They'll think him weak. A coward. But I doubt he cares.

He has his reasons for not laying hands on Selas, and she knows it. She's made him small without landing a single punch.

"I concede." Curi kneels and bows his head. "I wouldn't dream of challenging an elite."

"Get up you fool," Farnell snaps. "You'll challenge whomever we tell you to if you wish to stay in this program."

Curi's jaw flexes. He stands abruptly.

"Cam!" Someone cries.

This time I can't hold back.

I'm across the room in a flash.

Cameron is unconscious in the female gargoyle's arms. I reach for her, but the gargoyle steps away from me, cradling Cameron to her chest while shooting me a warning glare.

"We've got her," she grits out.

My instinct is to take my mate from her, but Selas is beside me, her hand on my arm, drawing me back, reminding me of what I can't have.

"Take her to the infirmary," Selas says. "The rest of you have a demonstration to watch." She looks up at me. "Let's teach the next generation."

You can't go after her. You can't be with her.

Focus.

I bare my teeth. “I won’t make it easy for you, Selas.”

“Do you ever?”

The double entendre makes me smile, but when I look up, I catch the Mason boy staring, a look of hopelessness in his eyes.

I remind myself that he’s a cadet. Young and foolish, that this is a training facility, and that Cameron will be in several situations where she might get hurt.

But it isn’t normal for a male gargoyle’s mate to be in danger.

Our mates are usually omegas who are coveted and kept safe in their dens.

This...There is nothing normal about this, and it will take every ounce of my will to keep my primal nature under control.

Because one slip could doom us both.

CHAPTER 27

CAMERON

The infirmary was empty. Hardly surprising, because gargoyles rarely got hurt, and if they did, they healed quickly. This room was for the odd emergency, but with me here now, it might get some use.

The female gargoyle tending to me seemed excited about having something to do. She cleaned the blood off my face, prodded the side of my head for a while, then shined a light into my eyes before standing back with a sigh.

She was petite for a goyle with silken dark waves and almond eyes, and either the air in the room was laced with a tranquilizer or she was exuding calming vibes.

She smiled and set the penlight down. "You'll be fine. You most likely had a brain bleed, but your gargoyle nature fixed it. If you were pure human, you'd be dead." She pressed her lips together. "Are you *sure* you want to be here, Cameron?"

"Yes. I'm sure."

"It's not going to get any easier," Sharniza said, her voice low. "You're going to get hurt. A lot."

I wasn't afraid of getting hurt. Not a fan of it. But not afraid. "I can handle it." I frowned up at her. "Do you want me to go?"

She rolled her eyes. "I'd like you to live."

"Aw, Shar, I knew you loved me."

She snorted. "Shut up."

The medic goyle clasped her hands together. "I do love it when the cadets make friends. Too many come here with the wrong attitude, like it's every man for himself and we must all be in competition, but you can't win a war without unity. You can't have your fellow warrior's back effectively if you don't care about them."

"Easy for you to say," Sharniza said, her tone bitter. "You're not the one who has to fight. You get to sit in a cozy den and knit booties for your babies."

The medic stared at Sharniza, stunned for a moment before her shoulders dropped, and a small smile lifted her lips. "Being an omega comes with its own challenges. Yes, we do get to stay cozy in our dens, but we're also responsible for ensuring our race survives. That the next generation of gargoyles are strong enough to continue the fight against the gray forces. It's no small responsibility."

Sharniza looked sheepish. "I didn't mean to offend."

"You didn't. We have our roles and our place, but you"—she looked at me—"this isn't the place for you. However, if you plan on staying, then I better stock up on supplies." Her eyes twinkled.

"Um...thanks?"

"Is she okay to go now?" Sharniza asked.

"Yes. You should be all healed up by tomorrow afternoon. Take it easy until then."

I swung my legs off the infirmary bed and made to stand.

"Oh, and feel free to come visit the den anytime. Just ask for Chlobe at the front desk and they'll ring me." Her eyes lit up with an idea. "In fact, you should join us for our monthly trip into Asteria. Next weekend. Sunday."

Asteria was one of the larger settlements filled with places to shop and known for export and trade. I needed some stuff. New clothes and the likes.

"Sure. That'll be great."

"Great, I'll add you to the warp roster and send you the details."

"We need to get to class," Sharniza said flatly.

I looked up at her stony expression, then back to Chlobe. "Can I bring a friend?"

I caught the edge of panic in her eyes before she staunched it and smiled. "If you like."

"Shar? Wanna come shopping?" I nudged her with my elbow meeting unrelenting muscle.

Shar smiled thinly. "Sure, why not?"

Chlobe's smile remained, but it now had a fixed quality to it. As if it was painted on. "I'll add an extra person to the warping. But feel free to pop in and see us before then." This she addressed to me, not Sharniza.

I wanted to ask why Shar wasn't included in that invitation but kept my mouth shut because I couldn't help but feel I'd made a faux pas by asking to bring Sharniza along on the shopping trip.

We left Chlobe to her empty infirmary and headed out the door, almost bumping into Varsa the caretaker.

He grunted and side-stepped to avoid a collision, shooting us an annoyed glare before shuffling off down the hall.

The corridors to the main building were silent and empty, most goyles either still in bed or in class. "What was that about?"

"I doubt he likes anyone," Sharniza muttered.

Huh? "No, not the caretaker. Chlobe. Things got weird when I asked if you could come shopping."

"Omega and alpha females don't mix. Unless they're mother and daughter, and even then, once the alpha matures, the omega doesn't have much to do with her. She's raised by the male influence."

"What? Why?"

"Just the way it is." There was a bitter edge to her tone.

"Just the way it is? Things are a way for a reason."

She came to a halt. "We all have our place, Cameron. Maybe you don't get that because you're a halfblood, but in this world, omegas stay with omegas and alphas with alphas. It's better that way. That way we aren't reminded of what we can't have."

Even though I'd told myself I didn't care about this world, I'd still wondered what life would be like as a pureblood. But now I was glad I wasn't a part of it.

Gargoyles may have super strength and power, extra sensory capabilities, and the ability to shift form and fly. They may be able to heal in a blink and resist damage, but as a half human I had one thing they didn't.

A choice in how I lived my life.

And there was power in that.

CHAPTER 28

SERATH

"You did good today," Selas says to me.

"Don't patronize me. You know this is the last place I want to be right now." I want to be on campus, stalking my mate. I want to be close enough to hear her voice and inhale her scent. "This cuff isn't working."

This mate bond is turning me into a primal mess.

"It's working fine," Willowman says. "If it wasn't, then you'd have claimed her already."

The observatory is bathed in rays of red and orange as the sun sets. It's beautiful. My favorite time of day because this is when my true nature surfaces. When our full power is released. When we can access our gargoyle forms and our baser forms, the primal beasts that each of us hide deep within. This is the moment that I usually lose myself as all the disconnected parts of me connect, but this evening, all I can think about is the bruise on Cameron's face and the blood on her lip.

The need to protect her and end whoever harms her flows through me in a sudden rush. My hands curl into fists.

Control it.

There is nothing you can do.

She chose this path.

She chose to be here.

Determined, willful, half human, and no match for the gargoyles Farnell will pit her against. She'll get hurt because he'll have no mercy. He'll treat her like everyone else and not give her an inch of leeway. It's why he's the best at what he does. Why our cadets come out strong.

But this is my mate.

Mine.

Focus.

You can't have her.

She won't make it here. Her body isn't as strong as ours, and death during training is a very real possibility. I press my knuckles to my chest and massage to get rid of the sudden burning sensation while craving the numb detachment that filled me before she arrived. The ability to step back, to assess a situation before acting is my strength, at least it always was before.

My role here. My purpose means everything. How can I lead my team when my mind and body are in such turmoil?

Cameron cannot be a distraction, but the fated mate bond has other plans. Plans that I'll need to fight.

"I'll work with her," Selas says softly. "I'll help her."

I glance up sharply, and she smiles.

"That is what you're thinking about, right?" she asks. "About Cameron and how she might get killed."

"That wouldn't be a bad thing," Orix mutters from his favorite seat, cat on his lap.

My body reacts instinctively to attack him. The cat hisses at me, as if sensing my intention, and Selas steps in front of me, placing her palm on my chest. "We can't let this come between us. We're a team." She shoots Orix a glare. "Have some fucking sensitivity. None of us know how difficult this is for Serath or Cameron. They're fighting nature right now, and nature is a powerful force."

"Hush," Orix soothes the cat, stroking between its ears, before meeting my gaze with an exasperated sigh. "Fine. I'll help train her too."

"You?" I can't keep the growl out of my voice. "After you tried to kill her?"

Orix rolls his eyes. "I thought we were over that. Look. I promised you I wouldn't hurt her, didn't I?"

He did. He made a vow. He doesn't make vows lightly. "I'm sorry. I trust you. Believe you."

He studies me for a long beat and then sighs. "I heard about this fated mate thing but seeing it...I'm sorry this is happening to you. I'm sorry it isn't the blessing it should be."

A wave of weariness washes over me. "You can train her too. After you apologize for trying to kill her." I give him a wry smile. "I think she'll need that."

"And how will that look to the other cadets?" Willowman points out. "Preferential treatment for the halfblood, especially from the elites, will bring up questions."

"Then we'll be discreet," Selas says. "We'll meet in secret somewhere secluded. I think I can give her some useful pointers. Two or three sessions should suffice."

"I agree," Prasan says. "We should help her." He looks at me. "Because it will help you."

The knots in my chest ease a little. I hate that I need them to do this. I hate that I've become this unbalanced male who can't focus.

I *need* to focus. "Have the Stone Council gotten back to us about the hybrid Graynite?"

"Nothing yet," Prasan says from the computer. "Although, outpost four and six have both reported grotesque attacks."

My heart sinks. "Did they neutralize them?"

"Yes."

Neutralizing grotesques always hurts. They're a breed of gargoyle. Watchers that fought with us against the gray, but the gray claimed them and turned them against us. The taking of our grotesques almost turned the tide in the grays' favor, but we pushed on and won the war, forcing the gray back into the hole it came from.

At least that's how history tells it.

Now that the gray is gone, we're left with rabid grotesques that constantly test the sanctity of our outposts, desperate to get into the major settlements and feed on humans. And then we have the graynites—powerful sentient creatures that surged out of the gray at the last moment before it was vanquished.

A final fuck you, from the entity from another world that hoped to turn our world to nothing.

The gray is gone but its influence remains, and I doubt that we'll ever vanquish it. "We need to know what they're up to. Has Alpha One checked in yet?"

"Not yet," Prasan said. "But the area they're in is an empty zone."

No signals, radio or otherwise. They're on their own. Gathering intel on the graynite stronghold. A city warded, walled and impossible to infiltrate. We've been sending teams in to test the barriers and the power of the wards for years, hoping to find a weakness.

If we can get in, we can wipe them all out in one fell swoop. "When is the deadline for check in."

"Forty-eight hours," Prasan says.

"If we don't hear from them in that time, I'm heading out there."

"I'll come with you," Orix says.

"Me too," Willowman adds. "You might need me."

"I'll stay here and keep an eye on Cameron," Selas says with a smile.

"We'll need to get approval from headquarters," Prasan points out.

The headquarters that barks orders while sitting in their offices. The place is run by humans and goyles together, coordinating our efforts at keeping the Rim safe. Most have never been out in the field, and yet, we're bound to take orders from them.

"Fine, do it now. Put in the request."

"I've been working on a transmitter that might be able to cut through the interference that the graynite shade creates. If we can weaken the shade, then maybe we'll get through the wards," Prasan says. "If they approve the request, then I'll come and see if I can plant it."

The shade...remnants of the gray and the power that runs through a graynite's veins. It powers their wards and keeps us at a distance, and it's something we've, to date, been unable to bypass or disable. Maybe Prasan's invention can change that. Either way, a mission gives me focus and takes me away from here, from Cameron and that...that's the best thing for the both of us right now.

CHAPTER 29

CAMERON

Arcana class was on the fourth and final floor of the main building, which was built as one huge central chamber with a glass-domed ceiling. The dying rays of the sun painted the granite floors a crimson hue and gave the whole area a warm, cozy look. Metal framework pressed to the glass, and I spotted delicate hinge work.

"It can open to let in gargoyles or let us out," Sharniza said. "The handbook says there's a warping spot right up there." She pointed to the red sky swirling with purple clouds.

It was easy to stand in the center of this space and ignore the many archways leading off from it, easy to forget about the gargoyles occupying benches set up against the walls. Easy to pretend that I was in the sky.

"Cam! Shar!" Touron called from across the room. "This way."

Sharniza and I joined him at the arch and followed him into the corridor beyond. Large plant pots lined the walls, each filled with lush foliage that left the air smelling sweet and floral.

"It's lucky I don't have a pollen allergy."

"Gargoyles don't have allergies, and we don't get sick," Sharniza reminded me.

"Room four zero one," Touron announced before pushing

open the door and leading us into a room where one wall was all windows and the other looked like it was made of reinforced steel. Seats were arranged at the back, and most were taken.

Curi sat head bowed and alone. His minions clustered with Saffe and two others. Looked like his refusal to fight Selas had made him a pariah.

I didn't like him. He was a bully. But his reaction to Selas had been weird. It would have been the perfect moment for him to step up and show the elites how good he was, but he'd backed down. It didn't make sense.

Palia and Ginia waved us over. They'd saved us seats.

"How are you feeling?" Palia asked me.

"Like I got punched in the head." I smiled wryly. "I'm okay, though."

The door opened, and Blake Yarrow walked into the center of the room. I glanced back at the door, expecting to see his sister, but she wasn't with him.

Yarrow clasped his hands behind his back and faced us, his expression unreadable, golden eyes bright against his warm brown skin. He looked older today, probably because he was in dress slacks and a button-down shirt.

Our gazes locked for a moment before his attention slipped to the bruise on my face. Yeah, it looked bad, and it would probably get worse before it got better.

He dismissed me and addressed the class. "Today I'll be testing your psychic shields. Every gargoyle has one, but not all of you know how to use it. My job is to teach you how to strengthen it, hold it in place, and use it to protect your mind against supernatural manipulation."

Palia put her hand up.

"Yes, Miss Lambert?"

"What supernaturals can control our minds? I don't know of any."

"There are a rare few who can." He smirked. "*If* they choose to." His eyes glowed bright, and Palia's hand shot up again.

She stared at it in horror. "Oh..."

Yarrow's eyes dimmed, and Palia dropped her hand back into her lap.

He'd done that. Made her put her hand up.

He nodded, happy to have made his point. "But it isn't witches you need to worry about. The main threat, the one you're most likely to encounter once you're on active duty, are the graynites. You'll learn more about them in your history class with Professor Mirrowind, but for the purposes of arcana, all you need to know is that if your shields are weak, a graynite can, and will, strip you of your soul." He let us sit in silence for several beats before continuing. "Graynites feed on souls because they have none of their own, and a gargoyle soul...well...It's a powerful thing. So today we'll test your natural aptitude. After that, we'll work on strengthening your connection with your shield. For those of you who make it to general or initiate, you'll be taught how to siphon arcana from the atmosphere to replenish and power up your shields, if need be."

He meant if we were captured by graynites. Wait, is that what had happened to the caretaker Varsa. He'd been siphoned and almost lost his soul? I needed to know what the graynites were exactly. My hand shot up before I could second guess myself.

"Miss Walker?" Yarrow waited.

"What is a Graynite? I mean, what kind of creature is it, exactly."

His mouth turned down. "No one knows. And that, cadets, is what makes them so dangerous." He rolled up his sleeves exposing corded forearms painted with gold glyphs that gleamed in the gloom.

When had it gotten so dark?

Yarrow didn't bother to turn on any lights, and with night spilling into the room, and our excellent night vision, we didn't need any.

"Mr. Mason, we'll start with you," Yarrow said. "Join me."

Curi crossed the room, and someone behind us muttered, "At

least he's not afraid of the witch."

Curi's shoulders tensed. He'd heard the comment, but he didn't respond, keeping his back to us all and his focus on Yarrow.

"All right, Mr. Mason. I'm going to push against your shields to test them. It may feel a little invasive, but don't push back until I ask you to, okay?"

"Okay," Curi said.

Silence fell as Yarrow closed his eyes and held up his hands. The glyphs on his arms began to glow, and the air grew thick and heavy.

"Do you feel that?" Ginia whispered.

I nodded.

Goosebumps broke out on my arms, and my scalp pricked.

Curi didn't move an inch.

"Now," Yarrow said.

Curi's shoulders rose as he exhaled, and Yarrow smiled and lowered his hands. "Good. Great work. Your shield is responsive. It's strong, and we can work on making it stronger. You can sit."

Curi reclaimed his seat, avoiding making eye contact with anyone.

Seeing him like this was almost uncomfortable.

"Miss Aziza," Yarrow summoned Sharniza.

He repeated his instructions and set to work. It took less than a minute for him to assess her, and the look on his face told me that Sharniza had some epic shield power.

I wouldn't have expected anything less.

She reclaimed her seat, and Yarrow moved on to the next cadet. Dayn's shield needed work, Saffe's shield was strong, and Palia and Ginia were called up together. Yarrow explained that they could work to expand their shields into a twin force if they wanted to.

"I'll work separately with you both on that," he said with a smile.

Finally, he called my name. "I doubt I have any shields. I'm only half gargoyle."

"Then we'll have to work on creating some for you." He took a deep breath and held up his hands. A prickle ran over my skin as his power tested me, delving past my aura and deeper to root out my psychic defenses. My head felt light, and then pressure built at the base of my skull. Panic bloomed in my chest as something in the deep recesses of my mind rattled.

No.

"Now," Yarrow said. "Push back."

The rattling intensified, and a dark foreboding swelled inside me.

Stop. "Stop!"

My mind was mine once again, and I sagged with my hand on my chest.

Yarrow watched me with concern.

A nervous laugh slipped from my lips. "I told you I didn't have a shield, didn't I?"

Yarrow looked as if he was about to contradict me, but then he nodded slowly. "Not to worry. We can build one."

I went back to my seat with a heavy heart because I was so out of my depth here.

Yarrow called the next cadet, but before he could start the test, there was a knock on the door.

"Yes?" Yarrow called.

The door opened and a small man, about four foot high, popped his head around the door. "Headmistress wants to see the Walker girl. Now," he snapped.

Yarrow didn't even flinch at the creature's tone. "Miss Walker, you're excused."

"What the heck?" Touron looked worried.

But this was perfect. I needed to see the headmistress anyway, and now I wouldn't need an excuse.

"I'll see you guys later." I grabbed my jacket and followed the tiny man out of the door.

THE HEADMISTRESS'S OFFICE was on the second floor. We passed several rooms with their doors open, occupied by human men and women doing administrative work. My guide turned down a second corridor lined with landscapes of pretty pastures and took me past a metal closed door with the words *File Room* printed on it. There was a palm scanner where the handle would be. Whatever was inside must be confidential and important. Next came a lounge with a kitchenette and finally a dark wood door with *Headmistress* printed on it.

The little man hadn't spoken the whole way here, and when we got to the door, he simply glared at me before storming off, as if I'd affronted him in some way.

O-kay. I knocked on the ajar door. "Hello?"

"Miss Walker, do come in," Miss Carter called.

I stepped from wood floors onto the plush carpeted interior of the office—a cluttered, cozy space filled with color. Squishy sofas, throws, patterned pillows, and books with bright spines piled haphazardly on bookcases came together to create an appealing space. Miss Carter herself sat behind a desk, scribbling furiously on a notepad. She waved me to the chair opposite her, never taking her eyes off her task.

I took the seat and waited.

"Okay. Done." She looked up with a smile. "If I don't jot things down, I forget half the time. Such a busy day today." She paused and studied my face with a wince. "That looks painful."

I resisted the urge to touch the bruise. "It's fine. I'll be fine."

"Yes...about that. I heard what happened in training class. That blow could have killed you."

Chlobe had said the same thing. "I'm only *half* human. I can handle it."

"Maybe this blow, but what about the next? What about a nastier encounter?" She clasped her hands and rested them on the desk, leaning forward earnestly. "Miss Walker, I admire your tenacity in coming to the academy. Your quick thinking helped you pass the entrance test and saved your life. However, you know, as well as I, that you don't belong here."

Hearing her say it so blatantly made my stomach ache. "I knew what I was getting into when I applied."

"Did you?" She gave me a stern, pointed look. The kind of look meant to root out lies. "The tests, the trials, the training, none of that is public knowledge so you won't know that we lost four gargoyles in the last six months. Cadets, *not* guardians. Two during basic training and two during initiate. Pureblood gargoyles died in training." She let that sit. "And you wish to continue?" There was an edge of exasperation to her tone, but it barely registered because she'd just given me the opening I needed.

"You left out the elite who died."

She blinked sharply. "Sorry?"

"The elite? Romi Basque was it? He died recently, didn't he? Accident they said?" She looked away and my stomach dropped. I'd been right. It wasn't an accident. "I was just confused as to what kind of accident could kill an elite." I gave her my wide-eyed, confused look.

"A terrible accident," she said. "The details of which are in a closed file, and nothing for you to concern yourself with."

Closed file. Confidential...

Dammit. "I'm not leaving here."

"I strongly advise you to reconsider. The longer you stay, the more chance that you'll be seriously hurt and the less chance I can get you out."

"Why do you even care?"

She tutted. "Because I'm human, and because you're part human. I can arrange for you to leave first thing tomorrow if you want. You can go back to your life. You'll be safe."

She meant it. She wanted me gone that badly. But was it really because she was worried about me? "Do you offer this deal to every halfblood that walks through those doors?"

"You're our first," she said. "And frankly there should be a law against letting you in. It isn't safe for you here." She threw up her hands. "But despite the human governing body's efforts, halfbloods are under gargoyle claim."

She *was* trying to help. Maybe even do the right thing, and if I had what I needed, if I felt they weren't lying to me about Romi, then I'd take her up on her offer and get the fuck out of this place, but I couldn't do that, because everything in me screamed that they were covering up the truth. So, I slapped on a little indignation.

"You think it's safe out there? With the tulpas, the shifters and the vamps. You think anywhere is safe while the graynites press in on our borders?"

She gave me a wry smile. "Right now, for you, out there is safer than in here, and you know it."

I kept my expression smooth. "Thank you for the offer. But I'm good. And if that's all, then I'd like to get back to class."

She held my gaze for several beats, her warm brown eyes begging me to reconsider. I looked back at her unmoved.

"Fine. You're dismissed. But if you change your mind, then come and see me."

I would as soon as I had what I needed.

And I knew just where to find it.

I walked slowly past the file room with the metal door and the palm scanner. What I needed was inside that room. Now all I had to do was find a way to get inside.

CHAPTER 30

CAMERON

Class was over by the time I got back. The cadets all gone. I could have gone in search of them, but my timetable was empty for the rest of the evening, and I'd had an overload of peopling for the day, so I headed back to the dorm, popped on some sweats ready for a jog, and almost bumped straight into Varsa, the caretaker on the third floor steps.

He held up his mop as if offering it to me. "It's dark outside."

"Yeah. I know."

"Dark and twisty."

I skirted him with a nod and a smile. "Thank you. I'll be fine."

His gaze emptied out for a moment, so it was like looking into glass.

"Varsa? You okay?"

He smiled, his gaze still dead and empty. "Perfect."

Gooseflesh broke out on my skin. "Great. Bye."

He'd been hurt by the graynites. Tortured and goodness knew what else. They'd broken him. These lapses in concentration weren't his fault, but damn it was creepy as fuck.

The forest trail was quiet, and the sounds of nature soothing as I ran along the winding track. The tempo of my sneakers hitting the ground, the beat of my heart, the whistle of the wind, those were the only things that mattered.

Everything else slipped away.

When I had a problem to solve or a conundrum to resolve, then running always helped. Running or hitting supernatural things. They allowed my brain to focus on the problem in background mode, and the solution usually presented itself at the most unexpected times.

So, I ran.

I'd almost completely zoned out and slipped into autopilot, when something landed in front of me with a thud.

I skidded to a halt with a shocked yelp as the female elite rose from her superhero crouch.

She flicked the tail of her braid over her shoulder before fixing her milky eyes on me. "We need to talk."

HAD I HEARD her right? "You want to train me?"

"Yes."

Who knew how long it would be before I could get into the secret file room in the main building. Training might come in handy, not to mention it would give me time with an elite. One who'd known Romi, who may even have been with him when he was killed.

Training was an excellent idea. "Thank you. I'd like that."

She smiled tersely. "Good. We'll begin tomorrow. There's a narrow trail at the curve in the main track, which leads to a small clearing. Meet me there tomorrow at six. We start then." She shot back up into the sky, leaving me with her instructions and a strange gooey feeling in my chest because there was no other reason for her to do this but Serath.

He'd asked her to do this.

Train me.

Give me a fighting chance.

Because he cared.

Because he was mine...*Whoa.*

Where the heck had that come from?

I turned and headed back toward the dorms.

I had a mate. A fated mate. Me, a halfblood.

I tried to shake off the thoughts, but they persisted.

The powers that be, the powers that governed gargoyle arcana had created one for me.

Shut up, brain.

I was one of them. A gargoyle. Not just a human. And after years of shunning this world and telling myself it didn't matter because I didn't belong, to find out now that it had claimed me in the most primal way possible was both comforting and terrifying.

But *he'd* never claim me.

I jogged up the path to my dorm and went straight up the steps.

And *I* could never claim him, not that I wanted to...

But knowing this potential bond existed meant I belonged, and that mattered.

Safe in my room, I shut the door on all the mate thoughts, stripped off my clothes, and headed for the shower. It was time to wash away the day.

THERE WAS NOTHING as refreshing as a hot shower, and when I padded back into my room ten minutes later, a glass of milk sat on my bedside table.

The ghost was back. "Hello? You can come out. I'm not afraid." I picked up the glass and took a sip. "Thanks for this."

A chill skimmed over my bare arms, and a figure materialized by the window.

The woman was probably in her twenties, but it was hard to make out her features properly with moonlight streaming through her body.

"Hi." I smiled. "My name's Cameron. You're Parker, right?"

"Melanie," she said softly. "My name's Melanie."

"Thanks for the milk and the coffee this morning."

She shrugged a shoulder. "It seemed like a nice thing to do, considering we're roommates."

Roommates? "This was your room?"

"It *is* my room."

O-kay, so this was a little creepy. "You've been here the whole time?"

"I'm here most of the time...when I'm not." She stepped away from the window into the gloom of the room, and I finally got a good look at her. Dark hair, gray eyes, and a cupid's bow mouth. She was pretty and dressed in an old-style nightgown. "Sometimes I go out there. I can get quite far now, but then I'm back here again."

I set the milk down. "Do you *want* to be here?"

She frowned. "I've got to stay. I'm waiting."

"Waiting? What are you waiting for?"

She gave me a wan smile and a one-shoulder shrug. "I can't remember, but it's all right. I'll know when it gets here...the thing I'm waiting for."

My heart went out to her. She was stuck here due to unfinished business she couldn't remember. I'd dealt with ghosts before. Some of them destructive. Angry and bitter. Clinging to life because they simply didn't want to admit theirs was over, but this ghost...she was sweet and lost.

"Why did you jump out of the window the other day?"

She caught her bottom lip between her teeth. "I was bored, and it's always fun to see huge gargoyles scream."

I chuckled. "Nice." I perched on the edge of my bed. "You worked here?"

"Yes, for several years." She walked back over to the window and looked out. "I know what they say about me. They say I killed myself, but I don't remember that, and I don't think I would do such a thing, but...there are so many things I don't remember. It's been so long."

"How long?"

"I don't remember." She gave me a dry smile as if to say, *see what I mean*. "It helps to speak to someone, but my last roommate didn't want to talk to me. She pretended I wasn't here."

"I'm sorry. Not everyone is comfortable being around ghosts. Supernatural monsters? Fine. Tulpas? No issue. But ghosts freak a lot of creatures out because they're a reminder of our mortality."

She considered my words. "But not you?"

"Nope. As long as you don't watch me sleep, I'm cool with you hanging out. In fact. It might be nice to have the company."

She smiled. "Thank you. I'd like that."

I finished towel drying my hair and reached for the milk again.

"Who's Romi?" she asked.

I froze, fingers grazing the glass. "What?"

"You said his name in your sleep a few times last night."

I arched a brow at her. "You were watching me sleep?"

She looked sheepish. "Only for a moment or two, you...You reminded me of someone and then...you didn't."

I sighed. Heck, what did it matter if I told her? She was probably the only safe person to confide in about my heritage. "Romi was my brother."

It felt good to say it. To just tell someone. And once I started, the whole story spilled out.

"Oh no." Melanie sat on the dresser, hands on her thighs. "We have to find out what happened to him."

"Yeah, that's the plan. But I have no clue where to start. Everyone I've spoken to so far says the same thing—unfortunate accident. The elites are a no-go zone. Serath made that clear, so now I'm stuck. Selas says she'll train me, but whether I'll be able to get her to open up to me is another issue. My only hope is getting into the confidential file room. But it's locked with one of those palm scanners so...yeah..."

"They have everything in the files in that room," Melanie said. "Allergies, blood type, all the confidential mission reports.

It's a wealth of information. I used to love cataloguing the details and reading about the missions and—"

"Melanie, wait. Did you manage the confidential files?"

"Yes. It was my job..." She frowned. "Until it wasn't."

And her room had been *here* in the dorms? That made no sense. She'd been human.

"I can help you," she said suddenly. "I can get into the office and find the files."

I sat up straighter. "You can?"

"Yes. I sometimes go there because it feels familiar. It's quiet in there. Safe... No palm reading scanner can keep me out," she said proudly.

"So, you can find his file?"

"I can look for it, yes. What's the family name? They always file under that."

I hadn't told her the family name yet, and I found myself hesitating.

"I can't help you if I don't know," she said.

Fuck it. "Basque. The surname is Basque."

Her eyes went round. "An original bloodline?"

"Yes. That's right."

Her frown deepened. "Basque..." She shook her head and smiled. "Romi. Basque. I'll find it, but I can't take the files out of the room. I can read them and...Oh, I'll have to find the files first, and the time away from here..."

"What is it?"

"It takes energy to stay away from this room for long periods."

"What kind of energy?"

"I usually siphon heat from the atmosphere so that I can materialize, and sometimes I take a little psychic energy from the gargoyles in the dorm, but that won't be enough. I'll need a big boost for this task. It involves being able to manipulate objects. That takes concentration, which drains energy fast."

Of course, it did. "Take what you need from me."

She smiled again and shook her head. "Even if I knock you

out cold, it won't be enough I'm afraid."

But if she had more willing participants...

I knew what I had to do. "Wait here. I'll be right back."

I headed out of the room and across the hall to Touron. I'd planned to keep my secret for longer than this, but nothing was going to plan, and if I wanted Romi's file. I was going to have to enlist the help of my friends.

I knocked and waited.

The door opened, and Touron stood there, towel wrapped around his slender hips, hair damp and the color of wet sand.

"Cam? Where were you? I looked for you."

"I went for a run. I needed some time."

"Is everything okay?"

"Yes... No, it isn't. I need your help."

CHAPTER 31

CAMERON

Sharniza and Touron eyed Melanie warily.

She waved and smiled before ducking her head.

Touron cleared his throat. "Great prank the other day."

She peered up at him with a wince. "I'm sorry. It can get tedious being trapped here."

"I'm sure you didn't bring us in here just to introduce us to your ghostly roommate," Sharniza said. "Or did you?"

"No. I need your help. Both of you. But I have something to tell you both first. Something about me that no one else can know."

"What is it?" Touron looked concerned. "You can trust us."

"She's known us for three days, Touron," Sharniza said. "She had no choice but to trust us with one secret, and I'm wagering that if she's sharing another one with us, it's because once again, she has no choice."

"You're right. I don't have a choice but to ask for help but, I do have a choice of who I ask, and I feel in my gut that I can rely on you both to keep what I'm about to tell you, to yourselves."

Sharniza nodded. "I promise."

"Me too," Touron added.

I swallowed the lump in my throat. "I didn't come here just to prove a point, or to find myself, or be a part of this world. I came here to find out the truth about my brother's death."

Touron blinked sharply. "You had a brother who went here? A pureblood?"

I nodded. "Yes, and his name was Romi Basque."

Stunned silence greeted my disclosure.

Sharniza was the first to break it. "Fuck. Well, so much makes sense now." She lowered herself into the dresser chair. "You're playing with fire, Cameron. Whatever happened to your brother is top secret. Confidential. Trust me."

"You know something..." I stared at her in dawning comprehension. "Of course, you're an Aziza, you must know something."

"All I know is that no one is talking. Whatever happened has been sealed and locked away. They don't do that with accidents."

"Then what?" Touron said. "What could have happened?"

"I don't know," Sharniza said. "But trust me, you do *not* want to poke at this."

"I don't have a choice. He was all I had. He was my family, and now he's gone, and I don't even know why. I deserve to know what happened to him." I blinked back tears. "Please. Will you help me."

"Yes," Touron said. "Whatever you need."

"Shar?"

She closed her eyes and exhaled. "What do you need from us?"

"HAVING YOUR ENERGY siphoned sucks," Touron said. "Sucks... Siphoned..." He giggled, a high-pitched sound that didn't gel with his regular baritone.

Sharniza snorted softly. "I think he's experiencing a lack of oxygen to his brain. Are those moths on the ceiling?"

The world was a soft haze, and each breath a bonus as I lay on the bed, unable to move. The drapes billowed as cold air blew in through the open windows. Sharniza's idea to clear our heads. She sat propped up in the corner by the dresser, breathing deeply as if that would help her recharge.

"I'm hungry," Touron said.

"I have some candy bars in my room," Sharniza replied. "Maybe we should have gotten them before letting the ghost feast on us. Give me a minute, and I'll see if I can get them."

"Cam?" Touron's face appeared above me. "Are you all right?"

"Mmmm..."

He was wreathed in a halo of soft light. I smiled up at him. "I'm sooo good."

He grinned goofily at me and reached out to brush a tendril of hair off my face. "I'm going to make you some coff—"

A roar shattered my ear drums as something flew into my room and landed on the rug by the bed.

Serath? Oh shit.

I needed to get up. Now.

Touron let out a yelp as Serath backhanded him across the room.

"Stop!" Sharniza bellowed.

I struggled to sit up. To check on Touron, and in the next instant I was lifted off the bed and crushed to Serath's powerful chest.

"Mine," he growled.

"No. Stop. Get off me. You don't understaaand—" The world dropped as we shot up into the night air.

Fuck.

Not again.

WE LANDED IN the clearing. The fucking clearing in the forest again. Serath kneeled with me cradled in his arms. His grip so tight I could barely breathe.

"Serath...you're crushing me..."

"He was too close. Touching you. On your bed..." His voice was a deep animalistic growl. "Mine." He gripped my jaw and forced my head up. His pupils were blown, his expression wild, teeth bared, jagged and sharp. "He was touching you." His tone was accusatory. He squeezed his eyes shut for a long beat. "One moment. I need one moment."

His heart beat hard and fast against me. There was nothing to do but wait for him to compose himself. Nothing to do but register every point of contact between us—his muscular thighs beneath my ass, taut and powerful abs pressed to my side, and the calloused pads of his thick long fingers that could crush my head if he wanted. The control...the absolute control he had in that moment made me liquid with desire but left my throat dry and aching.

He finally opened his eyes and looked down at me. His pupils were still large but not unnaturally so now.

"Hey..." I smiled up at him. "There you are."

He stroked my cheek with his thumb, and my heart fluttered, desire unfurling like a wicked twisted vine low in my belly. "You know I'm not into the overbearing macho types."

He let out a soft surprised laugh. "No?"

"Nope. I'm kinda into consent and conversation."

His gaze fell to my lips, flicked back up to my eyes, then back to my mouth. "Then...Can I kiss you, Cameron?"

Oh fuck. My stomach flipped, and heat spread through my groin, leaving me throbbing eagerly.

His nostrils flared, and he tucked in his chin and inhaled. "One kiss. Just...just a taste."

This was a bad idea. This whole fucking situation was dangerous as hell, but I wanted to feel him, wanted to taste him. I deserved this. I was owed this. He was mine, dammit.

One taste...What could it hurt? "Yes."

CHAPTER 32

CAMERON

My consent floated on a breath that a human ear may not have picked up, but Serath's preternatural senses heard me just fine.

His grip on me tightened a fraction, his body tensing as if he needed to brace himself, ready to hold back so he could stay in control.

The muscles beneath my hand flexed as he lifted me slightly before leaning in so that his mouth was mere inches from mine. My eyes fluttered closed.

"Do it. Please." I needed it. I needed to know.

His lips brushed mine with a tantalizingly feather-light pressure that stalled my breath. He did it again, and a soft whimper fell from my lips.

His chest vibrated in a purr, and he carefully pressed his mouth to mine. We breathed each other in, mouths parted, aching to lose control and devour one another. But like this, with him in gargoyle form and me in my human body, his sharp teeth would rip my delicate mouth to shreds if we lost control. Still, I needed more, I dipped my head and claimed his bottom lip, sucking on it softly.

He stilled, barely breathing, his arousal swelling against me, thick and hard. I wanted him between my thighs.

"No." He pushed me away slightly. "Careful." He looked down between us, at the huge bulge that begged to be touched.

But the beast inside me was awake now. Hungry for the feel of him. For the taste of him. "I want it."

He groaned. "Fuck."

Shit. Had I said that out loud?

His hand slipped from around my neck, down over my collar bones to my breasts.

I moaned and pushed my chest up against his hand. His eyes flared bright, pupils dilating. "We should stop now."

God that voice—a gritty thrum that had my clit vibrating.

"A-huh..." I grabbed his wrist and adjusted his hand, so he was cupping my breast. "We should definitely stop."

He squeezed and flicked my nipple though my top.

"Yes..."

The throb between my legs was painful now, slick, hot, and wet.

He growled and hauled me up, bringing me down on his lap so I was straddling him, pussy pressed to his hardness. A shockwave of pleasure shot through me, tearing a groan of satisfaction from my throat.

"Yes. Like this. Just like this." I rolled my hips against him, and he bared his teeth, tipping his head back and closing his eyes.

There was material between us, but I could feel him. The girth, the ridges. How would it feel inside...No. Don't think about that. Oh God...Fuck...

He gripped my hip and pressed a huge hand to the small of my back while I ground my wet pussy against his cock. Soft whimpers and deep growls filled the air as we chased our pleasure. I grabbed his hair, twining the long locks around my wrist to anchor myself to him as I rode him, imagining him inside me, pushing deep, stretching me wide.

Yes. Yes...

It was okay. This was okay, we could do this. Oh...fuck...Oh...

I came, body shuddering with release. Heat bloomed between

us as he found his release too.

We rocked together to milk the sensation. Our gasps and pants creating a symphony of their own.

"Fuck, Cameron. Fuck." He pressed his forehead to mine, breathing erratic and deep.

"What the fuck?" a male voice demanded from behind me.

Serath pulled me close and snarled at the intruder.

"Serath, calm down," the male said. "Let her go."

I glanced over my shoulder to find the silver-haired bastard who'd tried to kill me a few days ago glaring daggers at *me*.

"What did you do?" he demanded.

I met his glare with one of my own. "Fuck you, you wannabe murderer."

His mouth tightened. "Serath?"

"We didn't consummate," Serath said.

"And yet the air reeks of sex," Orix pointed out.

Another figure landed. Selas. Great, we had an audience.

"What happened?" she asked.

"Nothing." Serath stood, carefully, his arm around my waist so he could lift me up and set me on my feet. Shit. I wasn't wearing shoes, just socks.

"Serath?" Selas sounded disappointed.

"We didn't consummate," he ground out again.

"Obviously," she replied.

What did that mean?

"But you crossed a line." Orix jabbed a finger at him. "You're playing with fire." His voice vibrated with anger.

"And yet, I'm in complete control," Serath retorted. "I feel... better."

"There are other ways of ridding yourself of your blue balls," Orix retorted.

I turned with a low, menacing growl and pressed my back to Serath's chest. "No one touches his balls but me." The words were out before I could think and check myself.

Orix threw up his hands. "Great. Just fucking great."

"I didn't... I mean..." I was so confused right now. Torn between my human instincts of self-preservation and my gargoyle instincts to protect and claim.

Orix's lip curled. "You have no idea how dangerous you are, little halfblood. If you did, then you'd be encouraging him to get his rocks off elsewhere."

"Then tell me."

"We can't," Selas said. She looked genuinely sorry about it too. "But maybe we can help you in dealing with this connection. Maybe no contact is the wrong way to go about this."

"What do you mean?" Serath asked.

"Yes." Orix crossed his arms. "What *do* you mean? They should dry hump in the forest on a regular basis?"

"There was nothing dry about it," Serath said proudly.

My cheeks heated, and Serath stepped closer, his body heat soothing away my embarrassment.

"This connection is a soul bond begging to occur," Selas said. "The consummation happens through sex, which is why your primal instincts are to mate. The more we keep you apart, the stronger the urge will grow." She looked down at Serath's ankle. "Which could explain why the cuff failed tonight. I suggest we try an experiment."

"What kind of experiment?" Serath asked.

"You'll speak daily, on the phone. Satisfy the bond through verbal contact so that the urge to mate doesn't become unbearable. Maybe if you understand each other on an emotional level, it will help you control the mating urge."

"Or maybe it will make it worse," Orix snapped. "This is a terrible idea."

But it made sense. "We give the mate bond something, so it doesn't force us to give it everything."

"We can only hope," Selas said. She nodded at Serath. "Go now. I'll get her back to her room."

I turned to Serath, my heart in my throat as I looked up at the formidable male. "There's nothing between Touron and me. I swear it."

"You don't owe me any explanation," he said, but there was relief in his expression.

"I know. But I need you to know. Just...don't hurt him. He's my friend."

His shoulders slumped. "I'm sorry, I shouldn't have...I'll speak to you soon, Cameron." He reached out to touch me but changed his mind at the last minute, curling his fingers to avoid contact with my cheek.

He didn't trust himself to touch me, and I didn't blame him, because touching him felt too good. Too right.

He gave me a nod, stepped back, and then launched himself into the night sky.

Gone.

Orix shook his head, then followed Serath, but Selas remained.

"Let's get you back to dorms," she said.

"Cam? Cam?"

Sharniza?

A shadow flew over the clearing. "Down here!"

"Looks like you have a ride. I'll leave you in Miss Aziza's care."

"I'll see you tomorrow?"

She nodded. "You will, and Cameron...You can do this. I know you can."

She was talking about resisting the bond, and I nodded, lifting my chin with a confidence I didn't feel.

Because being with Serath, feeling his heat, his breath, tasting his skin...those were the only things that felt right, and resisting them was going to be one of the hardest things I'd ever done.

Selas slipped into the shadows, and I stepped into the moonlight, ready to greet Sharniza.

CHAPTER 33

MELANIE

The filing room usually feels safe, but not tonight. Tonight, there's an air of danger, probably because I'm here to steal something.

Information for my new friend.

Cameron reminds me of myself in some ways. I was curious and stubborn once. I used to have goals, and I would have gone to the ends of the earth to protect my loved ones.

What happened to that person?

What happened to me?

There are holes in my memory. So many holes that sometimes I feel as if I'll fade away, but then someone like Cameron comes along. Someone who sees me and for a little while, I have an anchor and a purpose.

Like tonight.

I rifle through the cabinets. Each one is locked, but I have all the passcodes. They never change them. It's only the door access that is ever updated.

I used to have access once.

But now I can simply pass through it. Wait...The filing order has been updated. They usually have everything in alphabetical order using surname, but it isn't like that any longer.

Everything is numerical now.

How can I find Romi's file?

Think. There must be a key somewhere. There's something about the numbers. Oh...they're cadet IDs. There's a book for that.

I find the folder with the IDs on top of one of the cabinets and scroll down the names to Basque. The ID is six digits. I memorize it and head back to the cabinets. It doesn't take me long to find the file. I draw it out. It's thick. Filled with mission reports. Excitement bubbles inside me because I'm about to find the information that Cameron needs. I can help her.

I flip open the file to the end, to the last report. Wait...This can't be right. How can...Oh God...

"Hello, Melanie."

I turn sharply, file clutched tightly in my hand.

Cold golden eyes bore into me. "What have you got there? Hmmm?"

CHAPTER 34

CAMERON

I'd dry humped Serath.

Or wet humped him, whatever. I'd climbed all over him, grabbed his hair, and ridden him till I came.

Stop thinking about it, dammit.

But the flashback kept hitting me as Sharniza flew me back to dorms, and guilt followed hot on its heels, because Levi...

Palia was right, this mate bond was too strong. I was glad I'd broken up with Levi before coming here, because if I hadn't, there was no way I'd be able to look myself in the mirror right now.

"Are you sure you're all right," Sharniza asked for the fifth time.

"I'm sure. I'm fine. Is Touron okay?"

"He'll live, but you know what this means?"

"What?"

"It means that Serath was peeping in on you," she growls. "Typical gargoyle male in heat, all possessive and irrational. They think with their cocks."

His cock was perfect. Argh, shut up, brain. "I'm good. We sorted it out. I just want to make sure Touron's all right."

"He's fine, trust me. But he's still not recovered from the siphoning, so I told him to hang back while I went looking for you."

If she'd found me sooner... My face grew hot again.

She swooped toward the ledge outside my window and landed carefully with me. "Wait...How exactly did you sort it out?" She locked gazes with me, her hazel eyes bright in her face as she lowered me to my feet. "You reek of coitus, you know. Please tell me you didn't."

Coitus? Who says that? "We didn't...We just...I don't want to talk about it." I turned to the room, but she gently gripped my arm to stall me.

"Did he force himself on you?" she asked softly.

"Force himself?" Touron appeared at the window, looking disheveled. His hair was wet, eyes bright. "What the fuck? I should have come with you. I should have—"

"You were still too weak," Sharniza snapped. "Cam, what happened?"

"He didn't force himself on me." I glared at her, indignant. "He would never." I wasn't sure how I knew that; I just...did.

"A fated mating brings on a heat," Sharniza said. "And a Gargoyle male in the heat of a fated mating can lose themselves to the beast completely. The primal nature is powerful, and it takes what it needs. Tonight could have ended very differently."

Orix's and Selas's reactions made more sense now. But Serath had controlled himself. Pulled himself back and been...gentle. That must have taken serious willpower, and me? I'd been all over him, pushing his boundaries and playing with the beast.

"He controlled himself, and he controlled me too." I stepped through the window and into the room. "Palia was right. This thing...it's strong. But we think we have a solution. We're going to be speaking regularly on the phone to try and....diffuse it."

"There are no phones here," Touron said.

"I guess they'll get me one. I don't know, but tonight, after we...after we spent some time together, the mating urge seemed to be under control. Selas believes if we satisfy the emotional side of the bond, the raw physical need to mate might ebb a little." I pulled off my dirty socks and sat on the edge of the bed. "Not that it matters, because once Melanie comes back with the information on Romi, I'm out of here." My heart sank as I said the words.

Touron's face fell. "I'll miss you."

I'd miss him too. I'd miss Shar and the twins. Even though I'd barely had time to get to know them all, I felt as if I'd known them my whole life.

Shar watched me with darkened hazel eyes. "Is that what you really want? To leave here?"

Risk of death aside, the academy wasn't so bad. I'd had friends outside of here—Fred and Teri, but I'd never allowed them to know the true me, so our connection had never deepened. Then there was Levi. A phantom ache filled my chest. Breaking up with him had been the right move, especially now I knew I was fated for someone else, even if we couldn't be together. It would only have hurt Levi to know this.

Outside of those three, there'd only been Romi, Ralph, and Derek. But Romi was gone, Ralph had his own life, and Derek... Derek was a tulpa desperate to be accepted by his own kind.

The lure of the outside world was tarnished compared to the bright sparkle of this place because there was a whole world of possibilities here. True friendships and a mate, that although I couldn't be with, proved that I belonged in this world, despite my physical shortcomings. Staying here felt right, and with Selas training me, maybe I wouldn't get my ass killed?

"Cam?" Touron prompted. "Do you want to leave?"

"No. I don't."

He exhaled. "Then you should stay, and we can figure out what to do with whatever information Melanie brings us. Together."

Together? My eyes heated. They'd help me too. Be here for me. I had no doubt.

"You can do this," Sharniza said. "With Selas training you and us on your side...You can do this."

Touron bumped her with his shoulder. "And you wanted to go it solo."

She rolled her eyes. "What can I say, you two are like persistent fungus."

The temperature dropped, and Melanie appeared by the dresser, looking gray and spectral so the only part of her that stood out were her inky eyes.

I sat up straighter. "Did you find it?"

"Yes." Her voice was a whisper. "I'm sorry, it says he died on a mission saving several humans from a cave-in. It was a large vampire nest in a network of caverns. The weight of the rock that crushed him caved his skull in. It says he died instantly."

"No..." Hot tears blurred my vision. "That makes no sense. Why hide it then? Why put it in a closed file?"

"The mission is marked classified," Melanie said. "It says that Romi went in, despite orders not to."

"That's an eviction offense," Sharniza said. "It would look bad for the Basque name for it to be common knowledge that he went against orders."

"So, they cover it up? They hide it?" I looked from Sharniza to Touron.

"It would seem so," Touron said.

I shook my head. "It doesn't feel right."

"I know," Touron said. "When my brother died, I didn't want to believe he could have been taken down like that. I didn't want to believe he could have been snuffed out in a way that made him seem so inconsequential."

But it was true. Romi's death had been an accident all along. "I need a minute."

"Better yet, get some sleep," Sharniza said. "You can make your decision about your future tomorrow."

"We'll stand by you, whatever you decide," Touron said. He closed the window and drew the drapes. "I think we can all use some rest."

I looked across at Melanie, who was fading away fast. "Thank you. For helping."

She gave me a watery smile and vanished.

The others left my room, and I collapsed onto the bed, rolled onto my side, and tucked my legs up to my chest. My mind warred with my heart on whether to stay or go.

"When I wake up, I'll know what to do." I repeated the phrase over and over, then closed my eyes and left the decision to my smart subconscious to solve.

Whatever my gut feeling was in the morning would be my final decision.

CHAPTER 35

CAMERON

The storm inside me had passed when I woke, and in its place was the calm, steady conviction that I'd be staying at the academy.

This was where I belonged. Where Romi had spent most of his life. He was gone, taken in the line of duty, and I hadn't gotten to say goodbye. There'd been no funeral. No closure. I hadn't allowed myself to grieve because I'd been so angry.

Angry that he'd been taken from me.

Angry that so much of his life had been kept from me.

I'd wanted there to be a reason. A conspiracy. Anything to make his loss make more sense than it did.

But now that I had my answers, it was time to face facts.

There was no conspiracy.

Just a cover-up to save the Basque name, and Romi... He was still gone.

Nothing would bring him back, but I *could* make him proud. I could become a guardian and walk in his shoes.

His home would now be mine, and in that way, I'd always be close to him.

I'd kept my identity a secret so I could get to the truth, afraid that if the gargoyles knew who I was, they'd be more close-lipped about Romi, but there was no need to hide anymore. I could tell everyone who I was. Fuck up Basque's name by coming out as his halfblood offspring, but...I didn't *want* his name. I didn't want the special treatment that would come with everyone knowing who I was. If I was going to do this, then I'd do it for me. Without the Basque banner.

I'd do it for me *and* for Romi.

There was no coffee waiting for me this morning. Melanie was probably still wiped out after her filing room break-in. I couldn't sense her presence, but I called out a thank you just in case she was here.

Although classes didn't start for a couple of hours, lounging in bed didn't appeal, so I showered, dressed, then headed down to the kitchens for coffee. It was coming up to midday, and the dorm was silent and sleepy. It felt weird being the only one awake, but it was also comforting to have the place to myself. I'd just poured myself a drink when someone stomped into the room behind me.

The little man who'd taken me to see Miss Carter stood in the doorway. "For you." He held out a package.

I took it gingerly, and he *harumphed*, his gaze going from my mug to the coffee pot behind me.

"Would you like one?" I held up my mug.

He snorted. "You think I have time to sit around and drink coffee?" He sounded like he wished he did.

"One second." I reached into the cupboard above the coffee pot and pulled out a travel mug and filled it with coffee. "Milk? Sugar?"

"I like it black and bitter," he snapped.

Like his soul, obviously. "Here you go." I popped on the lid and handed him the mug. "Now you can drink it without having to *sit around*. And thank you for the delivery, I appreciate it."

The angry wrinkles between his eyebrows smoothed out a fraction. "Yes, well. Bye."

He stomped off with his to-go coffee, and I sat down with the package. My name was on the padded envelope, handwritten in beautiful cursive. I tore it open and tipped out a mobile phone and a note in the same gorgeous script as on the envelope.

Dear Cameron,

This is for you. Keep it hidden in your room. We don't want the other cadets to ask questions. And call me after seven p.m. tonight so we can talk.

Serath x

He'd touched this envelope. Written this note himself. I lifted it to my nose and inhaled his woodsy scent. There was a hint of floral sage to it too. My stomach contracted and warmed.

I was so fucked.

THE DORM WAS waking up by the time I was done with coffee, so I filled two travel mugs for Shar and Touron, then headed back upstairs.

"Look, Curi, you brought this on yourself."

I recognized Dayn's voice.

"Fuck you, Lowther," Curi said. "You have no right to judge me. None of you do. You eat my food, sleep in my fucking mansion, come to every fucking event my family throws, and now you fucking shun me?"

"You froze," another voice said. Minion number two no doubt. "What would you have done if it was one of us who froze?"

Curi was silent. "Selas and I...we have history."

"Yeah? What kind of history?" Dayn asked.

"The it's-none-of-your-damn-business kind," Curi growled. "Because you and I, we're done."

"Curi, wait," Minion two said.

I pressed my back to the wall to get out of Curi's way as he stormed past without giving me a second glance.

"Fuck him," Dayn said.

"Easy for you to say," Minion two snapped. "Your father's friends with his. My family only got invites to the Mason affairs because of *my* friendship with him."

"Yeah?" Dayn said. "Well, then you should have thought of that before shunning him."

"But you said he was weak."

Dayn snorted. "Curi is a lot of things, but weak isn't one of them."

"Then why?"

"Because here, in the academy, I'm going to be the one leading, not Curi. If he looks weak, then all the better for me. Stick with me Bax and you'll be fine."

Shit. Now, they were heading my way.

I went back down the stairs a little before turning and starting back up. They passed by, and Dayn shot a sneer my way.

I would have given him the finger if my hands weren't occupied clutching coffee mugs, instead I returned his sneer with a flat look.

He snorted and smirked. "See you on the field, Walker."

What did that mean? The timetable said history and arcana today, and I had an extra session of arcana with Flora on my timetable after history.

I'd have to ask Touron and Shar if they knew.

"Cameron?" Palia ran up the steps behind me. "Did you hear what happened?"

"What?" I paused for her to catch up.

"Miss Yarrow was found unconscious in the main building this morning."

"Shit! What happened to her?"

"No one knows. She's still unconscious, but arcana has been canceled today. We're with Farnell on the outdoor training grounds."

"Wait, I've been up for ages. How come I didn't hear about this?"

"Did you check the notice board in the dorm hall?"

"Ah...no."

"Palia, ask her already." Ginia called from the floor below.

"Oh, yeah. We're headed to the coffee shop to grab a bite. Don't fancy cooking. They do the best toasties. You want to come?"

My stomach growled. "Do they take card? I didn't bring much cash with me."

"Yep. Card, cash, and some cadets have accounts open that their families cover."

Lucky for some. "I'll grab Touron and Shar and meet you there."

"Do you know where it is?"

I hadn't been there yet, but I'd seen it on the map. "I'll find it."

I hurried down the corridor, knocked on Shar's door and popped the coffee on the floor outside, did the same for Touron, then quickly unlocked my door and dropped the phone Serath had sent me into the bedside table drawer. Now, where was the satchel the academy had provided? I'd seen it when I'd scoped out the place. Ah, there it was in the back of the cupboard.

It contained a notebook and some pens—academic classes here were light after all. It was the practical stuff we needed to worry about, and that stuff would be tested...well, practically.

Touron's door was open when I stepped back out into the corridor. He was picking up his coffee. Shar hadn't surfaced yet.

"She's a heavy sleeper," Touron said before taking a tentative sip of his beverage. "But she should be up by now." He tucked a notebook and pen into his back pocket.

I picked up her coffee mug and knocked on her door again. Harder this time.

"One second." She sounded strange. Her voice higher pitched than usual.

She slipped out of her room a moment later and locked the door. "I'm ready."

I handed her the travel mug. "You okay?"

"Fine." She smoothed her hair back and tucked it behind her

ears. "My things arrived earlier. I was unpacking."

"O-kay," Touron said. "If that's what you want to call it."

Huh? It took a moment but then his insinuation hit.

Shar's cheeks flushed, and she narrowed her eyes. "I don't do that."

"Really?" Touron sounded impressed. "I do. Sometimes more than once a day."

My brows flicked up.

He met my gaze, unrepentant. "I have needs, Cam, and until they are met, I must make do with Veronica." He held up his hand and smiled at his palm.

"You're disgusting," Sharniza said with a slight smile.

"I am," Touron said. "But I'm your disgusting." He put an arm around each of us and moved us away from the door and down the corridor. "We have time to kill before class, so where to?"

A warm feeling bloomed in my chest. "The coffee shop." I smiled up at him. "I fancy a toastie."

He returned my smile, his gaze softening. "You're staying, aren't you?"

"Yes. Yes, I am."

CHAPTER 36

CAMERON

Stone Comfort was a one-story sprawling building with high-beamed ceilings, huge arched windows, and proper hardwood floors that could take the weight of a gargoyle in shifted form. All the seats were low-backed to allow for wings, and the tables were sturdy wooden affairs built to last—none of the plastic crap found in the human world.

Like all the buildings at the academy, this one was built to take damage. Built to last. And it was obviously the place to be early afternoon, which to gargoyles was early morning. The place was packed with initiates and general force trainees, and finding a seat would have been impossible if the twins hadn't saved us a table.

They waved us over eagerly, and I was acutely aware of the attention as we made our way over.

"Thc halfblood."

"No idea what bloodline."

"So fucking small."

"Could crush her."

"Ignore them," Sharniza growled from behind me. "Keep moving."

A leg blocked my path, and the owner grinned up at me

aggressively. "You should introduce yourself, halfblood," he said. "It's the polite thing to do."

I met his amber gaze evenly. "So's not blocking a lady's path with your boot."

"Ladies don't belong here at Stonehaven," he said. "Ladies don't make good warriors."

"It's a joke letting you in," one of the other gargoyles at his table said.

They were all big guys. Larger than the average cadets. The one blocking me had a buzz cut and a mulish jaw. And his companion had the sharp predatory features of a bird of prey. Both had amber eyes. Related maybe?

I made to climb over his leg, but he raised it, looking up at me with a smug smile. My instinct was to throat punch him, but I staunched it and backed up, intending to bypass him altogether, but the gargoyle at the next table blocked us with his leg.

Anger flared in my chest. "Move." My tone was lethally soft.

"Get out of the way," Sharniza said from behind me.

"Aw, do you need your goyle bitch buddy to fight your battles?" the mulish gargoyle said.

"Jay, she's an Aziza," his buddy whisper-hissed.

"Then she should know better than to carry dead-weight," Jay said. "Being a guardian is no joke. This program, this academy, is no joke." He stood to tower over me. "Letting you in makes a mockery of us all."

"*Letting* me in?" I squared up to him. "No one *let* me in. I earned my place here. I passed the entrance test just like all of you, so back the fuck off."

He leaned in, his expression a mask of menace and mockery. "Or what?"

"Back off." Touron shoved his shoulder, but the goyle barely moved, his attention fixed on me.

I wasn't strong enough to fight, what I was pretty sure was an initiate, and I didn't have the training to take him physically down a peg or two. But I could make him look and feel small.

"Fine, don't back off, stand there, towering over a female half your size. I guess whaling on the little guy makes you feel big, huh? It won't help you out there against the graynites, the shifters, and the vamps." I tapped my chin with an index finger. "Wait, have you ever even gone up against a shifter or a vamp? Do you know how to take one out? No? Because I do. It's what I've been doing for the past two years while you sat in your cushy mansion waiting to get your acceptance letter to Stonehaven, so don't fucking tell me what I deserve. If anyone deserves to be here, it's the likes of me."

Pindrop silence greeted my speech.

My scalp pricked and then a voice spoke up from behind me, abrasive and familiar, and a balm to my fired-up senses.

"Get away from her, Batiste. Now."

Jay stepped back quickly and tucked in his chin. "Elite Halle, I meant no disrespect."

"Yes, you did," Serath said. "I can see now you're not ready for an alpha position. You'll stay in initiates for another three months."

Jay looked up in horror. "Elite Halle, with all due respect, I was merely—"

"Enough!" Serath snapped. "Get out."

I finally dared to turn my head to look at him. His gaze zeroed in on me straight away, and that one look was like a punch to my chest. I exhaled sharply, and his husky eyes darkened. I was back in the woods with his hands on me and his mouth on mine. Our bodies rubbing together, desperate to connect.

A band of pain tightened on my thigh. "Look away," Sharniza whispered.

I dropped my gaze quickly to break the connection.

When I looked up again, the elites were heading out of the door with Jay and his companion in front of them.

One by one the other gargoyles went back to their meals, and now no one was looking my way.

We joined the twins at the table they'd saved for us.

"That was intense," Ginia said.

"No one else noticed," Palia assured me. "No one noticed how he looked at you. *I* only noticed because I know..."

"He left quickly," Sharniza said. "He did the right thing."

But a hollow pit had opened inside me. An absence of him. I needed to fill it. "I need food."

"We ordered a plate of toasties," Palia said. "They should be here soon, but you might want to get in some drinks."

Touron squeezed my shoulder, his expression grim. "I'll get the drinks."

I watched him head to the counter. "Is he okay?"

"He'll be fine," Sharniza said. "It probably took a lot for him to not jump in and pummel Jay, but he knew that if he did, then it would make you look weak."

"He's also kicking himself for not doing it anyway," Palia added. "Gargoyle males are so contrary."

I plonked my ass in the chair next to the twins, and Shar took the one opposite me.

"Everyone's buzzing about Miss Yarrow," Ginia said, neatly changing the subject.

"I heard," Sharniza added. "My cases arrived earlier, and I saw the boards. Strange thing to happen. I didn't think witches got sick."

"They don't," Ginia said gleefully. "Someone did something to her."

"Don't." Palia looked uneasy. "This place is meant to be safe."

"Obviously not for Miss Yarrow," Ginia said over the rim of her mug.

Touron returned with a tray of coffees for us. He looked less upset now. The food arrived a moment later.

Cheese and ham toasties made with thick cuts of ham and flavorsome fancy cheese. The bread was thick too. They probably had a huge toastie machine back there.

We ate in silence for a little while, the hum of conversation around us a pleasant buzz. I'd just finished off my toastie when three females walked in. They were smaller than regular gargoyle females, their bodies more rounded, faces softer.

I recognized Chlobe, so that meant these must be...

"Omegas..." Palia said with a sigh that had more than a hint of yearning in it.

The room fell into a hush, and every male eye went to these females. The air spiked with a musky scent. Touron sat up straighter, too, his chest heaving as if he was struggling to breathe.

I widened my eyes at Sharniza and mouthed, *What the fuck*?

She gave me a flat look and shrugged.

Chlobe spotted me. She whispered something to her friends, then made her way over to us. Our table was suddenly the center of attention.

"Cameron, you look so much better," Chlobe said. "I knew you'd heal fast." She smiled warmly.

I couldn't help but smile back. "Thanks for fixing me up."

Had Touron stopped breathing?

"No problem," Chlobe said brightly. "Oh, I added you both to the roster for the shopping trip." She turned the beam of her smile on Shar, who lifted a corner of her mouth in response, baring her teeth more than smiling.

Chlobe blinked sharply, looking taken aback.

"What time and where do we meet?" I drew her attention back to me.

"Oh, midday at the omega house. It'll be so much fun." She clasped her hands together. "There's this wonderful pasta place we always go to. You'll love it."

"I'm looking forward to it."

"Fabulous. See you then."

She headed back to her friends, taking the heat of attention with her.

"So, that's what it feels like to be an omega," Ginia said. "All the attention. The male pheromones are thick." She exhaled as if to blow them out of her nose.

Touron shifted uncomfortably in his seat. "I'm just going to...I need to..." He pushed his chair back and left.

"Say hi to Veronica," Sharniza called after him.

Poor Touron. "Is it like this all the time?"

"No," Palia said. "It's just so close to the omega moon that the omegas are probably giving off a pretty potent scent right now."

"Thank you." I patted her shoulder.

"What for?" Palia asked.

"For not using the P word."

She looked confused.

Ginia leaned in and whispered, "Pheromones..."

"Urgh." I threw up my hands. "You ruined it."

Chlobe and her friends grabbed their takeaway bags and left, and the atmosphere relaxed a fraction. The gargoyle behind the counter laid out some fresh scones.

My favorite. "Anyone for dessert?"

"No time," Sharniza said. "History in fifteen."

Dammit. Scones would have to wait.

CHAPTER 37

CAMERON

I thought I was done with sitting in a classroom listening to lectures when I'd turned eighteen. I'd opted not to go on to further education because I'd never seen myself as an academic, but two years later, here I was sitting in a lecture theater listening to a beautiful woman talk in a melodious voice.

Not so bad after all.

Mistress Mirrowind made it clear at the start of the class that we could interrupt with questions as they occurred to us. Then she'd smiled and my heart had melted a little, and I was sure I wasn't the only one enamored with the woman. There was a compelling aura about her, like you wouldn't want to disappoint her in any way.

Part of me recognized this was weird, but I couldn't summon the energy to care much for anything else but to listen and absorb the information she was imparting.

"Her hair..." Sharniza said softly. "It's so shiny."

"Look how small her feet are," Palina whispered.

"I bet she tastes like cotton candy," Touron said on a yearning breath.

Mirrowind looked up at us with a smile that told me she'd heard every word.

We all sighed in unison.

"The mageri were selective about who entered the city," Mistress Mirrowind said, turning her attention to the rest of the class. "The house Dracul and the powerful Raventhorn bloodlines made a deal with the mageri, and they have their place in the city. The fae would not sign their contracts and so are trapped in the Evergreen within the mageri wards."

"I thought the fae lived in Faerie," Palia said.

Mistress Mirrowind nodded, and her sleek silver-blond hair shimmered in the late-afternoon light spilling in through vaulted windows. "Yes, at one time they did. But their world was tainted by a darkness. One they were forced to flee from. I believe it was contained"—she pursed her lips for a moment—"eventually. But I don't know the details of how. I can say, however, that one breach into the fabric of a world can weaken the fabric of a connected world, and maybe the taint that infected Faerie was what allowed the gray to enter the human world."

"So, there are *no* fae in the rim?" Dayn asked.

"If there are any left, then they will be hidden."

"Are they a threat to humans?" Ginia asked.

"Not unless humans allow them to be." She smiled, flashing even white teeth. "Fae have rules, and they can get what they want by clever manipulation. If a fae takes a human, then the human has usually unwittingly made a deal with the creature."

"Can we extinguish a fae?" Palia asked.

"We are not so easily vanquished," she said, sapphire eyes twinkling.

We? *She* was fae?

The room went silent.

She laughed, a soft tinkling sound. "Oh, relax, dears. Not all fae are after your soul or your first born. Some of us are more concerned with the larger picture. The graynites threaten us all, even the fae." She widened her eyes. "After all, a soul is a soul, and a fae soul is powerful fuel." The light in her eyes dimmed for a moment, and my heart ached for her, even though I didn't understand why. "Now who'd like to see an accurate rendering of a Graynite." She flicked on the projector and plopped a slide in.

The white screen behind her lit up with the frightful image of a huge hunched-over monster with spines on its back, an elongated maw, and long thin fingers tipped with blackened claws. Its tail was thick and ridged with spines.

"Graynites are powerful creatures who have no soul, which is why they feed off the souls of others," Mirrowind said. "They came out of the gray in the same moment that the gray retreated back into its own world. We succeeded in closing the rift, but the graynites remained."

"What was the gray?" Ginia asked. "What was it *exactly*?"

"It was an atmosphere," Mirrowind said. "A smog, thick and dense, spilled into our world, and within it were creatures unlike anything you'd ever seen. They devoured while the gray itself eroded and killed our lands. The gargoyles were the only ones who could withstand the smog, their stone skin providing protection against the toxic effects of the air. The air of another world." She looked at the window, her eyes glazing over as if she were back there, back in the time when it happened. "So many died before they were able to close the breach. We evacuated, moving as many humans and supernaturals to the city as we could while the gray ate away at our lands." She blinked and she was back with us. "Anyway, you know the rest. The guardians found the breach in the gray and closed it, forcing the gray back into its own world along with all its creatures. But our world...what is now known as the rims, was left devastated. The mageri stepped in to help as much as they could, but they had a whole city of humans and supernaturals to deal with. From what I've learned, it was no easy feat wrangling them into order, but the creation of the wards around the city and subsequent Accords within, have brought order."

"Yeah, great for them, sitting in their bubble all safe and sound," Ginia said.

"Oh..." Mirrowind looked across at us. "My dear, the city is far from safe. It's had its own share of catastrophes, all narrowly averted, but still..."

"Is it true that there's a graveyard of the beasts somewhere far east?" a goyle at the back of the class asked.

"Yes," Mirrowind said. "But that sector is off limits, as I'm sure you're aware."

I had a question. "You said the gargoyles beat back the gray... but how?"

"With a mystical explosive created by the joint energy of the most powerful witches. When activated, it would force the rift to close in on itself. We knew that the creatures needed a certain atmosphere to survive—the atmosphere that came out of the rift, what we called the gray. We realized that if we shut it down, the gray would be forced to retreat, and what was left would die. Five gargoyles were chosen to deliver the mystical explosive. To fight their way through the hoard of infected and get to the rift. Does anyone know who they were?"

"I do," Dayn said, looking proud of himself. "Basque, Mason, Halle, Albion, and Aziza."

She beamed up at him and a stab of annoyance shot through me that he got to bathe in that smile.

"Correct," she said. "They sacrificed themselves to save us all, and in doing so blessed their bloodlines with the power to kill the graynites that managed to get through."

Wait a second. "Are you saying only those five bloodlines can kill a graynite?"

"Yes. That's correct. Any gargoyle can fight or wound a graynite, but only one of the five bloodlines can kill one. Most alpha teams have one of the five bloodlines in their troops, and the elite team is made up of all five. It's the only team that could potentially take down the Graynite alpha."

"They have an alpha?" Palia made notes furiously in her book. "What is his power?"

"We're not sure, but we believe he's like a queen bee or a queen ant. The colony can't survive long if he dies."

"So, if he dies then...they all die?" Palia set her pen down. "Cut the head off the snake..."

Mirrowind smiled tightly. "It sounds simple, but the graynites also have a hive. A fortress in an area of the rim that is warded with dark magic. Shade is a kind of power only they can use, and so far, we've been unsuccessful in breaching those wards."

And the five bloodlines together could stop him if he emerged. They could kill him and end all graynites but...But Romi was dead. "What happens now that Romi Basque is dead?"

I felt Touron's gaze on me but ignored it, keeping my expression innocently curious.

"He'll be replaced...Eventually," Mirrowind said.

"Eventually? I don't understand. I thought every alpha team had one of the five bloodlines in it? Can't we promote another Basque."

Her lips pressed in a thin line. "There is no other Basque. Romi was the last adult Basque in his prime. The next in line is just a child."

My pulse kicked up, and I dropped my gaze to hide my shock. My mind whirred. "What about Romi's father? He's an adult male. Can't he take over?"

Mirrowind gave me an indulgent smile. "Can anyone answer that question for Miss Walker?"

"He's passed his prime," Palia said. "Gargoyles age slow, but we do age, and there comes a point where we lose touch with our gargoyle beasts. It makes combat harder."

"So, we have no defense against the alpha?" someone asked.

The air of tranquility was shattered.

"The alpha hasn't been heard from or seen in a while," Mirrowind said. "He knows how important he is, and it's unlikely he'll surface anytime soon," she said casually. "The Stone Council has everything under control." She clicked off the projector. "Now, on to the forming of the Stone Council."

But my mind was still reeling with the news that Romi's death left me as the next adult Basque in existence.

It didn't matter.

It couldn't.

My father would have said something if it did, and like Mirrowind said, the alpha wasn't surfacing anytime soon. Plenty of time for the Basque child to grow up. Plenty of time for the Basque bloodline to produce more alpha and beta gargoyles. But my stomach continued to quiver long into the lesson, foreboding a cloud in the back of my mind, because wasn't it sod's law that shit hit the fan when you least expected it to?

I had to hope that the Stone Council had accounted for that, because if they hadn't and the alpha did emerge, then we were all fucked.

CHAPTER 38

CAMERON

There was just enough time after history class to change for training before heading to the outdoor pitch.

Farnell waited on the newly turfed ground, hands clasped behind his back, ice blue eyes watching us approach.

Up close and personal the pitch was massive, over a hundred yards at least.

"The crystals on the posts moderate the weather." Palia pointed at a post on the other side of the pitch. "Meteorological magic. Willowman's forte. I asked around." She looked proud of herself.

The crystals crackled with blue energy, as if preparing for a storm. "Farnell is going to make it rain, isn't he?"

Palia sniffed the air. "It smells that way."

"Gather round!" Farnell ordered from the edge of the pitch. "Today we're going to play a team-building exercise."

He crossed his arms and glared down his nose at us. "You"—he pointed to Saffe—"and you." He pointed at me. "Come over here." He pulled two flags out of a bag on the floor by his feet. One green. One red. I got the red flag. "Sharniza, Curi, Palia, and Bonet, you'll be together." Bonet, Curi's ex-minion looked to Dayn, who simply shrugged. "Dayn, Gina, Touron, and Waxen, you'll team up." Farnell nodded at Sharniza. "Red flag is yours to protect." Then to Dayn. "Green flag is yours." He pointed to a post a few yards away. There were a couple of holes in the wooden structure. "The flag bearer must get the flag into that post. But you've got to tag the post across the pitch first." Yep, there was another post far in the distance, so far it was barely visible in the growing mist. "The objective for the rest of you is to stop the opposing team's flag bearer by taking their flag. You'll play for thirty minutes, or until someone captures a flag. Only the flag bearer can carry the flag and you *cannot* carry your flag bearer." He glared at Sharniza. "Shifting and flight are permitted." He raised a finger to the sky and shouted. "Pluvia."

The sky roared, dark clouds blocked out what remained of the sun, and it began to rain.

For a moment everyone just stood around, looking stunned, then Sharniza locked gazes with me and mouthed, *run*.

I turned and ran, away from Dayn and his team, across the grass that was growing rapidly mushy.

Wings unfurled and flapped behind me.

Oh shit.

"Cam, get down!" Touron shouted.

I hit the grass, and the air above me rippled as a gargoyle flew past, missing grabbing me by a mere foot.

"Shut your mouth, Touron!" Dayn bellowed.

I rolled, jumped up, and ran again. There was no time to stop and look back. I had to use my instincts to guide me. Where was the post I needed to tag? There!

Movement to my right had me veering left.

"It's me!" Sharniza yelled. "I'm covering yo—"

A whirlwind of gray smashed into her, and the two gargoyles rolled in the mud—a mass of arms, legs, and wings.

I swerved away from her before adjusting my trajectory toward the tagging post. The rain fell in sheets, making it difficult to see, to breath, to think. The ground vibrated and the spot between my shoulder blades tightened. There was a gargoyle on my tail. A gust of air hit my back, and then a shadow fell over me.

My pursuer had taken flight.

I caught sight of Saffe in the air to my right, swerving and diving to evade Palia and Bonet. What was the point of this damn exercise? "Argh!" I dove at the ground to avoid the slice of talons and slid through the mud for several meters.

"Get back here, you rat," Dayn growled.

I rolled to my feet and risked a look over my shoulder to see him advancing on me. Shadows raced toward me from the left and right.

I kicked up my feet and ran, using the only thing I had to my advantage.

Speed.

I was fast, always had been, and these lumbering bastards weren't going to get me. I feinted left, then right to slide between Waxen's legs before scrambling to my feet once more.

The post was in sight. I grabbed it briefly. "Tag!" I turned and ran along the edge of the field, putting some distance between me and my pursuers, who'd expected me to double straight back.

They flew toward me.

A body landed in front of me. Bonet. He nodded my way, then launched himself into the air toward Dayn and Waxen.

I didn't stop to watch them tangle. My attention was on the final post.

Someone yelled curses from the air behind me.

"Grab her, Waxen!" Dayn bellowed.

Shit! Looked like Bonet had snagged Dayn, but Waxen had gotten away.

Wings beat close behind me. Gaining on me.

The post was so close now. I pushed harder, lungs burning with the effort.

Waxen landed several yards in front of me and blocked my path with his huge body.

Crap.

Sharniza cut ahead of me. "Stay behind me!"

We ran single file, and she body-slammed Waxen, sending him flying.

Yes, Shar! Fuck yes! We were so close to the winning post now that I could almost taste it, but the ground was slippery, slowing my pace while the goyles' large feet allowed them some stability, and shit, they were catching up to us.

"Keep moving," Curi ordered from the air above me. "We got you."

I was almost there, when something hit me in the face. Cold, wet, and blinding. The mud ball stole my vision. I stumbled, my ankle twisted, and a tearing sound filled the air.

I went down hard, fiery agony blooming in my ankle. I didn't have to look at it to know it was swelling fast. I'd torn ligaments. I swiped mud from my eyes as the air above me shifted, and Curi's bellow of rage told me he'd been taken out.

"Cam!" Sharniza cried.

The ground thundered as Waxen and Dayn ran toward me.

"Got you, rat!" Dayn called out with glee.

Sharniza was headed my way, but if she touched me, we'd lose. I had to do this alone.

For the team.

Fuck the pain. I pushed myself to my feet with a roar, scrambling for purchase in the mud for a second before bursting forward in a sprint. I blocked out the pain by channeling the rage that Dayn's words had evoked.

Rat? Motherfucker. I'll show you rat.

Shar's eyes widened as I ran toward her, then a grin split her lips. I raced past her.

The crunch of stone body hitting stone body rattled the air behind me.

Go Shar.

I caught sight of Touron several meters away. Shit. He was on Dayn's team.

"Stop her, Touron!" Dayn cried.

Touron broke into a jog toward me.

No. Fuck that. No. With a final burst of speed, I cleared the line and grabbed hold of the post. My fingers felt clumsy and numb, but I managed to slot the flag into place.

"Yes!" I fist-pumped the air. "Yes!"

Curi let out an uncharacteristic whoop.

Farnell approached with an unreadable expression. "Very well done, Miss Walker, now I suggest you get to the infirmary and have them treat that ankle."

My foot?

I looked down at the bulbous flesh straining and forcing the Lastonflex of my sneaker to expand to accommodate it. Pain hit me in a wave that made my knees weak.

"I've got you." Sharniza swung me into her arms. "I assume we can be dismissed," she practically growled at Farnell.

He looked down coolly at her. "You may. We'll discuss the merits of this exercise in our next session."

But Shar was already airborne with me clutched tightly in her arms.

"I'll meet you there!" Touron called out from below.

I held tightly to Sharniza, trying to block out the deep ache in my ankle. "We won. We fucking won."

"You did good," Sharniza said with a small smile. "You crazy bitch. You did good."

CHAPTER 39

CAMERON

My ankle throbbed dully as Touron gently lowered me onto my bed. Sharniza grabbed a pillow to prop my ankle up.

"I think one of us should stay with her," Touron said. "In case she needs anything."

"We can hang out with her until she's tired," Shar said.

"Hey." I waved my hands at them. "*She* can hear you and she's fine. I have the crutch, and Chlobe said the swelling should be gone by tomorrow even with the slower healing, so you guys are good to go get on with your evening." I glanced at the bedside clock. "It's only five, and the goyle day is just beginning." Shit... wait. "I'm supposed to meet Selas for training at six..." Serath had given me a phone, but he'd said to call him after seven, and by that time Selas would already be at the clearing.

"Can one of you please meet her in the clearing and let her know I can't make it."

"I'll go," Touron said.

"I'll grab us a bite to eat," Shar said.

My stomach rumbled in agreement with that plan. "Thanks, guys. You're the best."

I slumped against my pillows as the door closed behind them and replayed our win today. It was such a small silly thing, but it felt so good to not get crushed out there. My ankle throbbed in disagreement but fuck it. It was worth it.

I must have fallen asleep because when I opened my eyes the room was dark. A covered plate sat on my bedside table along with a couple of bottles of water.

The glowing numbers on my clock showed it to be seven forty-five.

Urgh. I sat up, wincing as the movement set my ankle throbbing again, and reached for the water. Damn, I was thirsty. I drained the bottle and peeked at the food. A doorstop sandwich.

My stomach growled angrily. Fine. I scoffed it down and was immediately thirsty again. Thank goodness Shar had left a couple of bottles for me. Feeling almost human, I leaned across to retrieve the mobile phone from my drawer. There was only one number programmed into it.

I hit *call.*

It rang twice before he answered. “Cameron.” He said my name like a prayer of relief. “How are you? Your ankle...”

A smile tugged at my lips. “It’s better. I’ll be fine by tomorrow. I’m sorry, I would have called earlier but I fell asleep.”

“Don’t apologize. Sleep is healing. But I’m glad you called.”

“Were you waiting?” Why did I ask that?

He exhaled softly. “Yes.”

My heart fluttered. “How’s your day been?”

“Uneventful.” He paused for a moment. “About what happened in the coffee shop today...I want you to know, not everyone feels that way. You *do* belong here, Cameron. You’re a gargoyle.”

My throat pinched. “Really? That isn’t what you said the first time we met.”

He sighed. “The first time I saw you I knew you were mine. I have a cuff on my ankle, which allows me to detect a potential mate. It heats when one is close. It heated that day.”

“So, you hoped I’d leave.”

“Yes,” he admitted. “For both our sakes. The cuff has since been modified to help mute the effect the bond has on me.”

"You were muted in the forest last night?"

He chuckles softly. "I know. I know. It needs work, but this... Talking to you like this helps. I think."

The clawing need that usually assaulted me in his presence was absent when we spoke like this. Instead, my pulse fluttered, and my belly quivered. "I think you're right." There was a sound like the wind in the background. "Where are you?"

"In the observatory tower. You can see the whole academy campus from here, and beyond the walls."

"Describe what you see." I settled back against my pillows, letting his voice wash over me.

"Mountains, capped by moonlight. Lush, dark canopies speckled with starlight. And the vastness of night spreading up and outward to infinity."

"I wish I could see it." My throat thickened. "To be able to fly...To see the world from that perspective."

"I'll take you one day," he said. "One day when it's safe, when this thing between us is under control, then I'll take you."

Silence settled between us, warm and filled with possibilities we both knew we might never be able to fulfil. I didn't want to think about that. Didn't want to dwell on all the ways this could go wrong. All the ways that we couldn't be together.

"So, tell me, what do the elite do exactly? Are you always stationed here?" I knew the answer to the latter question, of course. Romi had explained that the elites' homebase was the academy. They stayed here between missions and patrol, but he'd never fully explained anything about the patrols or missions, wanting to keep a distance between me and this world. Wanting to protect me.

But it was too late for that now.

"We have sectors we maintain," Serath said. "The furthest sectors of the Rim where the graynite threat is worse. Have you had your first history lesson yet?"

"Yes, Mirrowind explained the bloodlines and how only the five together can take down the alpha."

"Hmmm, that's what they say."

"You don't believe it?"

"It's never been proven. We've never had the chance to try, but that's the theory."

I wanted to ask more about the alpha and the graynites, but I also wanted to know more about Serath the man. "What's your favorite food?"

"Food?" I could hear the smile in his voice. "Hmmm... Let me see. Steak, medium rare, and lasagna. I'm partial to a good lasagna, any pasta dish in fact, and potatoes, I love potatoes. What about you?"

My smile widened. "Same. But add cream scones to that list. I love a freshly baked scone with cream and jam."

"There's this tiny bakery in Asteria that does the tastiest fluffiest scones. We'll have to go there one..." He sighed. "I'm sorry."

My pulse quickened because I wanted him to go on. I wanted to hear more. "No. Don't be. Let's...Let's pretend."

"Pretend?"

It was silly to play make-believe, but when make believe was all I could have with the male the cosmos had created just for me, then I'd take it. "This is our first date and we're making plans for more."

He was silent for the longest beat. Crap, now he thought I was being ridiculous. I should have kept my mouth shut.

"I'll cook for you," he said finally. "And we'll have dinner in the observatory with the night sky all around us."

I exhaled softly. "What will you cook?"

"Steak, medium rare, potatoes and roasted vegetables, then I'll fly you to Asteria, and we can visit the bakery at dawn for scones."

I wanted this. I wanted to do these things with him.

He continued to speak. To make plans, telling me about all the small settlements and the special places hidden there where we could go, his rumbling voice soothed away my doubts, allowing me to believe that all the things could be true.

That we could have it all.

SERATH

"CAMERON?"

"Hmmm, don't stop talking," she says sleepily.

She's tired. She needs to sleep so she can heal. I should end the call, but I'm loath to leave her. Like this, with the phone pressed to my ear and her voice in my head, I can imagine that I'm lying beside her. I can imagine that all the things we're saying are real possibilities.

I've never had anything or anyone that's wholly mine. Never been wanted in the way I know she wants me. Like this, with her voice in my ear, the yawning loneliness inside me echoes a little less, promising me a comfort and fulfillment that I can never truly have.

"I have a boogeyman," she says sleepily. "When I was a child and woke from a nightmare, he'd stay with me and talk to me until I fell asleep."

"Did you have nightmares often?"

"All the time...before." She yawns. "I can't remember clearly now, but...it was a monster. He wanted to get me, always trying to get me."

My chest tightens at the thought of her being afraid and my not being there to protect her. "You're safe here. Safe with me."

She laughs, a soft sleepy sound. "Am I? The things I want to do to you..."

My pulse quickens. "Cameron..." I want to inject warning into my tone, but it comes out as a plea. As if I *want* her to continue.

I feel her shut it down, and I can't help but be grateful to her. "I should get some sleep." She sounds reluctant. I could press her to continue the call, but we're swimming into dangerous waters, and she's right to pull back.

Stronger than me.

"Yes. I should get back to work." I look around at the dark, empty observatory. There's no need to tell her that we're practically grounded until we get another Basque. That all we can do is assist in small missions because the Stone Council fears losing another one of us.

We're stronger together, and with Romi gone, our bonds have weakened.

"Night, Serath," she says. "Speak tomorrow?"

"Goodnight, Cameron, and yes, tomorrow."

I end the call and stare at the tiny phone in my hand. Such a small device and now a lifeline. A connection to my mate.

If this is all I can have, then I'll take it and make the most of it, because the alternative...It's not worth thinking about.

"How'd it go?" Selas asks from the doorway.

"Good. It went well."

"I'm glad to hear it. Because I've just had some shitty news."

I take a final look at the starry sky, then turn away from my dreams and to reality. "Tell me."

CHAPTER 40

CAMERON

The weekend flew by, and I was back on my feet by Sunday and eager to do something. Training seemed like a good idea. Had Selas told Touron when we could meet again?

I dressed and stared at the empty spot where a coffee mug would usually be. Melanie had been absent the last few days. Well not absent exactly but uncommunicative. I'd felt her presence and even caught a glimpse of her in the corridor last night, but she hadn't visited since scoping out the filing room for me.

After everything she'd said about wanting company and being roommates, it was odd that she'd just stop talking to me. Had I upset her by asking her to help me? Had I done something wrong? And what the hell was I doing, worrying if a ghost wanted to be friends with me or not?

I grabbed a jacket and headed out.

Touron didn't answer his door, but Shar did, although she blocked me from entering. I stifled a stab of annoyance. "Why won't you let me come into your room?"

She frowned. "It's a mess."

She was lying. I should let it go, but it was bugging me now. "I don't care."

"But I do. I'll be out in a moment." She closed the door in my face.

Seriously?

She emerged a moment later and closed the door quickly behind her. "Your ankle looks better."

She was trying to deflect. Not having it. "We're friends, right?"

She blinked down at me in confusion.

"I mean, I didn't just imagine that, right?"

"Of course not."

"Then you can be honest with me. If you don't like people in your space, then just say so. I can respect that."

She exhaled and sucked in her bottom lip, as if contemplating something. "I'm keeping your secret, right?"

It was my turn to frown because where was she going with this? "Right..."

"Fuck it." She unlocked her door and pushed it open a little bit. "Go in."

Just like that? "Wait? Are you sure."

"Very."

I stepped into her room and froze.

Pink

Everywhere.

Pink, purple, and sparkly things, and oh, my God were those a pair of red stiletto boots?

The door closed behind me. "I like pretty things," she said flatly. "A lot. And if you tell anyone..."

"Mutually assured destruction. I get it." I looked up at her. "But, Shar, why are you hiding this? You're allowed to like pretty stuff."

"No. I'm not. I'm an Aziza. There are expectations for us. Especially the alpha females. We are raised to be warriors. There is no time for the softer things." Her throat bobbed. "I just thought... for a little while, until..."

Until she became a guardian.

"Fuck that shit, Shar. Wearing pink or heels, or makeup, won't make you any less kick-ass than you already are. I bet you could beat the shit out of any cadet, even if you were wearing these." I picked up the boots. "Nice leather by the way."

"They're surprisingly comfortable." The corner of her mouth lifted.

I put the shoes down and turned to her. "A goyle life is too long for you to stifle your wants and desires. You can have the best of both worlds. Be feminine if you want to. It won't make you weak. In fact, it makes you stronger because you'll probably be underestimated by an opponent or adversary."

She blinked and nodded. "It's not that easy, Cam, but I appreciate the sentiment."

Maybe in time she'd find the strength to go against the decades of brainwashing her family had put her through. I wasn't about to push.

"Let's go find the others and hit the coffee shop. I'm in the mood for a scone."

We bumped into Touron on the steps as he headed up to the third floor. His skin was flushed, eyes bright, hair tousled by the wind.

"Oh, hi." He slowed to a stop. "You're feeling better?" he asked me.

"Much. You're up early."

He shrugged. "I fancied a run."

I plucked a leaf out of his hair. "Into a bush?"

He plucked the leaf from my fingers with a crooked smile. "It came out of nowhere."

"I meant to ask about Selas."

He blinked sharply. "What about her?"

"Did she say when we could meet for training again?"

"Oh, yeah, starting tomorrow. She was sure you'd be healed by then."

"Urgh. I was hoping for a session today, but I'll hit the gym instead." I zipped up my top. "*After* my scones."

"You're going to Stone Comfort?" Touron asked.

"Yes," Sharniza said. "Want to come?"

"I need to shower, but I'll meet you there."

Shar watched him leave with a strange expression.

"What?" I nudged her.

She shook her head. "Nothing. Let's go.

THE GYM WAS empty when I got there at five. We'd ended up spending too much time hanging out in Stone Comfort. Palia and Ginia had joined us there with news on Yarrow. The witch was awake and had no memory of what had happened to her. She couldn't even recall going into the main building. But it looked like arcana classes would be back on the timetable this week.

I'd hung out with Levi, Fred, and Teri plenty of times, but it never felt this easy and comfortable, probably because I'd been lying to them about everything—what I was, who I was, and what I could do. Those omissions left a rift between us that never allowed the friendships to flourish. What was growing between me and my gargoyle friends, was organic and powerful.

I was connected here in a way I'd never felt in the human world.

I had to graduate, if not to initiate then to general forces. I *needed* to be a guardian, and yes, a guardian who couldn't shift and fly, might be seen as a liability to some, but what I couldn't bring in brute force and strength I could provide in stealth, speed, and tenacity.

So, while Sharniza and Touron headed back to the dorms for the weekend movie night—some creature feature with thirty-foot dinosaurs—I made my way to the gym for a workout.

My gargoyle nature made me stronger than a human, but not stronger than a gargoyle. It made me faster on my feet and gave me preternatural senses. I could form stone skin to protect against a blow, but when faced with gargoyle power that ability hadn't held up too well. There was no way I could take down a gargoyle with brute strength, so I needed to work on my agility and combat moves; the latter Selas would help with, but the former would come with training.

The gym had bars, a treadmill, and several sets of rings hanging from the ceiling. I'd get in a good workout of the muscles that would allow me to leap, climb, dodge, and twist.

My ankle was still healing, so the treadmill wasn't a good idea, but the bars and rings would work my upper body. There was an old cassette player on a bench by the wall. I pressed play, and a song I didn't know came on. It had a nice beat. Good to work out to. I turned it up and got to work, zoning out after a few minutes as I got into the rhythm of each exercise with the music as a backdrop to my exertion.

My biceps burned, and my shoulders ached, but it was a pleasant sensation because it meant my muscles were working.

The music stopped suddenly, jolting me out of my tempo. The tape was done. I dropped from the bar and turned to find two gargoyles standing by the cassette player.

The same two initiates from the coffee shop that Serath had told to back off. Jay Batiste with his mulish jaw and his buddy who reminded me of a bird of prey.

They were either here to work out and preferred doing it sans music, or they were here for me.

I hoped it was the former because I was so fucking done with altercations. I grabbed my towel off the floor and headed for the exit, but they moved quickly to block me.

Yep. It looked like they were here for me after all.

CHAPTER 41

CAMERON

Jay planted himself right in my path. There was a meter between us, but it wasn't enough. His aura was strong, his presence oppressive and aggressive, and it nudged the beast inside me.

No. Bad move. Keep it under control. Taking one of them on would be a challenge; there was no way I could take on both.

"What do you want, Jay?" I kept my tone unconfrontational, so I sounded like a barista asking someone what they wanted to drink.

"An apology," he said. "And maybe a little blood." He bared his teeth and pressed the tip on his tongue to one of his fangs.

"No. To both."

He narrowed his eyes. "I've been held back from a spot on the alpha team because of you."

"Because of me? No. You got punished for harassing a cadet."

"Cadet? You're no cadet. You're a halfblood."

"The two are not mutually exclusive."

"Huh?"

"She means you can be both," bird boy said.

"Shut up, Quaid," Jay snapped. "I know what she means."

Like hell, he did. But I wasn't about to argue with him. I recognized barely restrained violence when I felt it. He wanted a reason to snap and lose control. Any reason to whale on me.

I wasn't about to give him the excuse he needed. "Look, I just want to be left alone to train and get on with the program. If I'm as incompetent as you think, then I'll be out of here in a few weeks."

"She's got a point," Quaid said.

"No," Jay said. "She hasn't got a point. What she has, is Serath's dick in her mouth."

My stomach dropped.

"They're fucking," he continued with a sneer. "They must be. The way he looked at her in the coffee shop."

My cheeks heated. "What the hell?"

"Admit it. He's fucking you, isn't he?" He advanced into my personal space. "You're giving him your cunt for a place here on the program."

I reacted before I could think it through and punched him in the mouth.

His head bobbed back, the blow taking him by surprise. There was a split second of *what the fuck*, as he realized what had just happened, then his eyes glowed green and his body morphed into goyle form.

"Jay, no!" Quaid made a grab for his buddy, but Jay palm punched him in the chest and came at me.

I threw my towel in his face, and ducked past him, running for the door, but my ankle was still sore, so I wasn't fast enough.

He grabbed me by the nape and threw me across the room like a rag doll. I smashed into the bar, stone skin activating in time to prevent major injury, then landed in a crouch.

"Jay, stop it!" Quaid yelled. "They'll expel you for this."

"I'm already fucked," Jay growled. "My record tarnished, and all because of her." The final word ended on a growl as he tucked in his chin and rushed me again.

I grabbed the bar and used it to swing myself up and over his head, hitting the mat in a roll and coming up in a sprint for the exit.

"Get her!" Jay roared.

I slammed into a solid mass of muscle. Hands grabbed hold of my upper arms and held me still.

My head whipped up, and I locked gazes with Curi.

He stared at me in confusion.

"Mason. Good timing," Jay said from inside the room. "Bring her inside. Shut the door. We can teach the bitch a lesson. You know she doesn't belong here as a cadet, but we can teach her where she does belong."

Ice filled my veins and panic gripped my lungs in a vise, because there was no doubt in my mind what Jay was insinuating.

Mason's grip on me tightened. No. He wouldn't, would he?

His hold slackened. "Go," he said gruffly, then shoved me behind him and out of the doorway. "I'll deal with this."

He closed the door.

Wait...what the?

Don't look a gift horse in the mouth woman. Go.

But if I walked away now, then what would happen to Curi?

Fuck it.

I took a deep breath and yanked open the door to find Jay and Curi facing off.

Quaid stood to one side, looking uncertain.

He was obviously the smarter out of the pair of initiates.

"What the fuck?" Curi said to me. "I told you to go."

"I'm not leaving without you." He blinked in surprise, but I focused on Jay. "And you... What do you think will happen if you get into a fight with a Mason, eh? You might be able to salvage your reputation after being held back from alpha team, but touch *him* and it's your family that'll pay the price."

"She's right, Jay," Quaid said. "Look, let's just go. This is..."

"Stupid." I finished for him. "And you know you're better than this, right Quaid?"

He looked away. "I'm out of here, Jay. Do what you want." He strode past me and out of the room.

With his wingman gone, Jay deflated back to his human form. "This is your fault," he said to me again, but he didn't sound so sure any longer.

Curi gave Jay a final once-over, then walked over to me. "I'll walk you back to dorm."

CURI DIDN'T SPEAK as we made our way back to the dorm. He had a towel around his neck, a rucksack slung over one shoulder, and his blue hair was pulled back and tied in a knot ready for a decent workout, but instead he was walking with me.

He'd stood up to Jay for me, challenging my perception of him, and I needed to understand why he'd done it. "Why'd you stick up for me back there?"

"It was the right thing to do."

Curi doing the right thing...It didn't correlate in my brain, but then what did I know about this guy beyond a few shitty interactions? "But you hate me."

He sighed. "No. I don't."

I shot him a skeptical look. "Maybe I misinterpreted all the snarls, growls, and digs you've made then? Look, you wouldn't be the only one. I seem to have that effect on most of the males here."

He exhaled through his nose. "It isn't like that. It isn't about hating you." For a moment I thought he wasn't going to elaborate, but then he continued. "You confuse us. You have the look of an omega, and yet you act like an alpha. You want to fight alongside us instead of writhe beneath us."

"*Writhe*? Seriously."

The corner of his mouth quirked. "The only gray in our world is the one we fight. Everything else is black and white. Omega, alpha, sigma, beta, everyone has a place and there's a system. You confuse that system, and it affects some of us more than others. But give it time."

"Touron seems to be okay with me."

"Touron is from a civi family," Curi said. "He wasn't raised the same way as most of us."

"And how is that?" Curiosity had me slowing my pace.

"No, Walker, we're not doing this," Curi said.

"Doing what?"

"Disclosing shit. I intervened back there because Jay's an asshole, and what he was planning to do was way over the line, but that doesn't make us friends. Now, if you don't mind, I'd like to go back to the gym and get my workout in. I'm sure you can make it to the doors."

I looked up at the dorm house. We were already at the top of the path.

"Yeah, I'm good, I ca—"

He strode off, leaving me with a bunch of questions and the conviction that it was time to alter my assessment of the arrogant, abrasive gargoyle with the shockingly blue hair.

CHAPTER 42

CAMERON

The lounge was busy, movie still playing. My friends were squashed on the three battered sofas on offer. A couple of other gargoyles, not in our intake group, were stretched out on the floor.

On screen, a woman ran away from a dinosaur that looked like it was made of plastic. This was an old movie. One I had in the selection Romi had brought me.

My mood dipped. Romi...If he could see me now. Here.

If I could have come here when he'd been here...

I hated that we hadn't had the chance to be family in front of the world. Hated that I was still hiding my heritage from everyone.

At least my friends knew the truth.

I ducked out of the room before being spotted and headed for the stairs. Hot shower, food, then bed, and...Serath. The thought of him was like warm porridge filling my belly. I took the stairs two at a time and hurried to my room.

"Hello," Melanie said.

"Oh, fuck!" I jumped and clutched at my chest. "Melanie, fuck."

"I'm sorry, I didn't mean to scare you. I brought you some coffee."

There was a mug on my bedside table, but the film on the

surface of the drink told me it had been sitting there awhile. "Melanie, how long have you been waiting here?"

Her brow crinkled. "I'm not sure. I think I just got here, but..." She looked at the coffee. "That was hot a moment ago."

I kicked off my sneakers. "Where were you before coming here?"

She looked down at the carpet for several beats, then back up at me, her eyes wide with panic. "I don't remember."

Sometimes, ghosts who'd been earthbound for a long time experienced memory decay. They forgot about things that had happened while they were alive, but not where they'd wandered a few minutes or hours ago. It didn't work that way. At least I don't think it did. But then, I wasn't an expert on ghosts.

Melanie wrung her hands. "Why can't I remember?"

"It's all right. It'll come to you eventually. Don't worry. Look, how about we hang out? I'll jump in the shower and be back in a few minutes."

Her face relaxed. "Yes, yes, of course you're right. It'll come to me." She smiled warmly. "I'd like to hang out."

"Okay, I'll be out in a few minutes."

I showered and shampooed my hair quickly, then dried off and dressed in the bathroom before heading back into the bedroom.

My ghostly roommate was nowhere to be seen.

"Melanie?"

Nothing.

She was gone.

Something was off with her, had been for a while, and I doubt anyone had tried to help her. But that was going to change. There had to be a way to free her to cross over before she lost herself completely, and I knew just the witch to ask.

First thing tomorrow.

But for now...

I drew the mobile phone out of its hiding place and climbed into bed.

Serath answered on the third ring. "Hello, Cameron."

His voice sent tingles down my neck. I snuggled down under the duvet, not caring that my wet hair was making the pillow damp. "How's your day been?"

"Busy. You?"

"Not busy." There was no way I was telling him about the attack on me in the gym. If we were going to keep our connection a secret, then he couldn't be seen coming to my rescue all the time. Jay had noticed something between us in the coffee shop, even though I'd barely looked Serath's way. We had to be careful.

"You're thinking hard," he said. "Is everything all right?" His tone sharpened as he slipped into alert mode. "Did something happen today?"

"I'm fine. Just wondering where you'll be taking me on my date tonight."

He chuckled softly. "Actually, I have something for you. Go to your window and look on the ledge."

Wait, what? I climbed out of bed and padded to the window. The drapes were open, and the night looked in at me, starry, bright, and beautiful. A package lay neatly on the ledge.

"Do you see the package?" he asked.

"What is it?"

"That's for you to find out."

I loved the teasing note in his tone.

"Okay, one minute, I need to put you down."

"No. Take me with you."

I climbed out onto the ledge where cool air kissed my skin and ran its fingers through my damp hair, sending a delicious chill over me.

"You're beautiful," Serath said.

My heart forgot to beat for a moment. "You can see me?"

"I can."

"Where are you?" I scanned the night, peering at the nearest landing posts, but there was no one there. "This isn't fair."

"I didn't say I played fair, Cameron. Open the package."

I tucked the phone between my shoulder and ear, then picked up the neatly wrapped package. I wanted to tear it open but took my time. He was watching me. I wanted that. Wanted his gaze on me.

"So careful," he said in my ear. "So very meticulous, when I know that all you want to do is tear it off." His final words had a gruff edge, and the vibration shot straight between my legs.

I pressed my thighs together and swallowed against a suddenly dry throat.

What was with him tonight? Last night he'd been so... restrained, but tonight...

The paper fell away to reveal a crimson silk slip.

"Put it on for me, Cameron. Put it on, then come back to the ledge so I can see it."

My stomach flipped. This was dangerous ground. I should stop him, say something, but there was a liquid heat in my belly that felt right. I didn't want to lose that feeling, didn't want to lose this side of him.

"One second."

I ducked back into my room, hit speaker, and set the phone on the dresser, but I didn't step away from the window. Instead, I stood in full view and peeled off my PJs. Could he see me? Was he watching? The pulse in my throat thudded hard and fast.

He sucked in a breath. "Cam..." His tone was raw torment. "This is bad..."

I stopped undressing. "It is?" I kept my voice light and innocent. "Should I stop?"

"Don't stop, dammit," he growled.

That's what I thought. I peeled off my sleep tee and was rewarded with another low, agonized groan.

"Fuck...you're perfect."

I stepped out of my shorts next, leaving me naked except for my underwear. "I really hope you're the only one getting an eyeful here?"

He made a soft sound, part groan, part laugh. "Put on the

slip."

The material practically poured itself over me, caressing my skin in a way that heightened my senses and intensified the liquid heat low in my belly.

"It's perfect. You're perfect."

I ran my hands over the fabric that came just past my ass. If I took off my panties and bent over, I'd be on display, and for a moment I was tempted to do just that. But we were already pushing boundaries here.

"You're beautiful, Cameron." He sounded almost sad. "So very beautiful."

Beautiful? I hadn't been called beautiful before. My body was too muscular, too tall for most human male tastes. Even Levi, a halfblood like me, had only ever called me sexy, and that was only during sex. But then, if he had called me beautiful, I probably would have taken it with a pinch of salt, but when Serath said it, the *way* he said it...I had no doubt that he meant it.

"I have to go," he said softly.

"What?" I snatched up the phone, flipped the speaker mode off, and pressed it to my ear. "We went too far, didn't we?"

"No, Cam. It's fine. I just. I wanted to have this to take with me."

My scalp prickled. "Serath, what's going on?"

"I've got to leave on a mission. Tonight. And this...You in that slip of a thing, is the perfect image to take with me."

"But, where are you going?" Fear dug its claws into my lungs. "It's dangerous, isn't it?"

He chuckled, soft and low, making the hairs on my body quiver with need, even when my mind was screaming that something was wrong here.

"Serath, please, tell me the truth. Is there a chance you won't come back?"

"Cameron, in our world, there's *always* a chance that we won't come back."

Like Romi had never come back. "No. I'm not having it."

"What?"

"You'll come back. You'll come back because if you don't, then I'll come looking for you and probably get myself killed, so you'll come back to make sure I stay here. Safe. Do you understand me?" My chest heaved, and I breathed through my nose to calm myself against the wave of panic that the thought of losing him evoked.

He was silent for the longest time, and I was beginning to think the line had gone dead when he finally replied.

"I'll come back, Cameron. No matter what it takes."

"Serath, we need to move out," a male voice said from behind him.

"I have to go. Selas said to tell you that training is still on."

"She's not going with you?"

"Goodnight, Cameron. I'll see you soon."

He hung up.

I stared at the phone for several seconds, then closed the window and climbed into bed in the sexy crimson slip.

It was a gift from him; he'd touched it, and now that it was against my skin, it was almost as if he were touching me too. And this was crazy. It was insane to feel this way about someone I'd barely spent any time with, but it was real, and there was no running away from that. The question now was how we'd manage it because the conversations on the phone might calm down the physical mating urge, but a new urge was building. A new bond. An emotional one, and I had a gut feeling, managing that was going to be the hardest task of all.

CHAPTER 43

SERATH

Outpost ten is the closest outpost to Graynite territory. Home to two alpha teams, it's considered a hotspot, and it's one of the elite team's main bases. But after the loss of Romi, the Stone Council ordered us to pull back to the academy, a location hidden by powerful arcana and inaccessible to the graynites.

They're afraid to lose any more elites. We are the strongest of our bloodlines, which gives us the greatest potential to take down the alpha. We're essentially the most powerful weapon the Stone Council has...At least we were.

Without a Basque, we're nowhere near full strength. Without a Basque, we are no longer the ultimate weapon.

Willowman warps us to the base where guardians are out in force, running back and forth from the main barracks to the tower. The stench of blood is strong in the air.

Someone screams, high-pitched and feral.

My skin itches.

"Fuck," Orix says. "That sounds bad."

"Three injured," Willowman says. "One dead."

"We'll need to reinforce," Orix says. "Outpost six can send guardians. Prasan is on it."

He'd wanted to come with us, so had Selas, but orders from

HQ were clear. Only two elites, a Halle and an Albion, and the reason was simple: both of us had potential replacements who could step into our shoes immediately if we got taken down.

Orix heads to the tower to get a report from the alpha team leaders, but I head to the barracks where the sound of roars and screams intensifies.

"I'm going to check the wards," Willowman says before vanishing into thin air.

The barracks have been converted into a medic's den, and three gargoyles are laid out on the ground, one unconscious, the other two writhing and bleeding. Steam rises off pulsing red welts in their stone skin, and my scar burns at the sight.

I remember this pain. The agony. But my wound was confined to one area, whereas these males...they have wounds all over.

A medic applies a green poultice to the unconscious goyle. It should draw out the venom and allow him to heal. The others twist and cry out every time their medics touch their wounds.

"Add more, now," a female gargoyle orders. "Dammit, Braen do I have to do everything myself?" She growls and snatches the poultice bowl off one of the medics, and sets to work on the injured gargoyle herself, jaw set in determination.

"The poultice isn't working, Janna," the gargoyle working on the unconscious male says.

Janna's jaw ticks. "Keep applying it. It has to work."

I step into the room, and she glances up at me, her eyes flaring. "Serath..."

"Janna. Let me help."

"Nothing you can do here. Please tell me you brought Willowman."

"Someone call my name?" Willowman steps into the room and takes in the scene. "Fuck."

"The poultice isn't working," Janna says.

Willowman crosses to her and begins to examine the wounds. "Hold still," he orders the injured male who growls at him but obliges. They know what Willowman is capable of. He sniffs the wound and rears back. "This isn't the same venom."

"What?"

"It's stronger. We'll need a new poultice."

"Can you make one?" Janna asks.

A muscle in his cheek jumps. "I can, but not in time."

Janna's chest heaves. "You're saying..."

He nods. "Yes. I'm sorry. I'll head back to the lab and get to work right away." He grabs bandages off the side table and swipes them over one of the gargoyle's wounds before folding it and tucking it into his pocket. "It'll be agonizing if you let the venom run its course."

As if to illustrate his point, the unconscious gargoyle wakes up screaming.

Gargoyles roar and bellow regularly, but hearing one scream is gut-wrenchingly unnatural.

"I'm assuming your tranq supply is out," Willowman says.

"HQ haven't sent us a fresh supply," Jana replies. "I checked with the closest outposts, and no one has any."

Tranqs that worked on goyles were expensive, and we rarely needed them, and HQ rarely provided.

"Then you know what you have to do," Willowman says. "I'm sorry."

Janna's shoulders slump, defeat etched into her posture. "Give me a moment. Please."

Willowman and I exit the barracks.

"A new venom means a new breed of graynite," Willowman says.

"We don't know that for sure. They may have simply evolved."

"After what happened on our last mission? What you saw. You don't believe that."

Silence falls. The screams are gone.

Janna walks out to meet us a moment later. Her eyes are bloodshot, and her hands are fists. "The tower has the coordinates of the attack, but you shouldn't go out there."

"Orders are—"

"Fuck the orders," she snarls. "They know what's out there. We saw it and we told them. So why send you back out?"

I can't tell her the truth, because the truth is classified. "Secondary confirmation of graynite activity."

"Those things that attacked us weren't graynites," she says. "At least not the kind we know of." Her eyes darken. "They looked human, Serath. They *smelled* human. We thought they were in trouble, that they'd somehow wandered past our defenses into the hot zone. We thought we were helping them, and then...they were no longer human."

Just like the male who'd killed the werewolves. Human but not human. HQ knows about this because we reported it to the council last week and they know about what outpost ten just dealt with, but nowhere is it mentioned in the orders sent to us at the academy.

What the fuck are they playing at?

I'm torn between keeping the peace and revealing all, but there is a hierarchy for a reason. A structure that has kept our world safe for decades. I must trust that the council has its reasons.

"We'll be fine." I give her a nod. "We'll speak when I return. Willowman, how long will the poultice take to make?"

"At least twenty-four hours."

"Then come back for us when it's ready."

I take a breath and head for the tower, ignoring the vise around my chest because I'm about to head into what we call the gray zone, and the last time I was there, I almost died.

CHAPTER 44

SERATH

We fly over the twenty-mile strip of land adjacent to where the breach once opened, and to the area where the alpha team was attacked, past sparse woodland and along a winding road. There's a cart on its side, wheels pointing up at the sky. Blood speckles the ground.

Janna's report mentions the humans were riding in a cart. Humans that morphed into graynites. But there is no sign of them now.

We do a circuit, scoping out the land before hitting earth.

"No one's here now," Orix says.

We examine the cart for clues. But all we find is blood and venom residue. The ground is disturbed from the fight, but something niggles at me. I walk away from the cart, and it hits me.

"There are no tracks."

"What?" Orix asks.

"There are no wheel tracks."

Orix scans the ground. "You're right. So how did it get here?"

"They saw movement on the scanner because it tracks all movement of a certain size, right?"

"And we know that the animals in this zone are too small to trigger the scanners," Orix adds.

"So...Where are the tracks?" My pulse quickens. "There are none above ground, but what if..." I cross back to the cart and fling it aside. The gravel beneath looks too neat. "Look at this. There's a seam."

"It's a fucking door," Orix says.

We exchange glances. Our true mission is clear. We were sent here to find something vital, and this passage could lead us to it.

Orix nods, and I use a talon to pry up the door. It's heavy, and it takes a moment, but together we lift and slide it back.

There are steps below, leading into darkness. I give Orix a nod and am about to take the first step, when a low raspy chuckle drifts up out of the inky blackness.

"I wouldn't do that if I were you," the voice says. "You're meddling in affairs that don't concern you."

I know that voice. It belongs to the male from the ruins. The one who killed the mutts. "Come out where we can see you."

"You don't give the orders here, elite." He says it like it's a dirty word. "This is our terrain. Our domain. The same was said to the guardians that came before you. They were given the chance to leave. To walk away and they declined."

"Since when do graynites negotiate?" Orix says.

A bitter laugh floats up out of the darkness. "You're fools dancing to an out-of-date tune. Leave now. Last warning."

Orix and I step back from the hole in the ground, and it's Orix who replies.

"We don't take orders from graynites."

"Have it your way."

The ground beneath us rumbles.

Something is coming.

Orix roars as he morphs from gargoyle form to Chimera, lion jaws snapping and lizard tail swiping at the ground. His talons are set in padded paws that could crush a skull, and his wingspan is wider, the stone marked with feathered etchings. The Albion Chimera form is power and brute strength.

I suck in a breath and exhale, letting my own chimera free.

My wings twist and snap, becoming wider and serrated at the tips. My neck elongates and curves, vision switching to thermal through my dragon eyes, and my body tightens and streamlines itself into a pantherine form.

This beast beneath our gargoyle skin is a perk of being from one of the five most powerful bloodlines. This is what gives us an edge.

A shriek blasts out of the tunnel.

"Such a shame," the voice says. "Goodbye, elites."

The ground shakes, and a scaled gray form bursts out of the ground toward us.

Orix attacks, slamming into it and latching onto its hide to take it up into the air. There's no time to check if he has the beast under control because another comes at me.

My roar blasts it back a step but only for a moment. Our bodies collide in a flurry of claws, talons, and lethal teeth. I twist and smash my paw into its head, knocking it to one side.

It rakes at me with claws that can cut through a gargoyle hide given enough force. I catch the gleam of venom. New venom, the kind we don't have a cure for yet.

Fuck.

I fly back to avoid the swipe. And something lands on my back.

Watch out! Orix bellows in my mind.

Too late

I twist and flap my serrated wings. Blood sprays, the creature shrieks and releases me.

The one I had pinned a moment ago is up and rushing at me. My bellow knocks it back, and a tail swipe takes down the one running up behind me.

I need to kill one.

More incoming! Orix yells.

Fuck. I relinquish control to the beast, and for the next few moments my body acts on primal instinct, no thought except survival. No mission except annihilation. This is berserker mode, and I'm here but not here. I smell the blood, hear the screeches, feel the burn that rakes along my side. But I'm not in control.

Not until Orix's voice pulls me back.

"Serath, we have to go. We have to go now!"

I snap back into the driver's seat. We're several meters away from the hole in the ground. There are three dead humans on the gravel and a graynite standing over them. He throws back his head and screeches.

"Shift now," Orix orders.

I drop the chimera form, and pain shoots through me, sinking into my side like angry teeth.

"Human form now," Orix orders again.

I shift again, and I'm burning up.

The ground trembles. More are coming. My legs buckle. "Orix?" My vision fades.

I'm wounded. The venom is in my bloodstream.

Orix wraps his arms around me and launches himself into the air. "I've got you, brother. I've got you. You're going to be fine."

But he's lying because there is no cure. No way to draw the venom from my body, not for at least another twenty hours.

I'm dead already.

I close my eyes and picture Cameron in her red slip of a dress. I'm sorry, Cameron. I'm sorry I won't be able to keep my promise.

I'm sorry I won't be coming back.

CHAPTER 45

CAMERON

My bagel tasted like ash, and every bite sat like a rock in my belly. Stone Comfort buzzed with early afternoon activity and goyles grabbed a bite before classes, but everything felt off to me.

"Cam? Hello?" Ginia waved a hand in front of my face. "Are you listening?"

"No." I set my bagel down. "I can't focus."

"Serath?" Palia asked in a low voice.

"I have a bad feeling." I rubbed my breastbone with my knuckles.

"Indigestion?" Ginia asked.

Palia elbowed her. "Don't make fun. Mate bonds are powerful."

"She's not bonded yet," Ginia pointed out.

"It doesn't matter," Palia said. "I read that a fated mate bond is activated as soon as the mates have contact, consummation merely solidifies it. So, if she's feeling like there's something wrong then..."

I pushed my plate away. "I have to find Selas." I grabbed my jacket. "Tell Touron and Shar that I'll meet you guys in class."

"Cam, wait!" Ginia called out, but I couldn't wait. My chest was filled with dread.

Serath was in danger. I knew it.

SELAS

THE MESSAGE SCROLLS on the screen over and over, and each time I hope that I'm reading it wrong.

Prasan sits with his head in his hands. "I should have gone with them regardless of orders."

"We should all have gone together." My lips feel numb. "Is Willowman sure he can't speed things up?"

"He's positive. The gargoyle that died from the venom was smaller than the ones Janna had to kill. Orix says it took him fourteen hours to die. Serath is approaching twelve hours. He'll have to fight for another twelve hours to give Willowman enough time to get the anti-venom poultice ready."

"There's got to be some way to help him fight the venom."

Prasan curses under his breath, then begins to type, fingers flying across the keyboard.

"What are you doing?"

"Hacking into the city archives."

"What?"

"They gave me access a year ago for another mission, so I built in a back door just in case."

Hope quickens my pulse. "You think they'll have something?"

"We can only hope."

The bell above the door chimes and lights up. There's someone outside. "Are you expecting anyone?"

"No. Get rid of them."

I head for the stairs. The bell on each floor flashes, telling me that whoever is outside isn't going away anytime soon.

Fuck.

I hit the ground floor, annoyance a coiled serpent in my belly, and yank open the door, ready to shut down whoever dares to come over uninvited.

"Selas, thank fuck." Cameron says. "There's something wrong with Serath." She sucks in a sharp breath. "But you know that, don't you?" She pushes past me before I can gather my wits and block her entry. "Where is he? Is he hurt? How bad is it?"

"Cameron, you can't be here. You have to go."

Her glare is a hot brand on my face. "I'm not going anywhere until you tell me my mate is okay."

"He's hurt, Cameron. He's not going to make it."

She flinches as if I've slapped her, and her aura of anxiety ebbs and cools, like a blanket of calm has been dropped over it. "Take me to him."

"I can't do that."

"Yes. You can. You can take me to him. I need to see him." Her pain is a sharp pressure in my head.

"You can't go to him. He's in a restricted zone. I'm sorry. There's nothing anyone can do for him now."

"Yes, there is," Prasan says from the balcony above us.

My head whips up, gaze locking onto his blurry form. "You found a solution?"

"Yes," Prasan says. "And then she came right to our door."

CAMERON

THE ROOM THEY put me in smelled of Serath. There was a large bed with rumpled sheets where the pillow cradled the indent of his head. I held it to my nose, breathing him in where he lingered on the cotton fabric, and the knots in my belly eased a little.

A worn bedside table with a pile of well-thumbed paperbacks sat on the left side of his bed. Did he sleep on this side, or did he sprawl out across the whole bed?

I picked up one of the books, *Bram Stoker's Dracula*, an old, battered leather-bound copy, and *Mary Shelley's Frankenstein*. Books about monsters looking for love or acceptance. Creatures who would be considered outsiders.

I'd read these, too, and they were among my favorites.

I was tempted to open the drawer, to see what more I could discern about my mate but stopped, hand on the handle. This was his private space. His domain, and he hadn't shared this with me willingly. I'd been put in here to wait for his return so I could help heal him.

I wandered over to the window that looked out onto the campus. Stone Comfort and the training grounds were clearly visible far below. How long before he was back here? How long did it take to create a warp and transport a dying male?

My gut twisted. I couldn't lose him. And yes, that was crazy, because he wasn't mine, not officially, not primally, and he could *never* be, but still...the thought of him being gone, of no longer existing, was a claw raking my insides raw.

My feelings for Levi had grown slowly, creeping up on me and spreading through me like warm honey, but what I felt for Serath was an eruption of emotions and sensations. It was mystical and undeniable, and it was tearing me up not knowing if he'd survive his wounds.

Graynite venom, they'd said. And that was about all they'd said, aside from letting me know that my presence, my proximity to him would help him fight it off until they brewed up the antivenom.

And now I had to wait until they brought him—

The door burst open behind me, and Orix entered carrying Serath.

My mate was limp in his arms. Pale and unconscious.

"Serath!"

"Back up," Orix growled before laying him on the bed.

Serath's usual fresh forest scent was laced with the stench of decay and death. "Move." I shoved Orix out of the way and climbed onto the bed beside Serath.

"What the—" Orix reached for me and something inside me snapped. My vision bled red as I turned on him, teeth bared, chest vibrating in a warning growl.

"Back up," Selas said from the doorway. "Let nature work."

"What if they—"

"In his condition? Don't be stupid," Selas spat.

Orix threw up his hands and took a step back, muttering "*Fucking hell.*"

"She's in protective mode," someone said. "We keep the door open, and we check in and hope this works."

They continued to talk, but I zoned out of the conversation, my attention focused solely on Serath.

His face was speckled with blood. His torso covered in bandages that leaked black goo. He was slipping away. I could feel it. I needed to be close, to feel his skin against mine. My beast approved, purring in encouragement. I undressed quickly. His legs and torso were bare, boxers covering his modesty. Enough skin for me.

His eyes snapped open suddenly, and a low growl rolled up his throat. It exploded from his lips in a pained cry, and he began to thrash.

"Shit!" Orix took a step forward, but Selas held him back, her eyes on me.

"Cameron, it's up to you now."

Serath, bucked and writhed, lashing out at me as I tried to get close. I took a blow to the cheek and another to the side of my head before managing to slip under his arm and sling my leg over his thigh. He stopped fighting but continued to squirm in pain. I put my arm around his waist and pressed my body against his side to maximize skin on skin. He needed this. I wasn't sure how I knew this was the only way to help him; it was simply instinct.

He groaned and stilled. I pressed my cheek to his bicep and closed my eyes, focused on the undeniable thrum of energy between us.

"I'm here." My voice dropped an octave. "I'm here. Hold on to me. Stay with me."

My skin pricked, and warmth seeped into every point of skin-on-skin contact. My head grew fuzzy and floaty, and my limbs grew heavy, then darkness dragged me into its arms.

SELAS

IT'S BEEN SIX hours since we brought Serath back to the academy, and he's still alive thanks to Cameron, but the female has fallen into a deep sleep. Did Prasan's research miss something vital? What if this saves Serath but kills her?

She's a halfblood, a nobody in the grand scheme of things, but there's an energy about her, a sincerity and inner strength that I can't help but admire. Fate is cruel for not giving her all the tools to be the perfect guardian that I know she could have been.

"I'll take the next watch," Orix says.

A shadow darts across the floor. I tense and then relax as the feline Orix seems to have adopted rubs against my leg.

"Taz likes you," Orix says.

"You named him?"

"I know, I know, bad idea. But...he's so freeaking cute."

"You can't keep him here. You know that, right?"

"I know. I'll take him to the sanctuary soon."

Taz pads across to Orix who crouches to allow the feline to climb onto his shoulders.

This is what softens me toward this male. His care and empathy toward these creatures. The way his aura brightens when he's around them is beautiful.

"Did you speak to the Aziza cadet?"

"Yes, she's informed the academy that Walker is unwell. They'll believe it because Cameron is a halfblood."

We're playing a dangerous game. "If anyone finds out—"

"They won't. We won't let them." He looks over my head, into the room where Serath and Cameron are-face-to-face and entwined in sleep. His breathing is even and regular, and there's more color to his cheeks. "What if he takes too much?"

I'm surprised at his concern for the female, considering his prickly attitude to date. "He won't. His instinct is to protect her. His beast won't let him take more than she can handle."

"She's a halfblood, Selas. Does his beast even know how to deal with that?"

"She's his mate for a reason. We've got no choice but to trust that their primal sides will know what to do. You saw how she stripped and lay with him. She knew what he needed."

He exhales and shakes his head. "If their bond is this powerful without being consummated, then..."

"I know." It'll only get stronger. Harder for them to control.

"It's unfair. After everything he's been through..."

Serath has a painful past filled with holes and uncertainty—one he rarely speaks of—but we all know and understand how it's shaped him. There's been too much loss in his life, so much pain that he's learned to fly solo. Part of the team, yet apart from the team. No deep connections. No promises, and then she comes along. Validation from the universe, a promise that he's not allowed to keep because to do so would drive him insane.

"It might not be like that for Serath," Orix says, replying to my thoughts as if I've spoken out loud, reminding me of the bond we share. One that could have deepened and become so much more had I allowed it.

But although alpha females can love, we rarely get to keep the males we give our hearts to, and with Orix it would have been too painful to have him, only for him to be ultimately taken by an omega.

"You heard what happened to Dharius from outpost four." I look up at his face and imagine his beautiful features. Features I once tracked and memorized with my fingers. "They say he was frothing at the mouth when the Stone Guard took him away."

"The Stone Guard..." Derision drips from his tone. "Lackeys, nothing more."

Silence settles between us, thick and heavy with possibilities. His hand comes to rest on my shoulder, and my pulse skips a beat.

His sigh tells me he hears my reaction, hears the stutter in my heart and understands.

"I wish it could be different for Serath," he says. "I wish he could have this. Her."

Me too. "After this, he'll feel closer to her than ever. You know that right?"

"Yes."

"We'll have to be there to make sure that they don't consummate."

"They won't." He says it with such confidence that it makes me smile. "Three more weeks and she'll either be relegated to admin or scrape through to general forces and be posted far from here. We just need to get them through the next three weeks."

It sounds simple enough, but there's one huge problem.

A lot could happen in the span of three weeks.

CHAPTER 46

CAMERON

It was warm and perfectly cozy, and then it wasn't. I was being moved away from the warm place.

This was wrong.

This was bad.

The soft buzz of voices got loud and insistent before stopping altogether.

Sleep tried to wrap its arms around me, but the sense of wrongness kept me out of its reach.

I had to wake up.

Now.

"Cameron? Hey, Cameron, you awake?"

"Selas?" I cracked my lids to find her hovering over me.

"You can go now," she said.

Memory came back in a rush. Serath was hurt, and I'd been—

I sat up fast, reaching for him, but the bed beside me was rumpled and empty. Oh, God. Please don't have let him—

"He's fine. It's okay, he's fine." Selas cupped my shoulders and smiled reassuringly.

Thank God. "Where is he?"

"Back at the outpost."

I stared at her dumbly. "What?"

"You helped to keep him stable until we could administer the antivenom. He said to thank you."

He said to say... "Wait. He left again without saying goodbye?"

"It's for the best, Cameron. You know that. I'm sure you'll speak on the phone when he gets back in a couple of days."

Days? I wouldn't get to see him or speak to him for days? My throat pinched, and heat gathered behind my eyes. Disappointment, rejection, and finally anger. What the fuck? No. Hell no. Rage propelled me off the bed and across the room to the dresser where someone had placed my clothes. I tugged them on, fighting the vise around my lungs because this was bullshit. This weepy, fractured female wasn't me. Fuck her. Fuck her hard.

"Cameron?" Selas reached for me, but I stepped away from her.

If she touched me...if she was nice, then I might just lose my shit. "I have to get back to dorm."

"Cameron, please. I know this is hard but—"

Damn her. "Do you?" I stared into her milky eyes through a sheen of stupid tears. "Do you know? Have you any idea how fucking pathetic I feel right now, all these emotions that just..." I threw my hands up. "Came out of nowhere. They just...are. And then he asks you to thank me. *Thank me.*" My voice went up an octave. "As if I made him a coffee or painted him a goddamn picture. Fuck this. I have to get out of here. I can still smell him, and it's messing with my head."

Her shoulders slumped. "I'm sorry."

This wasn't her fault, and I was done yelling. "I'll see you around, Selas."

I made for the door.

"Cam, wait. I'll meet you in the clearing for training at eight tomorrow. I checked your timetable, and you have classes till seven."

I had no idea how long I'd been sleeping. "What day is it?"

"It's Tuesday afternoon."

I nodded and turned away.

"And Cam..." I paused on the threshold, waiting. "You did good. Thank you."

My mouth slanted in a bitter smile that she'd never see. "Yeah, glad to be of use. See you at eight tomorrow. Oh, and pass a message on to Serath for me, please."

"Of course."

"Tell him, I won't be calling him again. Tell him...it's for the best."

I hurried down the stairs and out of the door into the fresh air.

Fuck mate bonds.

Fuck feeling like shit.

I was done with it.

It was time to focus on me and my goals. It was time to learn how to kick some gargoyle ass.

THE FOREST CLOSED in around me as I ran, faster and faster, until I hit the clearing. There I stopped, threw back my head, and screamed at the almost full moon. Once. Twice. A third time, until the pressure in my chest was gone. I blinked back tears of disappointment because what did I really have to be disappointed about? No promises were made; in fact, the situation had been made crystal clear from the start.

I'd broken Levi's heart, and now Serath had bruised mine.

Karma sucked.

It was time to do the smart thing and listen to my head not my heart or the primal instinct that raged at me to go find him. To claim him.

Those voices would be put on mute. They had to be. For my sanity and for his.

The little game we had started would stop now.

Back in my room, I took the phone and shoved it into the depths of the wardrobe, along with the crimson slip he'd given me.

I stripped off my clothes that reeked of his room and jumped into a scalding shower. I'd missed classes, and I had some catching up to do, but I had friends who'd help me.

I may have lost Levi and Serath, but I had plenty more to hold on to here. And those were the things I'd focus on.

I dressed, grabbed my keys, and headed out in search of my friends.

THE NEXT DAY passed uneventfully, and I even succeeded in not thinking about Serath all afternoon, but as I jogged to my meeting with Selas, he was all I *could* think about. Probably because I was headed to meet his team member. An elite. And the association made it hard for me to block out thoughts of him.

I'd have to work on that.

Selas was in the middle of a kata when I got there. I stopped at the edge of the clearing not wanting to interrupt her flow.

She moved like silk, easy, light, and fluid, and she was going to teach me. Getting one-on-one time with an elite like this was an advantage I wasn't about to squander.

She finished up and turned to me. "You're on time. Good. I value punctuality."

"Same." I joined her in the clearing. "And I appreciate you giving me your time."

She smiled. "Good, then let's not waste it. I've seen you move, Cameron. You're fast, and you're light on your feet, and I'm sure you can hold your own against a human, vampire, or shifter. Your file said you were a hunter?"

"I was. Yes."

"You're no beginner when it comes to combat. I'm not going to insult you with teaching you the basic moves. What I *can* give you is an insight into gargoyle combat, the blind spots and the weaknesses that will help you in training against much larger opponents. But before working on those moves, you need to learn to connect fully with your gargoyle."

"I am connected."

"Are you? Can you feel her now, simmering beneath your skin?"

Simmering? "No. She comes out when I need her."

"When you need her, as in, when you're in danger, angry, or hurt?"

What was she getting at? "Yes. So?"

Selas tipped her head to the side. "She's not a guard dog, Cameron. She's a vital part of you, and I sense the disconnect between you. You hold back your primal nature, and I understand why. You've lived in the human world all your life, and maybe you wanted to hide what you were?" I didn't confirm or deny, but she nodded anyway. "You don't have to hide any longer. I can help you weave a stronger connection with your primal self, with your gargoyle half. It will make you faster, stronger, and more intuitive in battle."

Sounded good to me. "What do I have to do?"

"Meditate and move." She took up a starting position, one leg in front of the other, knees bent, arms out. "Move with me, Cameron."

The next forty minutes were spent learning the kata. Doing the moves repeatedly until I was floating, until my body moved without me telling it to.

A sense of calm settled over me, and a gentle vibration spread through my limbs. Was this the simmer she'd been talking about?

"There," Selas said. "Do you feel it?"

"Yes." There was a hum at my solar plexus and in my blood, a low-grade power that belonged to me, but usually only came out in bursts. It spread through me, settling and guiding my limbs.

"Good," Selas said with a smile in her voice. "That's enough for tonight. We'll continue tomorrow at seven."

There was a whoosh, and when I opened my eyes she was gone.

I guess I'd been dismissed.

If only I could dismiss Serath from my mind as easily as a gargoyle took flight, but there was no getting over a fated mate.

All I could do was steel my heart.

CHAPTER 47

Derek

"You have to howl," Maury says in his scratchy voice. "Howl and moan, and it scares them, and that fear tastes so good."

"The chase is my favorite part," Blink says. His single eye glazes over as he casts his mind to a specially horrifying memory. "And when I catch them and dig in my claws, and they scream..." He shivers in pleasure. "It's perfect."

"I just want to eat," Tiny hisses from the shadows, eight hairy limbs twitching. "Eat until I'm full...I'm never full."

All eyes turn to me.

I'm ready. I know just what I have to say to fit in, but the rehearsed words stick in my throat, and the truth spills out from inside. "I miss Cam..." My tone is mournful and filled with longing.

My face stings from a slap I'm not sure who delivers.

I barely flinch.

I'm used to this,

"You'll die," Maury rasps. "You'll fade away to nothing. She left you to die, do you understand? You're lucky the goyles don't care about Old Town. Lucky we get to feed and that the hunters here are shit. But you can't escape the fade if you refuse to hunt and feed. Stop denying your nature."

But Cameron doesn't know this. I never told her that tulpas

need belief to survive, and most feed on fear. But me. I have only Cameron who believes in me, and my food of choice is love. I can't tell the other monsters that. I can't reveal that my nature isn't the same as theirs. If I tell them, I'll be banished from this group, and these creatures are all I have right now, so I hang my head in shame as they laugh at my expense because there is nowhere else for me to go.

No one who'll validate my existence.

No one who needs me.

"You can come hunting with me," Tiny hisses. "I'll show you how. I'll teach you, and once you hunt, once you feed, then they will see you. They will fear you, and your power will grow."

I don't want to hunt. I don't want to feed. But if this is the only way to exist, then maybe I need to try. I have to survive until Cameron comes home.

She said she would.

She promised.

THE BLOOD AND the screams...

The horror.

No.

I can't.

I rock back and forth in the dark safety of Cameron's closet. She's gone, but her clothes are still here. Her scent is still here. A happy smell. The smell of sunshine and flowers.

My insides feel hollow as if the terror Tiny evoked has sucked something out of me. As if the screams of horror have hollowed me out.

I close my eyes and imagine Cameron's face. Her smile and her kind eyes. I imagine her hugs and the warmth that emanates from her beautiful heart.

Love.

Cameron is love, and she *will* come back for me.

I know it because we're bound. We belong together. I'm not sure why or how, but I know I'm hers and she is mine.

I'll just wait...wait as long as it takes for her to need me again so I can serve my purpose and fulfill my true nature.

To protect her.

CHAPTER 48

CAMERON

Thursday passed in a blur of classes, training, and a late-night gym session which Curi showed up for.

He worked out in silence and left when I did, trailing me back to the dorm like a protective stalker. He was watching out for me, which was a far cry from his attitude of a week ago, but I wasn't about to challenge him about it.

It was nice having the company. I could have asked Touron or Sharniza to come with me, but the gym was my space, my time to zone out and withdraw into myself, and having either of them there, would be a distraction because I'd feel the need to interact with them. I didn't have the same obligatory feelings toward Curi, and he was pretty good at blending into the background so that I mostly forgot he was even there.

I woke on Friday feeling achy and hot, as if I had a fever coming on. But I didn't get sick, despite what Sharniza had told Yarrow and Farnell when I'd missed classes earlier this week. The feeling passed after I showered, and the coffee Melanie had left for me, hot this time, helped shake off the last of the icky feeling.

I owed her some answers. Some help. I'd missed arcana this week, but I'd find Yarrow and speak to him after history.

There was a knock at my door. "Cam, you up?" Touron called.

"Yeah." I pulled the door open and did a double take.

Touron's sandy hair was brushed back off his face, accentuating his high cheekbones and strong straight nose. He'd forgone his regular T-shirt for a dress shirt, open at the neck, sleeves rolled up, and he was wearing slacks not joggers, and shoes...real shoes. Touron, messy-haired, grinning, mischievous Touron had somehow turned into a slick, mysterious, brooding gargoyle male.

He looked... "Wow." A grin split my lips.

His throat bobbed. "Good? I look good?"

"You look amazing, but isn't it a little much for class?"

"There are no classes today, Cam. It's the omega moon, remember?"

"That's today?" No wonder Selas had said our next training session would be on Monday.

"Yes, eligible males will visit the omega house so the omegas can get our scents, and they'll invite several of us to run with them tonight."

"By run you mean...fuck?"

Twin spots of color bloomed high on his cheekbones. "That's up to the omegas, unless...Unless it's a fated mate pairing, in which case they'll go into primal heat and...yeah, fuck."

"And you're an eligible male?" I bit back a smile.

He groaned. "Trust me, this is *not* my idea, but it's expected. We mate to keep our species alive. I've got to do this."

"Hey, it might not be so bad. You might meet *the one.*"

He gave me half a smile. "I don't think so."

"Why not?"

He gnawed on his bottom lip. "Because—"

"Hey, Touron, are you coming or what?" Waxen called from down the corridor.

Touron sighed. "I'll be down in a moment." Then to me. "Let's hope my scent doesn't attract anyone."

I leaned in and sniffed him. He smelled good. Like oranges and chocolate. "Oh, they'll be completely repulsed. I mean, yuk." I fake gagged, and he chuckled.

"I'll see you later."

Later.

He hurried down the corridor and out of sight. No classes meant a whole afternoon to kill, and I knew just who I wanted to spend it with.

Sharniza answered the door with bed head and a yawn. "No classes," she growled sleepily.

"I know." I slipped into her room. "But you and I are going to have a girly day. I say we bake cookies, make popcorn, and commandeer the TV room."

She arched a brow. "All the males will be busy preening for the omegas."

"Right, so why don't we gather all the alpha females for a movie marathon afternoon."

"You do realize that the only alpha females in the dorm are you, me, and the twins, right? In fact...We're the only female cadets on campus."

"Well, more cookie dough and popcorn for us then."

She shrugged a powerful shoulder. "Sounds good to me. Now go away and let me wake up properly with a bath."

Bath? "Did you say bath?" Be still my heart.

"Cameron, are you feeling okay? I know you've been under a lot of strain recently."

"Hush"—I grabbed her hand—"answer me. Did you say you have a bath?"

She looked wary. "Yes..."

I threw up my hands. "How is that fair?"

"You *don't* have a bath?"

"Nope. Just the shower, and I've been *dying* for a soak."

She grinned, flashing me her canines. "You can borrow mine anytime. In fact, use it now. I'll use your shower. I fucking hate baths."

"Now this is a fabulous start to girly afternoon."

THE URGE TO stretch came in waves. The ache in my muscles was back. Maybe I'd overdone it at the gym and in training. We'd just started our third movie, but I needed to get up and walk about.

"I'll be right back."

Sharniza barely took her eyes from the screen, and the twins didn't even flinch, too engrossed in the romance playing out on TV. This was a secret indulgence for them, and I wasn't about to spoil it and tell them that the girl got the guy. That in these movies she *always* got the guy.

I needed to splash some cold water on my face and lie down for a minute. I was halfway to my room when the boisterous sound of the males returning drifted up the stairs.

"Cam!"

I turned at my door and waited for Touron to catch up. His hair was disheveled, his eyes bright with mirth.

"How'd it go? Did you get picked to run tonight?"

He shook his head with a grin. "I guess my scent wasn't to any omega's liking." He slowed to a stop beside me, his nostrils flaring. "What have you been eating?"

"Eating? Oh, cookies and popcorn."

He leaned in and sniffed me. "Mmmm... No it smells like... fresh bread lathered in butter."

"O-kay." I backed away from him, and he looked up sharply, pupils dilating so I could see my reflection in his eyes. "Touron?"

He stepped away from me quickly. "I should shower. All the omegas and the scents. They're all confused in my head."

"We're having movie night if you want to join us."

He had his back to me as he unlocked his door. "Sure." Had his voice gotten deeper? "Later then." He stepped into his room and closed the door.

My neck twinged, reminding me I needed to lie down for a bit.

It was hot in my room, even with the window open. The full moon beamed down at me, filling my head with a warm fuzzy sensation. There was no need to turn on the lights. I splashed cool water on my face, then climbed onto the bed. The sheets were cool against my feverish skin.

Maybe I *was* getting sick.

It would be a first, but it was possible.

I'd have to go to the infirmary...I'd go in a moment. Just one moment.

The moon filled my head, bright and achingly beautiful. It called to me. Begging me to join in and play. To let its light fill me to the brim. It would be cool in the moonlight. The ache would stop. The fever would ebb.

This was a dream, so shoes didn't matter. I slipped from my room and down the dark corridor. The steps were blessedly cold on the soles of my feet.

The hall was empty and dark, too, but the sounds of a movie played somewhere in the distance. The dream felt almost too real. But it wasn't real because I wouldn't be floating if it was.

The night beyond the door beckoned, and I answered its call.

TOURON

CAM SHOULD HAVE joined us by now. I'd chickened out on knocking for her on my way down because for a moment she'd smelled too good, and the goyle inside me surged to the surface, wanting to push her up against the wall and inhale more of her delicious scent.

I'd had to get away from her and clear my head.

This is Cam. My friend. I don't want to have those thoughts about her.

But it's been almost an hour, and she hasn't come down. A human male twirls a woman around on the dancefloor, and her dark hair fans out like bat wings.

The female gargoyles are enthralled and so are a couple of the males, to be honest, but my focus is shot.

"I'm going to check on Cam."

"What?" Sharniza frowns. "She's not back yet?"

"No. I'll get her."

I slip from the room and head upstairs. Wait, is her door open? "Cameron?"

The room is empty, and the windo open, drapes billowing inward. A pair of sneakers lay by the bed.

"Cam?"

The bathroom door is open, too, but the washroom is empty. A sixth sense draws me to the window and there, far below, is a figure in gym shorts and a T-shirt. It's Cam. I'm sure of it. And she's headed into the woods.

Ice sluices through my veins.

I take the stairs back down, so fast I almost knocked Sharniza off her feet as she's coming up.

"What is it?" she demands. "Where's Cam?"

"Headed to the woods. There's something wrong with her. She left her sneakers behind, and she's walking in a zigzag."

"What?"

"We have to stop her."

Sharniza grabs me. "It's fine. It's okay. She won't be able to get in. Only omegas and invited males can get into the forest on an omega moon, remember?"

Why doesn't that make me feel better?

We hurry down the stairs and out into the night before morphing and taking flight.

"There she is!" Sharniza points. "Edge of the forest."

I swooped closer. "Cam!"

She continues to amble toward the trees.

"Cam, stop!"

"Don't worry," Sharniza says from above. "The wards will smack her on her ass any moment—"

The air fizzes and Cameron vanishes.

She's in the woods with the omegas. How is this possible?

"We have to get help," Sharniza says. "If she's managed to get into the forest, then the only person that can get her out is someone connected to her on a metaphysical level."

"Serath."

CHAPTER 49

CAMERON

The world came into focus in increments. Silver light, the prick of bracken against my soles, the whisper of icy air against my naked skin.

I was awake.

This was no dream.

What the fuck?

What was I doing in a forest clearing? Had I sleepwalked? How the heck had I gotten here?

The aches and pains in my body were gone, replaced by an energized fizzing in my blood. The feverish sensation, however, remained.

A low grumbling sound drifted up from my left and then another from my right. The sound of bracken being crushed and the thud of heavy steps running through the undergrowth, grew louder.

The forest was suddenly alive, and the air was thick with a sweet cloying scent.

Shit, shit, shit. The omega run had begun.

I had to get out of here.

Now.

I broke into a jog toward the trail. Something burst into the clearing and blocked my path. A male, formidable in gargoyle form, with red-rimmed, hungry eyes, fell into a crouch and growled with intention at me.

I held up my hands. "Hey, it's cool. I'm leaving. I don't belong here."

He sniffed the air, and his eyes rolled. "Rut," he growled.

It wasn't a question but... "No thank you." I made a dash to his right, and he leaped and landed in front of me, the impact shaking the earth.

I jumped back. "Fuck!"

"Rut!" Another male joined us.

The two faced off. "Mine..." the first one said.

They both turned to look at me.

"Choose," the second one demanded.

I backed up slowly, edging my way toward a trail, not the one I'd come by, but another, any other, just to get away from the males. "I choose..." I turned and ran.

Twin roars shook the world behind me, and the thunder of pursuit followed. I'd never come this far into the forest. The terrain was unfamiliar, the trail twisted and overgrown. Not a trail at all.

Grunts and groans of pleasure rose around me, and the distinctive aroma of sex saturated the air, spilling into my lungs with every breath. My core tightened, and my pussy throbbed, reacting to the pheromones in the air, but the terror of being caught kept me moving.

A root snagged my foot. I stumbled and threw out my hands to catch myself. My palms slapped earth.

"Yes, oh fuck, yes. More. Harder," a breathless female voice demanded.

Thwump, thwump, thwump.

The omega was in human form, naked tits rubbing on the ground, ass in the air while the gargoyle fucked her from behind. How was she taking his co—

"This way. I smell her."

I hoped they were talking about the omega, but just in case...I clambered up and away from the rutting pair, almost tripped over another couple, and barreled into a third where two males worked on one female, her cries of pleasure rising in a crescendo as she came.

I'd stumbled on the epicenter of consummation. The heady scent of pheromones filled my head and slowed my pace.

Nope. Not getting stuck here. Move woman.

I made it to the edge of the clearing before I was grabbed and hauled back against rock hard abs.

Hot breath kissed my ear. "So good. So, fucking good."

I knew that voice. "Curi?"

Someone growled from behind us, and Curi made a menacing sound that made my stomach tremble.

"Mine!" he snarled.

Hell no. "Curi, what are you—"

He pushed me up against the nearest tree and pressed his body to my back so I could feel him. All of him, thick, hard, and much too big. Panic swamped my thoughts for a moment, but the scrape of his talons against my hip bones snapped me back in control.

He was trying to get my shorts off. "Stop. Stop it. Look at me. Curi. Look. At. Me."

His grip slackened, and I took the opportunity to turn to face him.

His barrel chest blocked out the world. His thick muscle-corded arms caged me in place. His gargoyle form was monstrous and intimidating, but his eyes...they were the same eyes that had locked with mine days earlier before he'd saved me from being attacked.

"Mine," he said again. Softer this time.

"No." I locked gazes with him. "I said. No. I don't belong here. I'm not an omega."

His chest heaved.

"Curi, it's me. It's Cameron."

He blinked sharply, and his pupils contracted a little. "Cam...

fuck..."

"Where is she?" a male voice demanded from behind him. "I can smell her. I want her."

Curi's eyes widened. *Go*, he mouthed before turning to face the other gargoyles. His body blocked me from sight. "Mine," he said to them.

I slipped around the tree and threw myself into darkness.

The violent sounds of a tussle followed me. Curi and the males fighting over me? This was insane. I wasn't a fucking omega. Why the hell were they after me when the forest was filled with willing females?

Shit. The trees grew close together here.

I ran using my palms to slap the bark and stop myself colliding with the trunks, but my senses were wide awake, warning me of incoming danger. I swerved as a gargoyle rushed me from the left. He missed me and smashed into a tree, giving me a moment's head start. There was a clearing up ahead. Maybe the main clearing?

I burst into it and skidded to a halt, heart sinking.

Curi, pinned beneath a gargoyle knee, turned his bloody face my way. "What the fuck, Walker?" he demanded.

I'd doubled back without realizing, and now...shit, now I was surrounded by gargoyles.

This was bullshit. I hadn't signed up for this crap, and I was done running. "Snap out of it, dammit! I'm not a fucking omega."

Curi's nostrils flared, and he closed his eyes. "Fucking hell, Walker, rein it in."

Rein what in?

Was my anger making my smell stronger? Focus. Calm down. Breathe. "I'm not an omega. You don't want me, and I certainly don't want you."

The other gargoyles snorted and shook their heads, as if trying to clear their senses.

I was getting through to them.

A gust of wind blew past me, throwing my hair forward, and the gargoyles tensed.

"Cameron." Curi's tone thickened. "Run. Now."

Three gargoyles rushed me, but before I could move, a monolith of muscle landed between us with a mighty roar unlike anything I'd ever heard. Wings flared wide, then snapped tight, and Serath's woodsmoke and sweet sage scent smacked me in the face.

My heart shot into my throat. He was here. He'd come for me.

The gargoyles who'd been ready to jump me a moment ago froze.

He turned his head, offering me the shaved side of his profile. His jaw ticked. "Don't move, Cameron."

I locked my knees and waited.

"We do not take unless given," he said tightly. "We do not take unless it is our fated right to do so and willingly offered."

The gargoyles shoulders heaved as they took deep breaths and shook their heads, as if trying to dislodge bees.

Serath took one step back toward me. "There are omegas waiting to be pleasured. Find them and offer yourselves to them."

He snagged me around the waist and lifted me into his arms. My head fell back, gaze sweeping up the strong column of his throat to his hard unyielding jaw. He glanced at me once, and I caught the flare of his pupils before he launched us into the sky.

He'd come to save me, and despite all my intentions, I couldn't help but swoon at that. I blamed the damn romance movie fest. The stupid romcom session was about to get me into some serious trouble; I could feel it.

CHAPTER 50

CAMERON

Serath took us high before swooping down toward a watchtower. We landed, and he shoved me against the thick iron post, glaring at me with eyes that burned with inner fire.

He morphed back to human form but continued to tower over me. "What were you thinking?" His voice was a coil of barely restrained rage.

Thinking? I hadn't been thinking. "I fell asleep and woke up in the forest."

He took a step toward me, then spun away, standing with hands on hips. Muscle rippled across his powerful shoulders, tension moving up and down his back. "They wanted you."

"Yes. I don't unders—"

He was on me in an instant, body caging me to the post, husky gaze dark and wanting raking me over. "They wanted you because you smell..." He dipped his head and pressed his nose to the spot below my ear. "Divine." The word vibrated through me, and my pussy fluttered.

"I don't understand."

He cupped my breast and squeezed, tearing a gasp of shocked pleasure from me.

"They wanted what's mine." He kneaded me, and my knees

buckled. "Fuck, Cameron. Fuck." His scent spiked, and my mind emptied out.

I wanted him. I needed him right now. I turned my head, and he found my mouth, his lips hard and demanding punishing and biting. The coppery taste of blood licked at my lips, then his tongue sank into my mouth, rasping against my teeth and invading me until the only air was him.

Heat swept up from my toes to my head, the fervent need to divest and fuck assaulted me.

Now.

Here. "Need you."

"Yes."

"Inside me. Now."

I clawed at my shorts, and he ripped them off. Cold air kissed my slick skin. He tore his mouth from mine, dropped to his knees and grabbed my thighs, lifting my throbbing heat to his mouth.

I bucked as he claimed me, feasting on me like I was a succulent fruit. His tongue pushed deep inside me, and a guttural cry fell from my lips. He fucked me with his tongue, and I fisted his hair and rode his face, whispering incoherent sounds that blended into one until my orgasm built to its inevitable crescendo. I came with huge gasping sobs that left me bruised.

He rose to his feet and swallowed my cries forcing me to taste myself on his lips, sweet and fragrant.

My heart ached, insides twisting as we kissed deeply, the connection between us undeniable.

I reached for his arousal. Gripping it through his slacks. "This. Need it." My voice was a demanding growl, and he answered with a rumbling growl of his own before gripping my wrist to stop me touching him.

"We can't. Cameron...we can't do that. Ever."

Frustration formed a tight, painful spiral inside me. "Why? Why *exactly* can't we be together?"

He pressed his forehead to mine and sighed deep and weary. "Because consummating this bond with you will drive me insane, and...And it will *kill* you."

Kill me? That made no sense. "Why? How?"

"I don't know," he said. "It just...does."

I wanted to push, to argue, but what was the point? It wouldn't change the outcome, and my beast recognized that this moment with him was too precious to waste with questions. It would probably be our last time being close like this, so I let it go and leaned into him, closing my eyes and winding my arms around his neck.

"It isn't fair." My whispered words sounded petty and small, but I didn't care. My heart was too full of promise and loss in equal measure, of all that could have been and should be but could never be, and it brought out the selfish side of me.

"I know it's unfair," he said. "We must keep our distance."

I bit back a laugh. "You just had your tongue inside me. I'd hardly call that keeping our distance. "

His chest rumbled, and the vibration beat through me. My laughter died, mirth giving way to arousal.

"You taste so fucking good," he said his voice gruff with promise.

My stomach flipped. Hard. "I want to taste you too."

He made a low sound in his throat. "The things I could do to you...The things I want to do..." He exhaled and inhaled a couple of times to center himself. "This, tonight, was a one-off." He caressed my cheeks with the rough pads of his fingers. "A foray into the flames."

I lifted my chin. "But never again." Heart pounding because his lips were tantalizingly close.

His mouth brushed mine. "Never. Ever. Again."

"Serath!"

Serath tensed. "I've got this, Orix."

"Do you? Dammit, is she naked from the waist down?"

Serath snarled and covered me with his body. "Fuck off, Orix. I said I've got this. Do I look insane to you?"

Orix was right. I *was* naked from the waist down. "Um...

Serath, you tore my shorts and panties off."

"Get her some clothes," Serath called over his shoulder.

Long minutes passed in which there was nothing but my heart beating in time to Serath's and his warm breath ruffling the top of my head. I couldn't help but drag my hands up his sides and over his back, tracing the ripped muscle.

"Cam..." His voice was a low tortured moan.

"I'm sorry."

I was still throbbing for him, desperate for his cock, and my breasts felt full and heavy, aching for his touch.

"Hurry it up," Serath growled over his shoulder.

"Orix is on his way back," Selas said from somewhere behind him.

Serath shielded me with his body until a large shirt landed on the ground beside us. He snagged it and dropped it over my head. It came down to mid-thigh. Cotton not Lastonflex and it smelled of Serath.

"I'll get you back to your dorm," Serath said, voice low.

"I'll do it," Selas said. "Then we need to get her to the lab. We need to find out how she got into the forest in the first place."

Good point. We'd forgotten all about that vital fact in the heat of the moment. Oh, God. I'd just let him eat me out on a watchtower. Shit. Had anyone seen us?

My face heated.

"It's all right," Selas said. "You're okay." She flew closer. "We only just got here, and the other towers are unmanned."

"Serath, we should go." Orix hovered closer, wings flapping, every so often to stay airborne as he waited. "Now."

I didn't *want* him to go, but I *needed* him to leave. The push-pull of mind over primal instinct was almost unbearable.

Serath dropped a kiss on my forehead, lips lingering for a moment, then stepped away from me. "Just a few more weeks, and you can get on with your life. We can do this, Cameron."

I nodded and told him what he wanted, needed, to hear. "Yes. We can."

He morphed, then leaped into the air to join Orix, leaving me with the bitter taste of lies in my mouth, because after what we'd just done, after the moment we'd shared, I wasn't sure walking away would be that easy.

CHAPTER 51

CAMERON

We managed to get to my dorm room undetected. Selas waited on the platform outside my window while I ducked inside to grab some clothes.

I'd started explaining what had happened tonight, how I'd fallen asleep and ended up in the forest, but she asked me to wait till we got to the lab to save repeating myself. "Willowman should be up," she said from the platform. "He doesn't sleep much."

I locked myself in the washroom and rinsed off my muddy feet before dressing and pulling on socks and shoes.

My hair was a mess, windswept and knotted, so I ran a brush through it quickly and yanked it back into a ponytail. I looked flushed, my eyes too bright and big in my face.

I looked almost pretty.

"Cam?" Selas knocked on the door. "Are you all right?"

"I'm fine." I pulled open the door. "Let's go and find out what the hell is wrong with me."

WILLOWMAN'S LAB WAS in a cottage hidden behind the omega building. He had his own yard with a white picket fence and what looked like an impressive herb garden.

All the downstairs windows were lit a warm and inviting amber.

Selas led the way up the path and knocked on the door.

"It's open," Willowman called from inside.

The aroma of licorice wafted out as Selas pushed open the door and ushered me into a cozy sitting room that sported a crackling log fire. A tattered rug covered dark wooden floors, and a battered green sofa with orange scatter cushions faced the hearth.

Willowman sat at a worn wooden table with a cigarette in his mouth and a model set on the table in front of him. His shirt was open, leaving his tight abs on display. He looked rumpled and comfortable, and younger here in his environment.

His attention flicked from me to Selas, then back again. "What's happened?"

Selas pulled out a chair and nodded at me. "Sit." I obliged. "Cameron ended up in the woods tonight."

Willowman's eyes narrowed to slits. "Impossible. I checked the wards myself."

"I know, so the question remains...how *did* she get in?"

He fixed his golden eyes on me. "What did you do? How did you get in?" His accusatory tone rankled.

"I didn't *do* anything. Do you think I *wanted* to go into the damn forest and get fucked?"

"I don't know you well enough to guess your motives, Miss Walker."

Fine. "Look, I felt shitty, so I went to lie down. I fell asleep, dreamt about the moon and..." I shook my head. "It's fuzzy after that, but I woke up in the forest."

"You felt ill before. What symptoms?" he asked.

"Achy, feverish. Just ick. Look, I don't get sick. I've *never* been ill, so I just thought it was from training too hard."

Willowman rubbed his jaw, then relit his smoke and took a drag. "Strange. You were tested at the intake building. Blood tests show you to be a halfblood with alpha tendencies. Nothing abnormal there."

"But she got through the wards," Selas said. "Has a halfblood ever done that?"

"None has ever tried," Willowman said. "Maybe the wards mistook you for an omega." He didn't sound convinced, though.

"Did the gargoyles inside the damn forest mistake me too?" I glared at him. "They chased me."

"Omega run puts the males in a primal rut state," Willowman said.

"I know, but they said they could smell me. Since when do alpha females produce a scent to attract random males?"

"You're not an alpha. You're a halfblood with alpha *tendencies*."

I threw up my hands. "What does that even mean?"

"It means you might have been an alpha if you'd been a pureblood," Selas explained.

"The fact that you're Serath's mate means that you most certainly will be able to produce a mating pheromone," Willowman added.

"But it should be specific to him, right?" Selas asked.

"Right." Willowman looked intrigued. "I can take some samples. Blood, hair, saliva, and see what I can find, but halfbloods are...varied. There could be a host of reasons the males reacted to you in this way. The moon, the primal rut, and the air being saturated with pheromones could have confused them."

But he was wrong. "It happened earlier too. Before I went to sleep. Touron said he could smell me. That I smelled good. His pupils dilated."

"Touron?" Selas asked sharply. "What did he do?"

"He didn't *do* anything. He backed off and went to his room."

She looked away and nodded. "Okay, so the scent was there before you went into the forest."

Something clattered at the back of the cottage, and Selas's head whipped toward the inner door. "You got company?" she asked him.

He crushed out his cigarette in the small ceramic ashtray on the table. "It's just Varsa. I let him have the spare room."

"He's staying here?" Selas didn't look happy about it. "I thought the administration gave him rooms in the main building."

"He doesn't like the main building. He likes it here," Willowman said tightly.

She sighed. "But you can't be on hand all the time, and he needs help."

"There is no help," Willowman bit out. "And sending him to be around people he doesn't know would be severing the only connection he has to the reality he recalls." His jaw ticked. "Not happening. He stays here with me, and we're done discussing it." He looked across at me pointedly.

"We should collect these samples," Selas said.

"I'll grab my supplies." Willowman pushed back his chair and headed into a back room.

I waited until he was gone. "What happened to Varsa?"

Selas pulled out the seat beside me and parked her ass. "It's no secret on campus. A couple of decades ago Varsa was taken by graynites. We got him back, but his mind was...broken. They demolished his psychic seals and scrambled his brain."

"But they didn't take his soul?"

"No. Not all of it. But enough to leave him incomplete and confused. This place was his home for so long that it's the only place he seems to be able to function."

"The academy or this cottage?"

She gave me a sad smile. "Both."

Willowman returned with a black leather bag. "Roll up your sleeve. We'll start with bloods."

I tugged up my sleeve. "How long before you know anything?"

"A couple of days. We'll let you know what we find. In the meantime, if you feel odd in any way, come see me. If anyone asks why, say I'm giving you training in poultice making or something."

"Wait"—I winced as he jabbed me with a needle—"can you really teach me?"

He looked up in surprise. "You want to learn?"

"Look, if I make guardian, then I'll be grounded. Being able to make poultices that could help my team will give me an edge."

He studied me for several beats. "I'm not an easy man to work with, Miss Walker, I have very little patience for mistakes."

"I don't make mistakes, Mr. Willowman. Mistakes get you killed. I know that better than anyone. I've been hunting since I was eighteen, and I may be out of my depth in the gargoyle world for now, but I'm learning the rules. I won't always be a liability, trust me. I won't let myself."

He nodded. "Very well. We can start next week. I'll get the lessons added to your timetable and make it official."

He finished taking samples, and Selas walked me back to the dorm. We caught a few odd looks from some cadets out and about. Males who hadn't been invited to the party in the woods tonight.

"People are going to wonder what an elite is doing hanging out with a cadet."

"There are only a handful of female cadets on campus," Selas said. "If anyone asks, you can tell them I'm your unofficial mentor."

"Is that even a thing?"

"No. But maybe it should be." We came to a stop outside my dorm house. "This world, what we do, it's harder on us females. The alphas are told from a young age that they must put away feminine things and become warriors. The fact that we're barren means that being a guardian is our only hope of our lives meaning anything. For the omegas it's the opposite. They're told their only purpose is to mate and produce offspring. They're sent here to match with guardians, and they stay here until they've built their nests. After that they make babies. Lots of babies to keep our numbers thriving." She sighed. "Our lives are mapped out for us, and I know I would have liked to have someone to talk to about it. Someone who'd been through it all."

"My mother always told me to steer clear of this world. I guess she knew what it would mean for me to come here, but growing up in the human world and not being able to be my true self...it took a toll on me too. It's hard to build solid relationships when you're forced to lie to the people you care about."

"Cam!" Touron stepped out of the dorm entrance, and Sharniza appeared behind him.

Selas smiled. "You've made some solid friendships here. Gargoyles that will look out for you."

"They saw me go into the forest, didn't they?"

"Yes. It's the only reason we knew where you were."

I looked over at my friends, my heart swelling with love for them. They'd sounded the alarm to get help to me, but they weren't the only ones who'd helped me.

If Curi hadn't been there for me tonight, then Serath may not have gotten to me in time. He'd saved my ass twice now.

I owed him.

And I needed him to know how grateful I was.

CHAPTER 52

CAMERON

"Get lost, Walker." Curi made to slam his door in my face.

I slapped a palm to the wood to stop him. "I came to say thank you."

"Then say it and go." He glared at me with red-rimmed eyes.

We were headed out to Stone Comfort for Saturday afternoon brunch. Touron and Shar knew how Curi had stepped up to help me in the forest, and that I wanted to thank him, but it didn't look like he wanted my gratitude.

In fact, he looked like he wanted to hit someone.

"What the hell is your problem, Mason?" Touron said, coming up the corridor behind me.

"She's my problem," Curi snarled. "I lost my shot with my omega because of her."

Crap. "I'm sorry I—"

"Don't be sorry." He pushed the words out through clenched teeth. "Just stay out of places you don't need to be in."

His tone, his shitty attitude, had me flushing with indignant anger. "You didn't act like I didn't belong last night, did you?"

His face froze for a moment, then he grabbed me by my collar, hauled me into his room, shut the door, and slammed me against it.

What the—

He gripped my jaw, forcing my head up. "I could have taken you up against that tree. You reeked of sex. Of need. But I didn't, and now you throw it back in my face?"

Damn my temper. "I'm sorry. I shouldn't have said that."

"Hey!" Touron hammered on the door. "Open the fucking door or I'll break it."

I locked gazes with Curi, seeing doubt and turmoil and something else...Something I'd seen in the mirror plenty of times over the years.

Something that was only now ebbing.

Loneliness.

"I'm okay, Touron. We're just talking. I'll be right out."

The hammering stopped, and Curi seemed to deflate as if the possibility of an altercation had been the only thing holding him up.

His hand slipped from my jaw and settled on my neck. "This place will eat you alive if you're not careful, Walker. If it had been anyone else pinning you to that tree..." His grip on my neck flexed, and my breath snagged in my throat. "You were lucky I was there." He released me and stepped back.

"I know." I held his gaze. "I'm grateful, and that's all I came to say."

He tucked in his chin. "You should go now. I didn't get to rut last night, and you smell too good."

"Still?"

"Just get out, Walker," he growled.

I ducked out of the room and smacked into Touron's chest. He went to shove open the door, his jaw tense, mouth set in an angry line, but I pushed him back.

"It's fine. We're fine."

"He's an asshole," Touron said.

"An asshole who saved Cam's ass," Sharniza reminded him from the stairwell. "Let's go eat. I'm fucking starving."

We made our way downstairs, but I had to know. "Touron, do

I still smell...you know..."

He leaned in and sniffed me. "You smell normal to me. Why?"

"Nothing."

I guess my scent issue would remain a mystery until Willowman came back to me with answers. In the meantime, I'd keep my circle small and steer clear of the males, which thanks to our girls' shopping trip tomorrow would be easy enough to do.

I wasn't big on shopping, but I couldn't deny the fizz of excitement in my veins when faced with promise of a day out. After all it was the perfect distraction from thinking about Serath.

IT WAS EASY to push Serath from my mind when I was busy hanging with friends, working out, or watching a movie, but he was the only thing on my mind when I crawled into bed at four in the morning.

My gaze kept drifting to the wardrobe where the mobile phone was hidden. I could call him and hear his voice. He'd answer for sure. But then what? More angst. More reminders of why we couldn't be together. More pain.

I wasn't a masochist. But it was some time before sleep finally found me, and when it did, it took me into dreams of the male that belonged to me but that I could never have.

THE OMEGA BUILDING was a large sunlit space mostly due to the glass-domed ceiling that let in all the light. Gorgeous plants sat in large clay pots positioned carefully around the perimeter of the entrance chamber to create a lush, fragrant environment. An ornate arch led deeper into the building, where seating was arranged like a waiting area, and beyond that was a set of metal doors.

A woman sat at the desk by those doors. She looked up as we crossed the archway. "Miss Walker and Miss Aziza, good, you're on time."

She studied us with pale green eyes that seemed to be judging us before standing to greet us. She was tall for a gargoyle female, at least a foot taller than Sharniza.

"It was kind of Chlobe to invite you to come with us today," she said. "I'm Evelyn, the omega nest mother."

Evelyn crossed to the metal door and pressed her palm to the panel at the side before keying in a code. The doors opened into another entranceway. "Please wait inside. The ladies will be with you shortly."

We stepped through, and the doors closed behind us.

This second waiting room was decorated in pastel blues and purples. There were no windows, and it would have been claustrophobic if not for the huge landscape paintings that covered each wall. They mimicked the outdoors, giving the illusion of openness.

"They take the security seriously here." I parked myself on the nearest chair.

"Omegas are coveted and valued," Shar said stiffly. "We'd die out without them."

The inner door opened, and five omegas joined us. They were dressed for cold weather in jeans, sweaters, and jackets. Handbags crossed over chests or hung from shoulders. A couple of them looked surprised to see us, but then Chlobe pushed to the front of the group and rushed over to us.

"You made it. I'm so glad."

"Is that all of you?" Sharniza asked.

"Friday night took it out of some of us," Chlobe said with a mischievous smile. "Some of us chose mates and are still busy getting to know them."

In other words, they were still having sex.

Lucky for some.

The door we'd entered by opened, and Evelyn came in, trailed by Willowman. Today he was dressed in ripped jeans, a cream T-shirt, and a black leather jacket. His dark hair was artfully styled, and his golden eyes were ringed in kohl. He looked like a sexy rockstar. The man was a true chameleon.

"Hello, ladies," he drawled. "Ready for a delightful trip?"

One of the omegas giggled, the others preened, but Chlobe dropped her gaze, cheeks pinkening.

Someone had a crush.

I didn't blame her. Willowman was sexy-hot. Not my type, but definitely the type to turn heads.

"Yes, Mr. Willowman. We are ready," Evelyn said stiffly. "If you'd kindly open the warp."

"Of course, Evelyn," Willowman shot her a winning smile, which she ignored. "You have the return orb, correct?"

"I do." She patted her handbag.

"Good, and you all have your bags and coats." He raked everyone over. "It's not exactly warm in Asteria this time of year."

"Yes, Mr. Willowman," Evelyn said tightly. "They're prepared." She gave him a closed-lipped smile. "It's *my* job to make sure they're prepared."

Willowman returned her smile with a warm, toothy one of his own. "And you do it so beautifully."

Her cheeks grew pink, and she narrowed her eyes. "I know."

Whoa, subtext, subtext, subtext. I needed to know.

Willowman clapped his hands together. "In that case, gather round and prepare to be transported."

We huddled in a group, and Willowman did a circuit of us muttering an incantation. The air crackled and my skin pricked, then white light stole my vision. The world tipped, my stomach tried to turn itself inside out, and my eyes bugged, too big for my sockets.

I came to on my knees with someone patting my back.

"Oh dear. Oh dear," Evelyn said. "Are you all right, dear?"

"I'm fine." My throat was dry and raspy. "I guess warping and halfbloods don't mix well."

Shar helped me up. "Not just halfbloods. Plenty of gargoyles struggle with it. We'll get you some water in a moment."

We were in a pristine alley with the sounds of the street beyond teasing us to come see.

I'd never traveled more than a town over from Old Town, and although I'd read about the other places in the rim, this was my first time visiting one. Old Town had two sides—shitty and affluent. I'd lived in both. But the affluence of Old Town had nothing on this place.

We exited the alley onto dog-shit-free pavements lined with shiny store fronts and brightly colored awnings. Humans milled about, looking well fed and happy. The atmosphere was relaxed and peaceful.

"Market street," Evelyn said to me. "We shop here, and we eat over there." She pointed across the road to a restaurant that looked like it would cost you your first born to eat at.

It all looked and felt so...safe. "I didn't realize that places like this still existed."

"There aren't many left outside of the city," Evelyn said, "but there are two outposts close by, and the guardians visit here often. It keeps it relatively free of supernatural threats. The tulpas have mostly been extinguished." She clapped her hands. "Right, ladies. We meet at Gregari's in two hours. Do not be late." Her expression softened. "And have fun, dears."

She crossed the street to the restaurant, leaving us to our own devices.

"Where shall we go first?" one of the omegas asked Chlobe. "Ooo, the dressmaker's. She might have that new fabric in."

"Great idea," Chlobe said.

Yeah, dresses, not my thing, and I wasn't much for following the group, but I couldn't speak for Shar, so I looked up at her and shrugged.

"We'll catch up with you later," Sharniza said.

We split up, and the omegas headed up the road.

"You can go with them if you like," Shar said.

"And look at fabric? No thank you. Look, there's an accessories shop. I need some new hair ties."

The store was small but carried every kind of scarf, hair clip, hair tie, and several clutch bags. Shar's eyes grew round at the sight of all the sparkles, and we spent way too much time in the store.

I'd brought my card with me, so it wasn't an issue to pay for things.

Shar was hesitant to pick up anything at first, but after I grabbed a few things, she relaxed and started to shop.

We hit the dessert place across the road next for ice cream, then moved on to a shoe shop that happened to stock size eleven shoes for women.

"I don't know, Cam," Shar said. "When will I ever get a chance to wear these?"

"We'll make it happen. We won't be at the academy forever, Shar. Once we get our posting, there'll be opportunities."

She turned the silver pointy-toed sandals over and stroked the velvet material. "You're a dreamer, you know that?"

"Maybe. Or maybe I'm just an optimist." I shrugged. "Buy them, or I'll buy them for you, and then I'll be broke, and it'll be your fault."

She grinned up at me. "Fuck it."

I picked up some new clothes and essentials, then we met up with the omegas in a bookstore. The last half hour was spent browsing old books that had been beautifully rebound by the owner. Shar and I bought several between us with the promise of swapping once we'd read them.

The afternoon was topped off by delicious food and scrumptious dessert, all paid for by the academy, and by the time we made our way back to the alley, I was ready for a nap.

"Gather round, ladies," Evelyn said brightly. She pulled a crystal orb from her pocket and set it on the ground. "Closer, that's it."

We all shuffled closer to the orb, and Shar put her arm around me. "Just in case," she said. "But please don't be sick on me."

"I'll do my best."

Evelyn stamped on the orb, and bright light blinded me. Once again, my stomach decided it was time to do some acrobatics, but this time when I came to, I was crushed against Sharniza's bosom.

"Shar... Can't breathe..."

"Shit." She released me.

"What the...Where are we?" Chlobe asked.

It was dark, like night-time dark, except it had been late afternoon when we'd entered the alley.

"Where are we?" Another omega echoed Chlobe's question.

We were on a rise that sat above a shabby-looking settlement with winding narrow streets and battered-looking buildings. The moon was smothered by clouds so that it was hard to make out much detail.

"There must be some mistake," Evelyn said. "I..." She searched inside her bag, as if expecting to find a different orb in there.

"It's an outer eastern settlement," Sharniza said. "Look at the post." She pointed at a post halfway down the rise. It had a white circle pinned to it with a symbol I couldn't read from this distance. "That's a marker. These places are rife with threats and the last places to receive guardian help. We need to get to their local law enforcement building. They'll have a comms unit to contact the nearest outpost."

I'm glad she knew all this. But she was glossing over one huge fact. "Why did the orb bring us here?"

The flap of wings and an eerie screeching like gulls drifted on the wind. The hair on the back of my neck stood to attention. I looked up into the night sky just as the clouds parted and set the moon free to illuminate several winged creatures headed toward us. Too small to be gargoyles and too large to be birds.

"What are they?"

"Fuck," Shar said. "Grotesques incoming!"

CHAPTER 53

CAMERON

We ran down the hill toward the cover of buildings as the grotesque grew closer, dropping altitude with every passing second.

We hit the street, and Evelyn banged on the nearest door. "Open up."

Curtains twitched but no one answered.

"Move!" Sharniza morphed and kicked the door in.

Someone screamed. "You can't come in. Go away." A human woman hugged a child to her chest. "Please, you'll bring them to us."

"Where's your law enforcement office?" Evelyn demanded.

"Down the street. Turn left. Now go. Get out!"

We ran back into the street. The specks were getting larger. Closer. We were running out of time.

"Move," Shar ordered the omegas. "Run." Evelyn led the way and Shar brought up the rear.

"I'll be right behind you." I ducked back into the house. "I need a weapon. Anything."

The woman grabbed a poker and handed it to me.

It was better than nothing.

"Cameron, come on!" Shar boomed from the intersection.

I broke into a sprint to catch up, but as we rounded the corner, the grotesques dropped from the sky.

They landed on all fours, bat wings snapping at the air, taloned feet clawing at the ground. Their eyes glowed red and amber, maws too wide, nostrils flared and blowing mist. They were ugly as fuck and emanated a dark aura that made my stomach twist in warning.

The omegas screamed and ran back toward us, their bodies morphing to stone skin in presence of the threat.

Sharniza let out a bellow and dashed forward to cover the omegas. The grotesques screeched in response and ran toward us.

"Get away from my girls!" Evelyn darted forward, tweed skirt flapping, then tearing as she morphed and grew and fucking grew until she filled the entire street with her new form.

A snake. A huge fucking snake with a cobra-winged head and fangs. She attacked the grotesques, body whipping from side to side to keep them from getting past her.

But a couple flew over her head.

"We got it," Shar called out before body slamming the nearest threat.

"Get back!" I shoved Chlobe toward the nearest building. "Get under cover now!"

The second grotesque came at me, its eyes glowing blue, then green as they raked over me.

"Back off." I stepped forward, poker held firm in my hand.

The thing hissed, then lunged.

I swung the poker as hard as I could, connecting with its head with enough force to rock it back on its neck.

The impact ricocheted up my arm and jarred my teeth. I swung again. "Get." And again. "The fuck." It staggered back. "Away."

I'd forced it back, but my arm ached from basically smashing an iron rod against stone, and the thing was pissed.

It ducked and evaded the fifth blow, having learned my rhythm, then snapped at the poker, grabbing it between powerful teeth and whipping its head round to throw it, and me, but I let go and fell on my ass.

"Cam, get up!" someone screamed.

I rolled but the creature was too fast, landing on top of me and caging me with its body. The omegas' screams faded to background noise as the grotesque lowered its awful maw toward my face. Its eyes glowed blue, locking onto mine, and its chest rattled in ominous warning.

What the hell? What was it doing? Why was it just looking at me?

"Get away from her you bastard!" Sharniza snarled.

The grotesque was knocked off me by a whirlwind of stone-gray skin and powerful wings. Sharniza pinned it and punched it in the head over and over until it stopped moving.

"Girls!" Evelyn ran toward us back in human form and dressed only in an all-in-one Lastonflex body suit. Her tweed outfit and blouse were gone, torn to shreds when she morphed into... whatever that thing had been. Her skin was bloody, but I couldn't find any wounds, so either she'd healed or the blood wasn't hers. Highly likely considering the bits of Grotesque littering the ground behind her.

The whole episode couldn't have lasted more than five minutes but the carnage...

"Move," Shar said. "The station should be—"

"More are coming!" Chlobe pointed to the skies.

Sure enough, a fresh wave was on the way, larger than the first.

"Evelyn?" Shar looked to the nest mistress.

"Not this soon. I can't."

"Then we run," Sharniza said.

I ushered the omegas into the street. "Come on. It can't be far."

The grotesques were so close I could feel the gusts of air from the beat of their wings.

"Over here!" A woman ran out of a building a few meters down. "Move it!"

She stepped into the road, raised a rifle and shot at the sky. The grotesques swerved and dove to avoid the bullets giving us enough time to get into the building.

A station

The police station.

The woman with the gun hurried inside and slammed the doors shut. "Bertie, activate the runes now!"

A short, balding man behind the counter slammed a bloody palm onto a symbol on the wall. The lights flickered and dimmed before flaring.

"All good," the woman said. "All good. They won't be able to get inside now." She leaned against the door, hand on heart, eyes closed for a moment. "Second time this month. This settlement is going to shit." She pushed off the door and strode over to the counter. "Now who are you all, why are you here, and why the heck are there grotesques in my settlement?"

Evelyn stepped forward, tucking her hair behind her ears. "My name is Evelyn, and I'm responsible for these ladies. These are omegas and cadets. We're from the academy, and I have no idea why our warp orb brought us here, or why those creatures are after us."

She sounded disgusted and indignant and...scared, acting like she hadn't just turned into a huge killer stone snake and ripped apart a bunch of grotesques. Who was this woman?

"Bertie, send an urgent message to HQ," the woman instructed. "Let them know their omegas and cadets are here. Tell them we need an extraction now."

Bertie hurried off down the corridor.

The lights flickered.

"What's that?" Chlobe asked.

"They're testing the wards," the woman said. "Relax. You'll be safe here until HQ sends a team of guardians for you."

"I don't understand why we're here," Evelyn muttered. "The orb should have taken us home."

I exchanged looks with Sharniza. "Willowman gave her the

orb."

"Willowman doesn't make mistakes," Sharniza said.

I didn't want to believe that the man who the elites trusted would deliberately put us in harm's way. "Evelyn, did Willowman hand you the orb himself?"

"No...um...It was delivered yesterday. Cartwright, the academy grotesque...oh...

No." She shook her head. "Cartwright has been with the academy since it was formed. He wouldn't do anything to hurt us."

"Well, somebody sent us here on purpose, and those grotesques are after the omegas," Sharniza said.

"I don't know," Chlobe said softly. "The one that was on you"—she looked over me, her expression almost wary—"it could have killed you, but it didn't."

Ice gripped my nape. "Why would it want me?"

The lights flickered, and the room went dark.

"Jude!" Bertie came running down the corridor. "Power went down."

"Don't panic," Jude said. "The wards are mystical. They'll hold."

"No, it's"—Bertie gasped and leaned forward to brace his palms on his knees—"the power..." He sucked in a breath and coughed.

"Spit it out, Bertie," Jude snapped.

"It went out just as I...I sent the... message."

Jude's eyes widened. "Did the message go through?"

Bertie straightened. Hand going to his chest.

"Bertie did the message go through?" Jude demanded.

He shook his head. "I don't know."

A shrill ringing shattered the silence following Bertie's statement.

Jude hurried to the counter and snatched up the phone. "What?" She went still and silent, listening. "Okay." She looked over at us and hit a button on the phone.

A cultured male voice drifted out of the speaker on the phone.

"Hello, all. My name is Ignus. I'd like to apologize for the theatrics, all the argh and grrr. In hindsight the grotesques may have been overkill. You see, we were expecting you to be accompanied by *actual* guardians."

Sharniza's lip lifted in a soft snarl.

"What do you want?" Evelyn said. "If you're working for the graynites then you know they have no use for omegas."

"Oh, I know perfectly well. But it isn't the omegas we came for." My scalp pricked as every eye turned to me. "We came for the halfblood."

CHAPTER 54

WILLOWMAN

The blood samples are clean. The results are the same as what we have on file. There's nothing in Walker's saliva to suggest any anomalies.

I'm stumped.

I'll need to go deeper, but I don't have the equipment here. I'll have to send the samples to HQ for deeper analysis, but if they run them through their database, it might reveal that Cameron is Serath's mate.

We can't risk that, which means a trip on my part, because there is one other place, one other person who may be able to give us the answers we need.

I'd downplayed my concern so as not to cause the girl panic, but I have questions and I need to satisfy them.

I reach up to grab the cooling case where the samples need to be stored, and my hand brushes something smooth and cold.

What? Why is there an orb up on that shelf? It should be in a box with all the other orbs I haven't used yet. But this one crackles with power.

Familiar power.

A signature for a warping.

I hold it close and open my senses to read the destination

woven into it.

A return warping. The one I'd created for Evelyn, but if this orb is here, then...

What orb do they have?

CHAPTER 55

CAMERON

The speakerphone crackled in the silence that followed Ignus's declaration that he was here for me and not for the omegas.

"I imagine that you're all quite shocked," he continued. "Believe me, so was I when I was given this most important task. I wish I could tell you more, but...Oh, who am I kidding, I don't care about any of you enough to tell you much of anything. The only person I care about is the halfblood."

This was bullshit. "Who the fuck are you and what do you want with me?"

"Ah, Miss Walker, so good of you to speak up. Like I said, my name is Ignus, I work for the graynites, and I've been tasked with bringing you in. As to why, that is something you'll need to ask them. Now, here's the deal—you come out and your friends get to live, but if you refuse, then we'll come in, kill everyone, and take you anyway."

"You can't get past the wards," Jude said.

"Ah, about that. Your wards will be unraveled in about... twenty minutes. No, wait. I have an update. Make that ten. My people are good. So tick-tock. I'm watching the door."

He hung up.

"He's bluffing," Jude said. "These are high level wards

provided by HQ."

"We can't simply assume he's lying," Evelyn said. "My obligation is to the girls. If they want the halfblood, then they can have her."

"Don't be ridiculous," Sharniza said. "We *never* give the graynites what they want."

"She has a point," Jude said. "If they want her, then she must be important in some way."

They were discussing my fate as if I weren't there. As if I didn't get a vote. "Enough." Everyone turned their attention to me. "This isn't your decision. It's mine. If that message didn't go through, then no one is coming to save us. If Ignus isn't bluffing, then everyone in here will die, and he'll get me regardless. So, we need to be smart. Is there any way for you to check if the wards are stable?"

Jude chewed on her cheeks. "I don't know. Guardians installed them, said to activate them with human blood. Said they'd last for a day at least once activated. Enough time for back up to arrive, if need be, but nothing about checking if they're stable."

The phone rang again, and Jude went to answer, but I waved her off and grabbed the receiver.

"Hello?"

"You have five minutes left," Ignus said.

"Wait. How do I know you'll let them live."

"You don't," he said simply. "But what other options do you have?"

"You could be bluffing."

"I could be. But you can easily check that."

"How?"

"The anchor symbol will be fading." He hung up.

I set the phone down. "Where's the anchor symbol?"

Jude pointed at the wall with the bloody handprint, then frowned. Wait...the symbol...it's faded.

"Fuck."

"What?" Sharniza asked. "What does that even mean?"

"It means I have to go out there."

She stared at me in horror. "What? No."

"Listen to me. The ward is failing. Is there another way out of here aside from the obvious? Think. Anything."

"There's an old hatch in the basement, leading to a network of tunnels. But we don't use them. It's too dangerous. The tunnels are unstable, and we boarded up the hatch years ago."

"We'll take the risk," Sharniza said. "Where do the tunnels lead?"

"Several places," Jude said.

"The old library route is the least damaged," Bertie supplied. "Jude, isn't there an old comm unit in the basement there?"

"Yes!" Jude perked up. "If we can get to it, we can radio the nearest outpost for help."

I nodded. "Good then we have a plan. You take the tunnels, and I'll stall."

"No way," Sharniza said incredulously.

"Yes. You know it's the only way. I need to buy you guys some time."

Sharniza looked like she wanted to argue, but then her shoulders slumped. "Dammit."

Jude pulled a map off the wall. "Here's the old post office. You can get into the tunnels through there and meet up with us." I took the map and tucked it into my pocket.

The phone rang. Final call. I answered. "I'm coming out."

A MAN DRESSED in a suit stood in the middle of the street, slender, wiry, looking like any average human. *This* was Ignus? This guy was working for the graynites?

A grotesque stood either side of him, like stone bookends waiting for instruction.

He stared at me for long seconds that made my skin itch in discomfort. There was something too probing, too familiar about the way he was looking at me.

"Nice to put a face to a name," he said finally.

"I wish I could say the same for you."

He pursed his lips. "Ooo, sassy. I like it."

I shrugged. "I have my charms." Had they gotten into the tunnels yet? Was it safe to run?

"I'm sure you do, and now you can come with me, and we can explore those charms together."

Ick. "I'll pass on the exploration, thank you."

"You don't get to decide that, Walker." He held out his hand. "Come to me."

Did he think I was a dog to be ordered about?

I tensed, ready to make a break for it. The skies were clear of threat, but three grotesque were stationed on the street and two on the roof of the building opposite. I wagered they needed me alive, so they'd chase me, but if I kept close to the buildings it would be hard for them to fly down and grab me.

"Come, and we can go," he said.

My feet itched to run. "Go where?"

His thin mouth curved in a taunting smile. "To see your brother of course."

The *oomph* drained out of me as my pulse skipped a beat, then settled into a canter. "What? What did you say?"

"To see Romi, your brother. He is your brother, right?" He canted his head questioningly.

I swallowed the lump in my throat. This was bullshit. He was fucking with me. He'd somehow found out who I was, and he was using that knowledge to throw me off balance and—

"Did they tell you he was dead?" he made a faux sad face. "Did they make you cry?"

Oh, God. "Romi's alive?"

This time his smile was all teeth. "Come with me and find out."

"You're lying. Tell me the truth."

His expression hardened, all mirth gone. His mouth turned

down, nostrils flaring and dark eyes bleeding into the whites, giving me a glimpse of the monster beneath the pretty facade. "I don't have to do anything, Walker. You'll come with me regardless."

"Fuck you, freak." I turned and broke into a sprint.

I got maybe ten meters before my feet came to halt.

"Stop. You're going to stop."

My head vibrated, and his voice burrowed into my mind.

"Turn around and come with me."

No. No, I didn't want to go with him. I needed to run away, so why was I walking back to him?

"That's a good girl."

My head buzzed with his words as his instructions controlled my limbs.

No. No. No.

This couldn't be happening. I didn't want this.

He laughed and held out his hand. "That's a very good girl."

Derek

"I'M SCARED, DEREK. I'm scared he'll come for me in my sleep."

I won't let anyone hurt you. I promise. I sit by her bed and hold her hand. My fingers glow, and that glow passes up her hand, over her arm, and covers her, cocooning her like a shield. Nothing can hurt her now. Her mind will be safe. Her body will be safe.

"I love you, Derek," she whispers as she slips into dreams.

I close my eyes and dream with her.

No. No. No. I don't want this.

Stop.

Let me go.

I snap out of the memory and stare at my hands. They're pulsing with light.

Cameron's in trouble.

CAMERON

FIGHT IT. CAM, you can fight it. Please. Stop.

But I couldn't. He was in my head. In control of my limbs and I was being drawn closer and closer to him. He smiled smugly and took a step toward me.

A crack like thunder ripped the air, followed by a flash of light, then darkness filled the space between us. It pulsed, then exploded toward Ignus, sending him flying onto his ass.

His hold on me snapped, and I staggered back, staring at the hooded figure standing in front of me. "Derek?"

Derek smiled, his mournful eyes lighting up. "Unnnng Hrrrggg arghh"

You need me.

Something clicked in the back of my mind, and tears blurred my vision because he was here to protect me from the monster, just as he'd always been there to protect me from the nightmares.

Ignus ran at him, but Derek stood firm and pushed out his hands slamming Ignus with another wave of power.

"Angga ingg," he said to me.

Run now.

So, I did.

The grotesques leaped into the air to follow. I ducked my head and pushed harder, sprinting with everything I had to put distance between us. Had the others gotten to the library yet? Had they called for help? How long would it take to—

Talons snagged the back of my top and lifted me off the ground. "Argh!" I twisted, kicked, and fell to the ground before scrambling to get up and continue running.

It hit me again, knocking me off balance this time, instead of trying to pick me up. I hit the ground on my side, jarring my hip. My stone skin numbed the worst of the blow, but I'd lost my advantage. The grotesque had me pinned.

"Nice trick," Ignus said from behind the beasts. "But your tulpa's no match for me. Now get the fuck up. I'm done playing."

"You've also lost your pretentious accent, you wanker."

He growled and made a grab for me, but the heavy beat of wings had him faltering.

A blast of icy air raked over me, then Serath was bearing down on Ignus. The elites were hot on his tail along with several other guardians. My heart leaped into my throat, beating so hard that words were impossible.

The cavalry had arrived.

"Fucking hell." Ignus clenched his teeth. "Until next time, Walker." He brought his hand down and something smashed. The spot where he'd been standing lit up bright blue and when the light died—he was gone.

The grotesques took to the air, and the guardians followed, bringing them down one by one.

Serath landed in a crouch, then strode toward me, his husky gaze filled with fire. I didn't have time to pull myself up before he'd scooped me into his arms. He held me tight for long aching seconds. His heart hammering against me. My goyle nature reveled in the contact, wanting to melt against him, but my human side, the rational side, was stuck in a loop, hearing Ignus's words over and over. *I'm taking you to see your brother...Did they tell you he was dead?*

I shoved at Serath's shoulders, wanting to see his face when I asked him. Wanting to look into his eyes and read the truth.

His grip slackened enough for me to pull back and lock gazes with him. "Is it true?"

"What?" He scanned my face.

"Is Romi still alive?"

His expression closed off but not before I caught the flicker of unease in his eyes.

My stomach quivered with hope, fear, and a concoction of emotions that I couldn't define. "Serath, tell me. Tell me the fucking truth. Is Romi alive?"

He set me down, his jaw clenching. "Why are you asking me this?"

"Just answer me."

"Why do you care?"

"Because he's my brother!"

My words echoed up and down the empty street.

Serath stared at me in shock, as if seeing me for the first time. "You're Romi's sister? But...how?"

"Because Basque fucked my human mother and then made her sign a contract never to tell anyone. Because I wasn't good enough. And no one knows. No one but the people I've told myself. But he did. Ignus knew somehow."

He fucking knew, and now everything I'd come to know and believe was in question.

CHAPTER 56

Cameron

The room at the academy was twelve by eight with a small window, a desk, a chair, and an empty filing cabinet. I'd been locked inside it for over an hour with no explanations.

I didn't know if Shar and the others were okay. I assumed so, because leaving the omegas behind wasn't an option for the academy, but still, it would be nice to be told. Nice to be let out of this fucking room, which might as well be a cell.

Ignus's words swam round and round in my head. I needed to know if they were true. Was Romi alive or not?

The lock rattled, and the door opened. Miss Travani entered. I hadn't set eyes on her since our first meeting at the gates on my arrival, but she looked just as coiffed and pristine as she had at that meeting, her classic nineteen twenties bob gleamed in the shitty overhead light, which also happened to make her skin look sickly pale against her dark red lipstick.

"Miss Walker, so sorry for the wait," she said.

I didn't have time for pleasantries. "Why am I locked in here? I didn't do anything wrong."

"No. You didn't. But after the attack, we needed to gather a little information on what happened."

"I told the elites what happened."

"Yes, that the grotesques and their master were after you."

"They were and he was."

"And we needed to understand why."

I sat up straighter. "You have answers?"

"It isn't for me to relay that information."

I was so sick of this shit. "Just fucking tell me who he was and why he wanted me. No, forget that, just tell me, is my brother alive or not?"

She blinked sharply and her nostrils flared a little. "Please, Miss Walker, calm down. You'll have your answers momentarily. But not from me."

"Then who?"

"From your father."

HE WAS HERE? Basque was here? And she knew. Of course, she knew. I mean, I'd confessed to being Romi's sister so...

"Your father will see you in the headmistress's office now," Travani said.

"He is not my father."

She pressed her lips together. "Unfortunately, we do not get to choose our sires or how they subsequently choose to treat us." She held open the door. "Regardless of your feelings—or lack of—toward him, he is the only creature able to answer your questions."

And I needed those answers. I stood slowly. "In that case, lead the way."

Breathe, Cam. Breathe. Do not lose your shit.

The main building was as silent as a grave. Predawn was downtime; most everybody would be climbing into bed soon, so there wasn't anybody about to see me being led to Mistress Carter's office. Miss Travani knocked on the door to the study, then pushed it open and stepped back to usher me inside.

Panic seized me. I was about to meet the male responsible for half my DNA. The male who'd abandoned me and my mother, who'd wanted me out of his life so badly that he'd made my mother sign a contract to ensure my true heritage never came out.

I hated this man, and yet, in this moment, I couldn't help but *want* to see him. To look into his eyes and maybe see myself reflected there. I hated myself for that weakness.

"Go on," Miss Travani said kindly. "You'll be fine."

I swallowed past the dryness in my mouth and entered the room. Gray light flooded the space, washing out the color and making everything look ashy. Mistress Carter watched me from behind her desk, a small smile playing on her lips that looked suspiciously like pity. That smile added steel to my spine as I finally allowed myself to register the male standing at the window with his back to me.

His shirt stretched across his back, not Lastonflex, but normal cotton, and he wore dress trousers and leather shoes, as if he weren't concerned about having to shift. Which, based on what Palia had explained about the effects of aging on gargoyles, in Mirrowind's class, made sense. His hair was ashy-blond in the gray pre-dawn light but would probably be white-blond like mine.

"Lionel?" Mistress Carter said softly.

Basque turned to face me.

I wasn't sure what I'd been expecting. Stern angry features maybe? Someone who looked cruel? I'm not sure. I do know that I hadn't expected to see warmth, or the tentative smile that lifted his mouth.

"Cameron. It's good to see you."

Good to see me? Ribbons of emotion tangled in my chest. "Are you joking right now?"

His lips made a thin line. "Yes. I can see why you may feel that way."

"You can? Oh, good, because I was beginning to think I was delusional and that I'd imagined the last twenty years of being ignored."

"You have every right to be upset. To hate me even, but please, allow me to explain."

"Frankly, I don't care enough about you to wonder why you left me. All I want to know is if my brother is still alive."

His jaw ticked. "Up until last night, we weren't sure. But after what you reported, I believe that he may be."

His words knocked the wind out of my sails. I grabbed at the back of the armchair and doubled over, eyes hot with the threat of tears.

He was alive.

Romi was alive.

"Please, sit down. Miss Walker," Mistress Carter said kindly.

I slipped onto the armchair, grateful for the wooden support. "How? What happened to him? Where is he?"

"He was taken during a mission," Basque said. "We're not sure where he is, but if he is alive, then it's likely they have him at their stronghold."

He was alive, and the relief mingled with fear for him, for what they might be doing to him. "I don't understand why they'd keep him alive."

"There are many reasons." Basque said, "Romi is an elite, therefore he has information that they could use against us, but his psychic shields are impeccable. He's strong."

Numbness swept over me. "You think they're torturing him, don't you?"

Basques mouth turned down. "Yes. If he is alive, then that is exactly what they're doing, and if Romi breaks... If they take down his shields, then—"

"Your precious information will be in their hands." I gave a bitter laugh. "Your son is in danger, and that's all you can think about?"

"No, Cameron. I couldn't care less about the information. My concern is for my son's soul and what it would mean for him to lose it."

"Lionel?" Mistress Carter looked up at him, shocked.

"It's all right, Regina. She needs to know the truth if she's going to succeed in the task we have for her."

My pulse throbbed hard in my throat. "Tell me."

"If the graynites succeed in breaking through Romi's shield, they will strip him of his soul." He pressed his lips together. "And a gargoyle without a soul is a Graynite."

HIS WORDS TOOK a moment to sink in, and even then, my brain refused to accept what they meant. He watched me in silence as I processed this information.

I needed to know if I'd understood him correctly. "Are you telling me that a Graynite is simply a gargoyle without a soul?"

"It's a little more complicated that," Basque said tightly. "But that's all you need to know for now."

But I wasn't done yet. "Were all graynites once gargoyles?"

His jaw ticked. "Yes."

I sat back in my seat. "Fuck. And no one knows? The cadets? The initiates? The elites?"

"The elites are aware of the fact."

"But how? How did this happen? History and—"

"You're told what you need to know in order to do your jobs."

"Wow. Hold onto the information and control the masses. Nice. I mean that's never backfired before, has it?"

"Do you think telling the guardians that we expect them to kill creatures that were once just like them is going to help them be effective protectors to the human race? Do you think allowing them to feel empathy toward these creatures will be beneficial? One moment of hesitation is all that it takes for them to bring you down. They feed off souls, Cameron. Human, supernatural or Gargoyle, it matters not to them. They're a threat, and they have my son."

"How did the graynites come to be? How did it start? I need to understand what I'm dealing with here?"

"It began with a curse," Mistress Carter said, gaze flicking to Basque to check if it was okay to continue. He nodded. "We were dying. Losing against the gray and so the gargoyles made a deal with a powerful force."

"What force?"

She shook her head. "That information is classified. I...*We* don't know. All we know is that they were given the power to fight the gray, but the cost was their souls. A whole army lost their souls. The gray was defeated and the graynites were born."

The graynites that they said came out of the gray just as it was pushed back through the rift. Not monsters, but heroes *turned* into monsters by a curse. "How can you live like this? Knowing only half the truth?"

"Because the truth of the past won't change the present," Basque said. "When the graynites took Romi, it was no fluke. They took what they believed to be the only adult Basque in existence. They hoped to put us at a disadvantage against the alpha, which means that the alpha planned to surface."

"But then they found out about me somehow..."

"Yes. Basques have never been very fertile. Our bloodline is dying out, so when you were born, I knew your life would be at risk from the graynites if they found out about you, and so I sent you away with your mother and hid you best I could."

Which was why my mother had never registered me. "But then I surfaced and registered, and my blood went into the system."

"Yes. Basic tests are done at the intake center, but the samples get sent to a lab where they're tested further. We believe there may be a mole in our midst. If they get their hands on you, then we'll be left without any way to kill their alpha."

"So, what? You want me to hide out here and cower? They have my brother."

"And I know how much you mean to him. How much he meant to you."

"How could you..." Oh...Oh shit. "*You* told him about me, didn't you?"

He looked sheepish. "Not directly, but I may have left some paperwork lying around for him to find."

"You knew my mother died..."

"I'm sorry." His throat bobs. "She was a sweet woman. A decent woman. When you called that day, you sounded so much like her that for a moment...for a moment I forgot..."

My throat pinched. "We have to do something. We have to get Romi back."

"There is only one way to do that," Basque said. "Only one way to free Romi and stop the graynites once and for all, and that is to kill the alpha."

He made it sound easy. "The alpha who's hiding behind wards? That alpha?"

"We're close to cracking his wards, but without an elite team at full power that knowledge is useless." He gave me a pointed look.

My scalp prickled. "Wait... are you saying—"

"Yes, Cameron. I want to claim you as my heir. As a Basque. And I want you to fill Romi's place on the elite team."

He was insane. "I'm a halfblood."

"You're a Basque, and even at halfblood your blood is more potent than most."

Mistress Carter coughed into her hand.

Basque lifted his chin. "What? It's true. Look at her. She made it here, didn't she? She survived a grotesque attack and fought off a Graynite." He sounded almost...proud.

But hang on..."Ignus is a graynite?"

He gave me a small tight smile. "Classified intel for elite status only."

Bastard. Way to bait a gal. I wanted to save Romi, but I wasn't delusional. I knew my limits. "I'm no elite."

"Not yet," Basque said. "But you will be. Your training will be fast-tracked and intensified, and in a few weeks, you'll take the official elite trial."

"What about the initiate exam?"

"There'll be no need for that," Mistress Carter said. "As the only Basque available to take the elite spot, you'll be allowed to skip it."

"A few *weeks*? Will Romi survive that long?"

Basque's nostrils flared, and he lifted his chin, eyes blazing. "My son is strong. Basque blood is powerful. I have faith in him." His shoulders heaved. "And I have faith in you, Cameron. You can do this."

There was a knock on the door. "Come in," Basque called.

Selas entered the room followed by Prasan, Orix, and finally Serath. He kept his gaze fixed ahead, but I knew he sensed me because his hands curled to fists, and his neck muscles flexed as if he were fighting the urge to turn his head to look at me.

"Elite team, thank you for coming," Basque said. "You've been debriefed, but now I'd like to introduce you to your new trainee, Cameron Basque. My daughter." The elites finally looked my way, and a jolt passed through me at the intensity of their regard.

"Mr. Halle," Basque said. "As elite leader, I'm putting you in charge of my daughter's training."

Halle? That was...

Serath's shoulders tightened. "With all due respect, Mr. Basque, I believe that Selas would be—"

"I've studied the team stats, Mr. Halle, and my decision is final. You will *personally* train her in preparation for the elite trial."

Serath's fists tightened. "Sir, the elite trial is—"

"The only way she can bond to the elite team," Basque interrupted. "The *only* way." He gave Serath a stern look, and the elite's jaw ticked. "By all means involve the other team members in the training, but I want her under you."

Under him...Oh boy.

He had no idea how bad that would be. But we couldn't let him find out. I looked across at Serath and plastered a polite smile on my face. "I look forward to working with you, elite."

He finally turned his head to look at me, his expression a mask of polite indifference. "And I you, Miss Walker. And I you."

CHAPTER 57

CAMERON

The sun was up by the time I got back to the dorm. I hadn't expected Basque to hang out for a get-to-know-you session, but being dismissed so abruptly stung. Fuck him. I'd done without him for two decades. I didn't need him. He'd held back the elites, though.

Probably discussing my training plan *under* Serath.

Fucking hell, the last thing we needed was to be thrown together like that. How would I focus on training if...*urgh*. I'd have to find a way. Romi's life was at stake. My focus would be on becoming good enough to pass this elite trial.

Questions sprang to mind now, like how had we ended up in the eastern settlement? Basque said HQ had a mole, but did our diversion to the outer eastern settlement mean we had one here too?

Shar, Touron, and the twins were waiting for me in my room. Melanie hovered by the window, looking spectral and mournful, but her expression brightened at the sight of me.

"You're all right!" She clasped her hands together. "We were so worried."

My gaze tripped from face to face, and gratitude thickened my throat. "You guys..."

Touron crossed the room and pulled me into a hug.

I hugged him back, inhaling the fresh cotton scent of his Lastonflex top.

He released me, and Shar took his place. I wasn't a hugger, not usually, but I'd make an exception today.

"I thought he got you," Shar whispered. "Back at the settlement when you didn't make it to the library. I came back for you, and I saw you on the ground just as the guardians showed up. You were almost at the edge of town by then."

"You fought him off and ran," Ginia said. "How did you do it?"

How? Crap. "I didn't...It was Derek."

"Derek? As in your boogeyman tulpa?" Touron looked confused.

"He showed up when Ignus got into my head to control me and make me come to him. I couldn't fight him off. He was burrowing deeper and deeper into my head, and Derek appeared and blasted him. He saved me and told me to run." But where had Derek gone? Guilt tightened my gut. Where could he...Wait...

I hurried to my wardrobe and pulled it open. A pocket of darkness clung to the back recess. Could it be... "Derek?"

The shadow moved, and glowing mournful eyes looked up at me. "Jrgggg ak mmmm?"

Can I stay here?

I fell to my knees, blinking back tears. "Yes, buddy. Yes, you can stay. You saved me."

"Rggg taj dun."

"Yeah, you always save me." And I'd left him behind. Forgotten about him for a while. Never again. "I love you. I'm so sorry for leaving you."

"Illuuuurvve uuuug."

"Do we get to meet him," Touron asked.

"That's up to Derek."

His eyes went round, then he nodded hesitantly.

I opened the door a little wider. "Derek, meet my friends."

He peered at them, then ducked back into the gloom. “It’s okay. They’re nice. I promise.”

“Hey.” Touron stepped forward. “I’m Touron, and these are the twins, Ginia and Palia.”

They both waved.

“I’m Sharniza.” Shar stepped forward, and Derek looked up, his eyes widening at the sight of her. “Mmmmrggg.” He ducked his head.

Pretty

“What did he say?” Sharniza asked.

I bit back a smile. “He said—”

“Nnnng.”

Don’t

“He said, nice to meet you.”

“You too,” Sharniza said.

“Mfffg yar frggg,” Derek said.

“Okay.” I closed the door. “He said he needs to rest for a bit. I think holding off Ignus took it out of him.”

“But how did he do it?” Palia asked. “He’s a tulpa. A boogeyman, and he just went up against a...what even is Ignus?”

“A graynite.” I held up my hand to stem the questions. “I don’t know how, but he is. That’s what Basque said anyway. And I have no clue how Derek managed to hold Ignus off, but I’m going to find out.”

“So, what happened in the office? What did Carter say?” Sharniza asked.

I took a deep breath. “It wasn’t Carter that wanted to see me. It was my father. Lionel Basque.”

WE TALKED FOR an hour before yawns and sleepy eyes forced us to accept that it was time to turn in, but we hung out for a little longer, lounging around my room and watching the sun grow brighter while feeling its weakening effects on our bodies.

"We should get some sleep," Ginia said. "Classes are in a few hours."

Palia stood and yawned. "And we have a new class added to our timetables."

"Urgh," Touron groaned. "What is it?"

"No idea." Palia shrugged. "There's an announcement saying we have a new instructor joining the academy and new timetables will be available shortly."

"Might not be on your timetable, though," Touron said. "You're training with the elites."

"She'll still need to know the academic stuff," Palia pointed out.

"We'll find out soon enough, but for now, shoo, all of you. I need sleep. Halfblood here, remember?"

My friends drifted off to their own rooms, and I closed the door with a sigh and then spotted Touron's blue hoodie on the end of my bed. I'd give it back to him later.

I kicked off my shoes and crawled onto the bed.

There were no more secrets now. By the time I woke, everyone would know who I was. Everyone would know I was training to become an elite. The next few hours would be my last as the halfblood with an unknown sire.

Romi was alive, and tomorrow I'd begin the training that would get me closer to saving him.

Someone knocked on the door.

"Urgh." I grabbed Touron's hoodie and shuffled to the door, yanking it open. "You could have waited till—"

A large, tattooed male stood on my doorstep. My breath stalled and then exploded from my lips in an exhalation.

"Levi..."

He tipped his head to one side and gave me his signature crooked smile. "Did you miss me, princess?"

Oh shit.

Cameron's journey continues in
The Stone Secret.

GARGOYLES
OF
STONEHAVEN

THE
STONE
SECRET

USA TODAY BESTSELLING AUTHOR
DEBBIE CASSIDY

The Stone Secret

The secrets of Stonehaven won't stay buried for long.

I've barely had time to wrap my head around the revelations doled out by my gargoyle sire when a knock at my dorm door brings a blast from the not-so-distant past back into my life.

I thought I'd left Levi behind.

I was wrong.

He's here for me, and things are about to get complicated.

But convincing Levi that I've moved on without revealing that Serath is my fated mate isn't the only challenge I'm facing.

With the elite trials mere weeks away, I need to make sure that I'm physically and mentally prepared, and that involves training directly with Serath—the object of my forbidden desire.

Focusing won't be easy, but I'll need to find a way, because failure is not an option.

Failure, means death.

ALSO BY DEBBIE CASSIDY

The Veritas Legacy
Wicked Onyx

Gargoyles of Stonehaven
The Stone Initiation
The Stone Secret
The Stone Curse
The Stone Survival

Labyrinth of Gods
Lost and Stolen Gods
Damned and Broken Gods
Restless and Insurgent Gods
Wrathful and Avenging Gods

ABOUT THE AUTHOR

Deviyanee Cassidy is a *USA Today* Bestselling Author of Paranormal and Fantasy Novels. She writes under the pen name Debbie Cassidy. Born in the UK, and raised in a small town, she spent most of her time reading and dreaming up stories. After studying psychology at university, she worked various jobs before finally pursuing her passion for writing full time.

Deviyanee has drawn upon her cultural experiences, and Indian Mythology when creating some of her worlds. Her books are filled with action, vivid descriptions, multi-layered plots, and heart stopping romance. They feature strong female protagonists who find themselves drawn into supernatural worlds filled with magic, danger, and romance.

Deviyanee explores themes of personal growth, redemption, and the struggle between good and evil. She's been praised for her engaging characters, intricate world building, and emotionally resonant storytelling.

Learn more at: debbiecassidyauthor.com

PAGE
&
VINE